LET'S FAKE
A DEAL
A Sarah Winston Garage Sale Mystery

Sherry Harris

KENSINGTON PUBLISHING CORP.
www.kensingtonbooks.com

KENSINGTON BOOKS are published by

Kensington Publishing Corp.
119 West 40th Street
New York, NY 10018

All Kensington titles, imprints, and distributed lines are available at special quantity discounts for bulk purchases for sales promotions, premiums, fund-raising, educational, or institutional use.

Special book excerpts or customized printings can also be created to fit specific needs. For details, write or phone the office of the Kensington sales manager: Kensington Publishing Corp., 119 West 40th Street, New York, NY 10018, attn: Sales Department; phone 1-800-221-2647.

KENSINGTON BOOKS and the K logo are Reg. U.S. Pat. & TM Off.

First printing: August 2019

10 9 8 7 6 5 4 3 2 1

ISBN-13: 978-1-4967-1698-9
ISBN-10: 1-4967-1698-1

Printed in the United States of America

Electronic edition:

ISBN-13: 978-1-4967-1699-6 (e-book)
ISBN-10: 1-4967-1699-X (e-book)

To Bob

To the least fake man I know,
Love you.

CHAPTER ONE

Two police cars squealed to a halt at the end of the driveway, lights flashing, front bumpers almost touching. I stared at them and then at the half dozen people milling around the garage sale that had started fifteen minutes ago at 7:30 a.m. Everyone stopped browsing and turned to stare, too. Doors popped open. Three officers jumped out. Unusual in these days of budget cuts and officers riding alone that two were together. I didn't recognize any of them because I was in Billerica, Massachusetts, just north of where I lived in Ellington.

"Who's in charge here?" one of the officers called. His thick shoulders and apparent lack of neck looked menacing against the cloudy late September sky.

"Me. I'm Sarah Winston." I gave a little wave of my hand and stepped forward. It seemed like the carpenter's apron I was wearing with SARAH WINSTON GARAGE SALES embroidered across the front was enough to identify me.

The officer put out a hand the size of a baseball glove to stop me. "Stay. The rest of you, put everything down and see the two officers over there."

What the heck? I stayed put, having had enough experience with policing through my ex-husband's military and civilian careers in law enforcement to know to listen to this man no matter what I thought. Several people glanced at me but did as they were told. I stood in the center of the driveway all by myself. One by one people spoke to the police officers and scurried off. Five minutes later it was me and the three cops. Thankfully, it wasn't hot out here like it would be in August.

"What's going on?" I asked.

"Do you have any weapons?"

"No." I looked down at the carpenter's apron tied around my waist. It had four pockets for holding things. "There's a measuring tape, some cash, and a roll of quarters in the pockets." Ugh, would he think that was a weapon? I'd heard that if you held a roll in your fist and punched someone, it was as good as brass knuckles. "Oh, and my phone. Do you want to see?"

"Put your hands on the back of your head and then kneel," he ordered.

I started to protest but shut my mouth and complied. Something was terribly wrong. Thank heavens I'd worn jeans today instead of a dress.

"Now lay face-first on the ground."

I looked at the distance between my face and the ground. I couldn't just flop forward. It would smash my nose. I hunched down as much as I could, rolled to one side, and then onto my stomach. The roll of quarters made their presence known, digging into my already roiling stomach. The driveway was warm and rough against my cheek. A pair of highly polished black boots came into sight. I felt the apron being untied, and I was quickly patted down. Then I was yanked up by the big officer. My carpenter's apron looked forlorn laying on the driveway.

"Please tell me, what's this about?" I asked again.

The big guy glared down at me, hands on his hips. His left hand was a little closer to his gun than made me comfortable. If this was an effort to intimidate me, it was working on every level.

"We had a tip that everything being sold here was stolen."

CHAPTER TWO

Cold. Cold like someone had just dumped one of those big icy containers of liquid over my head. The kind they dumped on the winning coach at a football game. Only I wasn't the winner here. The cold reached through my skin and gripped my heart. "Stolen? That's not possible."

"Is anyone else here?" the officer asked. His nameplate said JONES.

"Yes. The two people who hired me are in the house." I pointed, thumb over shoulder, to the large two-story colonial house behind me.

"Do they have any weapons?"

"No. No one has weapons. It's a garage sale. I won't let anyone sell weapons at the garage sales I run." I stared at the officer, hoping I'd see some sign in his face that he believed me. I didn't. "I was hired to run this garage sale. It's my job."

"By who?" The other two officers headed to the house. One stood by the front door and the other went around the side of the house toward the back.

Why did this guy sound so freaking skeptical? "A young couple. Kate and Alex Green." I remembered the day we met at a Dunkin' Donuts in Ellington. I'd instantly labeled them as hipsters with their skinny jeans, flannel shirts, fresh faces, and black-rimmed glasses. Kate and Alex had been shy but eager at the same time. Alex had just gotten a job at Tufts University in tech services. "They just moved here from Indiana and didn't realize how expensive everything is. They owned a huge house in Indiana but once they got here realized they were going to have to downsize."

I almost chuckled thinking about their wide-eyed explanation of how the money they got for their home in Indiana would only buy a small cape-style house far from Boston in this area. Sticker shock was a real thing for anyone who moved here.

"Once they realized they had to get rid of two thirds of their stuff, they decided to reduce their carbon footprint," I said, "and to buy one of those tiny houses. Me? I couldn't live in one. Not that my one-bedroom apartment is that big, but those loft bedrooms? You have to climb up some little ladder. The bed's just a mattress on the floor. How do you make the beds without hitting your head?" I shuddered. "Claustrophobic, don't you think?"

Officer Jones stared at me. I was rambling. Just answer the question he asked, I reminded myself.

"So where did all of this stuff come from?" he asked, sweeping his arm toward the carefully set out tables full of items.

"From the Greens. They put it all in storage when they got here from Indiana." I remembered their excited faces as they told me that they'd moved into a one-bedroom apartment in a complex on the north side of Ellington to prepare for their new lifestyle.

"I priced everything at the storage unit, and then they moved it over here. This is their friends' house." I waved a hand at the house. "And their friends decided to sell some stuff, too. Stuff I didn't know about." I pointed to a group of tables that held computers, TVs, and cell phones. Then over to a bunch of furniture. "They priced all of the electronics. Personally, I thought their prices were a little bit high, but I don't usually deal with electronics."

"What do you usually *deal* with?" Jones asked. He stepped in closer. His coffee breath swept over me.

He sounded like he expected my answer to be "drugs." I glanced toward the house, hoping the Greens would be out here in a second to explain all this to Officer Jones. How they owned all of this stuff and it was some kind of terrible mistake. But the only person by the house was the officer knocking on the door.

"My favorite things to sell are antiques, furniture, linens, old glassware, but I sell pretty much whatever my customers want me to. And you wouldn't believe the stuff some of them want to sell." Officer Jones didn't crack a smile. "The rest of it they said to price as people expressed interest. Personally, I think everything should be priced in advance, but the customer is always right." I shut up. I was volunteering too much again.

"I'll need you to let us into the house so we can talk to the Greens," Officer Jones said. He glanced over at the officer standing at the front door.

"I'd be happy to," I said as we walked to the front door. "They went in to make some coffee for everyone since it's chilly out here. Then they were coming back out to help run the sale." If they worked the sale, then I didn't have to hire anyone to help me, which meant we all pocketed more money.

The officer by the door stepped aside as I opened the door but followed Officer Jones and me into the foyer.

"Kate?" I called. "Alex?" No answer. "The kitchen is just down the hall." They should have heard me. Why didn't they answer?

The two officers exchanged a look. One that gave me prickles of discomfort.

"Miss Winston, would you mind stepping back outside while we take a look around?" Officer Jones asked.

The prickles turned into waves. I called to the Greens again. Nothing. "I'd be happy to wait outside."

Officer Jones looked at his fellow officer. "Go with her."

The other officer didn't look happy, but Jones's message seemed clear. *Make sure she doesn't take off.* I went back out onto the porch and walked down the steps to the sidewalk that led from the driveway to the house. The other officer followed me out. We stood awkwardly while avoiding looking at each other. A few minutes later Officer Jones came back out along with the officer who had gone around the back.

"Where are the Greens?" I asked, trying to look past the officers toward the house.

"No one's in there. The place is empty," Officer Jones said.

Empty? Although empty was better than him saying there was someone dead in there. "I saw them go in there a half hour ago." It hit me that it didn't take a half an hour to make coffee. But I'd been busy enough that until now I hadn't realized how much time had passed. I paused. "By empty do you mean empty of people?"

"Empty of almost everything," the other officer said. He didn't look at me, but at Jones. They both looked at all the furniture on the lawn.

"This didn't come from the house, did it?" I asked. I didn't have to wait for an answer. I could tell by the expression on the officer's face it must have. How could I have been so naive?

I turned to look at the house again. It had one of those historic plaques by the door that said it had been built in the early 1700s. Where *were* the Greens? If only the plaque could tell me that. The house was a colonial style from the early eighteenth century. It was at the top of a hill. I'd read a bit about its history. The house had been a place where the townspeople went during Indian attacks. It had a tunnel that led from the basement to the nearby woods that was a last-resort escape route if things went south. The woods were long gone, and in their place were rows of small houses with small yards.

"There's a tunnel. From the basement to someplace around the back. Maybe they went out that way," I said. The officers just looked at me. "If this is all stolen, they're the ones that did it. Shouldn't you send someone after them? They *stole* the stuff."

The smaller officer stepped away and talked into his shoulder mike.

Jones turned to me. "Do you know where the entrance to the tunnel is?"

I nodded. "Yes. Do you want me to show you?"

* * *

Minutes later I was down in the basement or cellar or whatever people from New England called them. Basements were few and far between where I grew up in Pacific Grove, California. This one had rough dirt walls and wasn't fit to be a rec room or man cave. It was creepy enough to be a madman's cave, though. Damp air flowed around us with its musty, rotting smell.

Jones and the two other officers studied the primitive-looking wooden door with its rusty lock, hinges, and doorknob. It was set into the back wall of the foundation.

"So if you didn't know anything about this house, how did you know this was here?" Jones asked.

"I noticed the historic plaque by the front door the first time I came over, so I read about the history of the house online."

"When was the first time you came over?"

"Two days ago. To see where I could set everything up."

Jones and one of the other officers looked at each other. All of this exchanging looks and no explanations was making me very nervous. Cops. Jones reached over and turned the knob on the door to the tunnel. It moved easily in his hand, but as he pulled on the door the hinges groaned, resisting. The door snagged on the rough dirt floor. Even only open an inch, the smell of stagnant air pushed me back a couple of steps.

"I don't think I need to be here for this," I said. I

was afraid of what was on the other side of that door. Spiders, rats, bats—with my luck a dead body.

But Jones lifted the door just enough to clear the spot where the door had snagged. We all peered in but saw nothing but darkness.

CHAPTER THREE

Jones flipped on a powerful flashlight. The tunnel went for about twenty yards before the darkness took over again. Lots of spiderwebs hung, but they looked recently disturbed to me. I shuddered thinking about having to plow through them.

"Let's go," Jones said.

"I'm not going in there," I said. "No reason to. Could be dangerous, and you don't want to put an innocent civilian in harm's way." I accented the *innocent*.

Jones stared down at me but must have seen the sense in my words. If anything I told him was true, the Greens had fled down the tunnel to escape. They could be waiting farther down beyond where we could see. "You two go down," Jones said to the other two officers. "We'll go to the backyard and try to figure out where you'll come out."

A backyard in daylight sounded good to me. We hustled up the steps, around the house, and into the backyard. There was a large deck leading down to a beautifully landscaped yard. A hedge of boxwoods made a natural fence that separated the flattest part of the lawn from where it dropped steeply to the houses below. We skirted the boxwoods and peered down the steep slope.

"It looks like there's some kind of entrance down there," I said, pointing.

From up here we could see a rickety door in the hill. Maybe something awful had happened to the Greens. "Maybe they were kidnapped," I said to Officer Jones. I didn't want to believe that sweet couple had stolen goods.

"If there even are people named the Greens."

"There are." I looked at Officer Jones, but he wouldn't look at me. The kidnapping story didn't ring true even to me. It was wishful thinking on my part. Most of the stuff that sat out front were items the Greens had had me pricing in a storage unit they had rented. They said it was theirs. I clenched my fist.

"Seems kind of odd to have a garage sale on a Thursday," Officer Jones said. "I thought most people had them on the weekend."

Even that sounded like an accusation of some kind. "It's when they asked me to do it. The customer's always right."

Officer Jones stared at me until I looked away. In this case the customer had been far from right, the lousy, cheating Greens.

A few moments later the door below us swung outward, and the two officers blinked in the light. After they looked around, they climbed the hill toward us.

"Did anyone come out ahead of us?" one of the officers asked.

"No," I said. Jones gave me a look like this was his show and I'd better sit back and watch.

"Anything in there?" Jones asked them.

"Nothing but cobwebs and rats. A few footprints in a damp spot."

"They looked fresh," the other officer added.

They all turned to me, and I didn't like the looks they had on their faces, like I was some kind of great prize they'd just won at a state fair. I put my hands out as if I could somehow ward off their thoughts.

"I don't know what's going on here. But I didn't steal that stuff." I gestured toward the front of the house. We headed back that way. Nothing had changed out front. The Greens weren't standing there waiting to explain themselves.

"Do you know what kind of car the Greens drove?" Jones asked.

I thought about it. "I met them at the Dunkin's on Great Road in Ellington the first time we met. I didn't walk in or out with them, so I didn't see what their car looked like. After I finished pricing things at the storage unit, they showed up there in a big box truck they'd rented from somewhere."

"What company did they rent it from?" Officer Jones asked.

I shook my head. "I'm not sure. It wasn't one of the big-name places. I didn't pay that much attention. There was no reason to at the time." Back when I'd thought they were honest, trustworthy innocents from Indiana. "I have their phone number. In my phone. Over there." My carpenter's apron looked abandoned and lonely on the driveway.

Jones nodded and walked me over. He picked up the apron and pulled out my phone, looking at it suspiciously before handing it over. I pulled up the number and gave it to him. "Why don't I try calling? Maybe we can get this all straightened out."

Part of me still wanted to believe that the Greens were the people they portrayed themselves as being. Jones let me try to call them. I put my phone on speaker. The call just rang. There was no "Hi, this is the Greens" or any other sort of message. It went to voice mail after it rang five times. Officer Jones reached over and disconnected.

"Give me the best description of the so-called couple you can," Jones said.

"I took some pictures of the sale earlier, before I opened. Maybe they are in one. Can I look?"

Jones nodded and I started swiping through pictures.

"This is the only one," I said, holding out my phone. It was disappointingly bad. They both wore nondescript hooded sweatshirts, one black, one gray. And they were looking down at something on one of the tables. Plus they were way across the yard from me. At least the house was in the background, so he could see I'd taken the picture here and wasn't making people up. I made the picture bigger and cropped it to focus on their heads. Alex had a small birthmark on his right cheek that looked like a comma.

"This doesn't help much," I said. I was so disappointed, but I pointed out the birthmark, which was a blurry blob. Officer Jones squinted at it as I described them. It was my best shot. I was still uncertain whether he believed me or not. I was leaning toward not.

After I finished describing them, Officer Jones used the mic on his shoulder to call someone. He repeated my descriptions. I assumed he was putting some kind of APB out on them. Maybe the all-points bulletin meant he believed me even though he seemed pretty skeptical.

"And where's the storage unit?" Jones asked.

"It was on the west side of Billerica." I gave him the address.

After he wrote it down, he tilted his head back and glared down at me. I wanted to grab Jones by the collar and tell him *You've got to listen to me, I'm innocent, I'd never do this*. But I'm guessing he heard that a lot. So I stood there waiting for his next move. I hoped it didn't involve handcuffs and hearing the Miranda rights read to me.

I broke first—no big surprise. "I didn't know any of this was stolen." Maybe if I said it often enough, it would get through his thick head.

"Turn around," Jones said. "Hands behind your back."

"You've got to be kidding," I said. But one look at his face told me he wasn't. I complied.

"You're under arrest for receiving stolen property," Jones started.

The snap of the handcuffs startled me. They were hot like they'd been out in the sun and tighter than I ever imagined. My ex, CJ, and I had had some fun with his handcuffs back in the day. But this was nothing like that. A man across the street stood on his porch, arms folded. Officer Jones had said someone had tipped them off. I had a feeling the man on the porch was that someone. Other people clumped in small groups down the street.

Jones started reading me my Miranda rights. *Miranda rights!* Soon I was in the back of the squad car, then at the station, fingerprinted, mug shot taken. *Mug shot!* It would show a tearstained face. I'd been stripped of my personal belongings and booked.

Jones had asked a lot of extra questions besides the ones about my address and name. Where did I get the stolen items? Who else was I working with? At least I knew better than to answer anything that would incriminate me or sound like a confession. Just the facts, sir. Jones wasn't happy that he couldn't trick me into saying more. One phone call and then into a holding cell. Nightmares do come true.

CHAPTER FOUR

"What were you thinking using your one phone call to call me?" Scott Pellner asked. It was almost ten. He stood outside my holding cell. The one I still couldn't believe I was locked in. Fortunately, it was a slow day here and I had the place to myself. Pellner had his arms across his chest and must have been on duty, because he was wearing his Ellington Police Department uniform. He had these deep dimples that didn't soften his face, and frankly his look and body posture scared me a little. Pellner was only a couple of inches taller than me, but unlike me he didn't have an inch of fat on his muscled body.

"I thought maybe you could vouch for me. Tell Officer Jones that I'm not selling stolen goods."

"You think I can just wave some magic police wand and make this all go away?"

I nodded. "Something like that." My voice rose at the end, making it more of a question than a statement.

"I swear I spend more time with you than my wife sometimes. And get you out of more messes than my five kids combined."

Ouch. That hurt. "I'm sorry. I just figured you could talk policeman to policeman to them. You know I wouldn't sell stolen goods if I knew they were stolen."

"Don't say things like that in here. It sounds fishy, and who knows who is listening." His dimples deepened even more. At this rate his whole face was going to be sucked into them. At last his face relaxed. "I do know that you wouldn't knowingly sell stolen goods, but it doesn't mean you're not a pain in my neck. You should have called a lawyer. Not me."

My hand went to my mouth. "You think they are going to keep me here?"

"They might. I looked you up in the system before heading over here. In Massachusetts anything above $250.00 is a felony."

Oh, no. There was way more than two hundred fifty dollars' worth of stuff at the garage sale. "They think I committed a felony?"

Pellner nodded. Tears started rushing up into my eyes. I blinked as fast as I could. I hated crying in front of people. I always feared once I started crying, I wouldn't stop. That all the hurts and scares of the last couple of years would just overwhelm me and that the tears wouldn't end until I was just a hollow shell of the former me.

"Please explain to them that I didn't steal that stuff or even know that it was stolen."

"I'm a cop, not a miracle worker. They've probably looked you up online. They saw the stories. Possible connection to an art theft, old woman's death, missing manuscripts, to name a few things."

I'd had some brushes with the law, but I'd never

been arrested. "But none of that is true," I wailed. "I helped solve those crimes. I didn't commit them."

Pellner patted my shoulder through the bars. "Fortunately, I called Vincenzo DiNapoli for you. He's on his way."

I clenched my jaw and nodded. "Thank you," I managed. I couldn't believe things were so bad I needed Vincenzo. He was a lawyer, sometimes for the Mob according to stories I'd heard. He'd gotten Mike "the Big Cheese" Titone off the hook, helped a friend of mine out, and had helped me out of a jam. I didn't like being in a position of needing an expensive lawyer. Who did?

"Officer Jones said they were tipped off. Do you know by who?" I asked.

"It was a neighbor. Apparently, whoever lives in the house you were set up at rents it out on SuiteSwapz. The neighbor knew they were out of town and realized the furniture out on the lawn was theirs."

I remembered the man on his porch across the street watching my arrest. I suspected he was the tipster when I'd first spotted him. Now I was certain it was him. I needed to talk to him and maybe his other neighbors.

"Uh-uh." Pellner shook his head. "Whatever it is you're thinking, don't do it."

"What?" I asked.

"That innocent act isn't going to work with me. Stay out of this and let the police handle it," Pellner said. He leaned in. "This time is different. You have charges against you."

"I know." It hammered through my soul with every heartbeat.

"Getting involved with these people wasn't smart, Sarah."

As if I didn't know that. "I've never had to do a background check on anyone."

"Maybe it's time to start," Pellner said.

"Why would the Greens do this? Why risk it? If they'd just stuck to selling the stuff from their storage shed, no one would have caught on."

"All my years in law enforcement and I still don't understand the criminal mind."

"They would only make a thousand dollars at most. On a good day. *If* they were very lucky." My mind spun in vicious circles. "The things they were selling weren't that valuable." I bit my lip. "They were willing for me to go to jail for a *felony* for them." Why me?

"I will vouch for you," Pellner said. "Not sure how much it will help."

"Do you know Jones?" I asked.

"Yes. Our sons are rivals on their respective football teams."

Of course they were. "What happens next?" I asked.

"Vincenzo will show up. He should be able to set up bail and get you out of here. They'll set up an arraignment. Normally, it would be tomorrow, but the judges are all in some statewide conference tomorrow, so it won't be until Monday."

"An arraignment?" Words I'd heard all my life suddenly sounded terrifying. "Then what?"

"That will be up to the DA." He winced right after the words came out.

Oh, no. The DA. I was dating Seth Anderson, the district attorney for Middlesex County.

"Seth is going to find out about this?" I hadn't even thought that far ahead yet. I'd been so freaked out up to this point. Bad to worse. Frying pan to fire. Pick your cliché. What would Seth think? Even worse— what would his mom think? Seth's mom would never accept me now.

"Are you, uh, seeing each other?" Pellner asked.

"Sort of. A dinner here or there." I downplayed our relationship for reasons I wasn't quite sure of. Maybe because it was humiliating to talk about Seth with Pellner because Pellner was a friend and former co-worker of my ex-husband's. My face heated as I tried to hold back the tears and emotions that wanted to explode out of me.

Pellner put his hands up in front of him. "Don't start crying. Please." There was an edge of desperation in Pellner's voice. "I'll go give Seth a call and explain the situation."

I nodded. "That's very thoughtful of you." Better for Seth to hear it from Pellner than one of his staff.

"Just hang in there. We'll get it straightened out."

Vincenzo DiNapoli showed up within thirty minutes. Vincenzo's charcoal gray suit hung perfectly on his tall frame. A purple tie popped against his white shirt. His dark black hair was streaked with just the right amount of gray. As he walked toward me, his gold pinky ring with a big ruby glinted in the light. My heart rate went down a notch just seeing him.

Soon after we were standing in front of the bail clerk. Officer Jones and Pellner were there, too.

"Gentlemen. Sarah," he said. Vincenzo sounded like he was here to pay a social call.

He shook hands with Officer Jones. "Dave, I heard your son is being scouted by some great colleges."

Vincenzo knew Officer Jones? That had to be good.

Jones smiled. "He is." He glanced at Pellner with a bit of a superior smirk on his face. "Everyone from Boston College to USC has been by."

The look or news didn't faze Pellner.

"He has a big decision ahead, then," Vincenzo said. They chatted about the pros and cons of various football teams for a few minutes while I stared in amazement. "I don't want to keep you, Dave." Vincenzo turned to the bail clerk. Somehow, I only had to pay a forty-dollar fee and was released on my own recognizance. But only after they set an arraignment date for Monday morning.

Seconds later I was sliding across the smooth leather of Vincenzo's Mercedes and greeting his driver. Vincenzo settled in once I was out of the way. The driver took off immediately.

"What happens next?" I asked Vincenzo.

"Jones is an overzealous idiot," Vincenzo said.

I was shocked. He seemed to like the guy while we were in the station. "So the charges will be dropped?"

"We have a good case, and your association with the district attorney won't hurt us any."

"But what if being associated with me hurts Seth?

He's running for reelection. It's a tight race with that older candidate who keeps mocking Seth's youth."

"Seth has proven himself in the past year." Vincenzo frowned.

"What? Why are you frowning?" I'd rarely seen Vincenzo frown.

"I don't want you to worry about it."

"How can I not? Just lay it out there for me," I said. I sounded way more confident than I felt on the inside. On the inside I wanted to make like an ostrich and bury my head in the sand.

"Okay." He glanced at me. "In Massachusetts, if the goods were stolen, which it sounds like they were, the prosecution doesn't have to establish the identity of who stole them originally. Just the fact you had them could be enough."

My lip started to quiver.

"But the definition of possession will work to our advantage. We will challenge the fact that you were the one in actual possession of the goods. The prosecution will have to prove that beyond a reasonable doubt. We need to find the Greens." He paused. "And by we, I don't mean you. I have an investigator who I'll have work the case."

"Is that it? Is that all they will need to do to convict me? Prove I was in possession of the items?" What if no one found the Greens?

"No. They also have to persuade the jury that you knew you were selling stolen goods. A person can't be convicted if she only acted foolishly. You believed the clients who hired you were honest people. I think we have a good case to prove that."

"Oh great, the world will know I acted foolishly."

Vincenzo gave me a sideways look. "Okay," I said, "it's better than being convicted."

He nodded.

"Is there anything that will help the prosecution's case?" I asked.

"Yes, unfortunately."

"Tell me. I'd rather know what we are up against. My imagination is way worse than the reality."

Vincenzo nodded. "The test of a defendant's guilt in a case like this is subjective. The prosecution can try to prove you knew you were selling stolen goods based on their price. For example, if you are selling a diamond ring way below its actual value, that could provide sufficient circumstantial evidence that you knew the item was stolen."

Oh boy. I slumped into the corner of the seat. If Vincenzo thought that, I was in bigger trouble than I thought. "But it's a freaking garage sale. Everything is sold below its normal value."

"And we will point that out. We have an excellent case. I don't like to lose, and I don't plan to start losing now. If the police contact you, get hold of me first."

I felt like we'd been down this road together before and not just the one to my house. His driver pulled up in front of my building.

"My car is still in Billerica where the garage sale was supposed to be." I'd been so relieved to get out of the police station, I'd completely forgotten.

"Give me your keys and I'll have someone drive it over to you within the hour."

I handed over my keys and got out of the car. "Thanks."

CHAPTER FIVE

As soon as I got home at noon, I tried calling the Greens. Still no answer. I grabbed my laptop and searched for any communications from the Greens. Surely, I must have some e-mails. Nope. Nothing. Texts? No. Now that I thought about it, all our conversations had been over the phone, so I had a record of our calls. I called. Again and again. No answer. I left messages even though by now I figured they wouldn't be calling me back.

Maybe the number was for a burner phone or a stolen one or they used caller ID spoofing. It was then it sank in how very clever they were and how much trouble I was in. While I wanted to give in to the nerves and go all hysterical wailing female, I didn't have that luxury. I had to find them before they left town and disappeared forever.

Next, I went through Tufts University's website searching for Alex Green. I even called the school after I couldn't find him on their website. They hadn't ever heard of him, which at this point wasn't too surprising. Did Kate have a job? I can't remember ever discussing that with them. I combed through a bunch of social media sites. Green was a common name, as were Kate and Alex. I spent over an hour sifting through profiles of people who were Greens, just not the ones I wanted. Why hadn't I looked them up online before I'd first met them? It was because they'd seemed so trustworthy. A lack of presence on social media would have been a warning, a big red flag telling me something was wrong. I ended up being friends with lots of my clients on various social media platforms. I berated myself again for being so lax.

I made a fluffernutter sandwich of white bread, peanut butter, and marshmallow fluff. It was my go-to meal because of my lousy cooking skills. Fluffernutters were a staple in New England homes and schools. It baffled me that it hadn't spread across the country. I made a pot of coffee to go with it.

After I ate I started searching virtual garage sale sites in the area. I went to mine first. Maybe that's how they'd first stumbled on to me. Wait, what *had* they said to me? I couldn't remember much more than they said I'd come highly recommended. Apparently, I'm such a sucker for flattery it had clouded my judgment. Then again, they had the fresh-faced, very friendly, Midwestern thing down to a T. They also had mentioned my website. I went to it. Sometimes people left comments, but as I suspected they hadn't left a trace of themselves there.

In a last desperate attempt, I searched my reviews on other websites. They were mostly good. I had high ratings. What would the Greens have said anyway?

"Completely naive."

"Excellent fall guy/gal."

"Sarah's great at selling stolen goods. Four stars. Highly recommended."

Ugh, that kind of thinking was getting me nowhere. I had a meeting this afternoon at four with a potential client and wanted to wash off the stink of the morning. After Vincenzo had my Suburban dropped off, I took a shower and lay down with cucumbers on my eyes to try to make some of the puffiness go away. After resting and with a lot of makeup, I didn't look too bad. At least I hoped I didn't. I'd been tempted to cancel the meeting and do some more wallowing, but I worried that I was going to need every last client I could scrounge up once word of my arrest got around.

On the way over to meet my client I decided to make a quick stop at the Dunkin' Donuts on Great Road, where I'd originally met the Greens. Normally, I drove through the drive-through. But I parked and went in. Part of me hoped they would be sitting in there with a simple explanation of what had happened. No such luck. I ordered a coffee from a young guy who worked lots of hours here and was often working the drive-through window.

I no longer had to ask him to leave room for cream, he just did it. "Anything else?" he asked.

He knew how much I like their donuts. "No food, but I do have a question. Have you ever seen this couple in here?" I handed him my phone. *Please, please, please say yes.*

"No." He handed the phone back to me.

"Thanks for looking."

"Yeah. The picture isn't the best. I'm not sure I'd recognize them even if they came in every day."

"He has a little comma-shaped birthmark on his right cheek," I said.

He handed me my coffee. "Sorry. That doesn't sound familiar."

I took my coffee and carried it to a table. One where I could watch the entrance and the drive-through. This wasn't a busy time of day. I could sit here for a few minutes before I had to head to my appointment. But of course the Greens didn't come in. After I finished my coffee, I went to the bathroom. Maybe the Greens had seen me come in and had hidden. That, too, was a dead end.

At four o'clock I stood on the doorstep of a cape-style house in Ellington for my meeting with a potential new client. I wore a black pencil skirt with a tailored white shirt, hoping I looked professional and not like someone who'd spent the morning in jail. The morning clouds had left, the sun warmed the air, and on any other day I'd be enjoying the changing leaves on the trees.

The door opened after I rang the bell. I smiled and worked hard not to stare.

"Hi." A blond woman who looked to be in her early forties answered the door. "I'm Kitty Thompson."

She had on a bright pink fifties-style poodle skirt, only instead of a poodle there was a silhouette of a Siamese cat. Her blouse was a lighter shade of pink and was embellished with black cats. Her glasses were a cat-eye style with rhinestones on the corners, and her fingers were bedecked with rings with cats on them. She had a white headband in her blond hair that looked like sequined cat ears. I maintained my pleasant smile while wondering if this was the proverbial crazy cat lady. If there was one thing I'd learned since I'd opened my business a year and a half ago, it was there were all kinds of quirky people in the world. And as long as they paid me, I could overlook that. I added a new caveat to the philosophy. And as long as they actually owned the goods they were selling.

I introduced myself.

"I've heard so much about you," Kitty said.

She was about to hear a whole lot more when the news of my arrest hit. I wondered if she'd still want to work with me then. Instead of stepping back to let me in, she stepped out on the small porch with me. Two planters that looked like cat heads were filled with bright yellow mums.

"Follow me. I want to show you my vision."

Oh boy, from past experience the clients I'd had with "visions" had been difficult to work with. So I was leery of clients with visions. Heck, I was just leery of clients right now. "Sure," I said. I'd been working on my poker face recently, so I hope I passed.

I followed her down the driveway to the curb, where we turned and looked at her house.

"What do you see when you look at my house?" she asked.

What the heck was the right answer here? "A charming, well-kept cape," I said. Kitty frowned. "In a lovely neighborhood with a mix of Victorian-, colonial-, and cape-style houses. It's a wonderful area of town," I added. And it was. It was within walking distance of some restaurants, Whole Foods, and Marshalls. It's probably better for my pocketbook that I had to drive to those places. Kitty was still frowning.

I squinted at the house, thought about Kitty and her apparent love for cats. Then it clicked. "The dormers kind of look like a cat's ears. The windows eyes. The door a mouth." That was a stretch, but I had a good imagination.

"Yes." Kitty bounced on her toes. "I'm going to sell some of my collection of cat things so I can make my house look even more like a cat."

CHAPTER SIX

What? A cat house? I worked hard not to let my jaw drop. I didn't think her neighbors would love that idea, but I'm not sure what they could do about it.

"I'm going to install a little round pink window above the door for the cat nose. And then I'm going to round the roof so it will look like the top of a cat's head. I'm working with a gardener who is helping me with some kind of viney plant to wrap around rods for the whiskers. Don't you just love it?"

"It's very inventive," I said. Her poor neighbors.

"If my backyard was bigger, I'd do some kind of addition in the shape of a cat's tail. But the yard is too small and the alley is in the way."

Kitty looked so sad I started to feel bad for her. "So what do you have to sell to fund this . . . project?" I asked. Whew, I almost said lunacy.

Kitty started bouncing again. "Come on in." I followed her up the sidewalk. "I can't wait for you to meet Duchess and Toulouse." I smiled politely. "Get it?" she asked. "Two of the cats in the Disney movie *The Aristocats*?"

"Of course," I said. I had some vague memory of watching it

"It's one of my favorite movies along with two oldies, *That Darn Cat!* and *Thomasina.*" Kitty opened the door and ushered me in.

We stood in a small foyer with a staircase in the middle and rooms to either side. The pink wallpaper was printed with sleek black cats with their tails curled up. The wall leading up the stairs had paintings of cats in matching brown frames. I climbed up the stairs to study them.

"Those are the fur babies I've owned over the years."

"Who is the artist?" I asked. "They're very good." Very lifelike. "I can almost hear them purring."

"I painted them. It's one of my hobbies."

"Is this what you do for a living?"

"Oh, no. I'm an accountant," Kitty said. "I work with numbers all day long."

"I think you could make a lot of money painting people's pets."

"Do you really?" Kitty started bouncing again.

I wanted to put my hands on her shoulders to stop her. "I do. Are you planning to sell these?"

"I couldn't. They are my heart."

I nodded. "Okay, so why don't you show me what you are thinking about selling." I trotted back down the stairs.

"You are going to have to help me. I don't want to part with anything. But between you and me, the place is getting a little crowded."

"I have to warn you I can be tough." I grinned to soften my words.

"That's just what I need."

Two cats pranced out just then, one orange and one gray. Kitty picked up the orange one. "This is Toulouse." She thrust him into my arms. I hadn't told her I was allergic yet. "And this sweet girl is Duchess."

Toulouse started purring, and I cuddled him close for a minute before setting him down and trying to subtly wipe my hands on my black pencil skirt. "They are adorable. You just have the two cats?"

"Yes. I'm not one of those crazy cat ladies." Her cat earrings swung as she said it. "Toulouse is the more social of the two. Duchess is leery of strangers and sticks close to me."

"Obviously," I said.

"Follow me," Kitty said. We walked through room after room decorated with cat items. Toulouse followed us, but Duchess had disappeared. There were throw pillows, curtains, rugs, clocks, lamps, dishes, glasses, placemats, refrigerator magnets—all decorated with cats. There was even a coat tree that looked like a cat. You could hang your coat on the whiskers, ears, and tail. And that was all on the first floor.

We headed up the stairs. Up here it was shower curtains, tub decals, soap dispensers, bedspreads, pillowcases, more throw pillows, paintings, lampshades, and even a cat night-light. In Kitty's office there were cat paper clips, curtains, and a desk chair upholstered in a pink fabric with white dancing kittens. Instead of spots in front of my eyes, I had cats in them. You name it and it came with cats on it. I felt like I'd fallen asleep and woke up in kitty city. More surprising is that Kitty made it work for the most part, and the place was pretty cute.

"Is that it?" I asked when we came down from the second floor.

"There's the basement," Kitty said.

Moments later we stood in a low-ceilinged unfinished room. The walls were cement block. It was dingy, musty, and I just wanted to get out of there. Boxes were stacked floor to ceiling and made it even creepier.

"How long since you've opened any of these boxes?" I asked.

"Awhile." Kitty looked reluctant.

"Define awhile," I said.

"At least a year. Maybe two."

"It's all filled with cat items?" I asked.

Kitty nodded.

"Then this can all go." I gestured with my hand.

Kitty gasped. "All of it?"

"Do you want to redo the outside of your house or not?" I asked. I headed back upstairs and blinked in the bright light of the kitchen. There was a whole wall of cat clocks. Most of them had eyes and tails that moved. Individually, I loved these kinds of clocks. But together they were a bit much—make that too much.

"You're right," Kitty said when she came upstairs. "The project is more important."

"Think of all the cat lovers you will make happy," I said as I walked to the front of the house.

Kitty grabbed my arm. "I hadn't thought of that."

She smiled. "I'll be helping other people, too. Thank you, Sarah. You have a great cattitude."

I laughed politely. "I'm going to need you to go through the upstairs of your house and put stickers on the things you absolutely can't part with. I'll come back tomorrow." If I wasn't in jail. "And help you make the tough decisions."

"Okay. Can you come up with a great name for the sale that will draw more people?" she asked.

I thought for a moment. "How about the Biggest, Most Cat-tastic Garage Sale Ever?"

Kitty started bouncing. "Yes. That's purrrrrr-fect."

I managed not to shake my head as I left. I just hoped this wasn't going to be a cat-astrophe.

I stopped stock-still when I got home. Seth sat on the top porch step of the house I rented an apartment in. It was almost five. Pellner must have followed through on his promise to call him. He was focused on his phone. A small frown formed as he stared down. He was still in a suit with the tie loosened, and his dark hair looked like he'd run a hand through it more than once. I hadn't expected to see him. I knew he had some fund-raiser for a senator tonight. Seth had asked me to go with him a few days ago, but I had said no for a couple of reasons. Earlier in the week I'd promised a friend that I'd meet her, and I still felt awkward at fancy social events with the rich and famous. Especially the ones his mom attended.

I hoped that it was a good sign he was here and that he wasn't waiting to tell me my bail was being revoked. Seth was the kind of man who would deliver bad news in person. Might as well get it over with instead of standing here. I took a couple of steps before Seth looked up. His happy look stopped me again. Sometimes being around Seth made it hard to breathe. He had thick, broad shoulders and intelligent brown eyes. Seth stood and trotted down the stairs. Two seconds later he hugged me to him. I wrapped my arms around his waist under his suit coat, inhaling his soapy, lovely scent.

"Are you okay?" Seth asked.

"As much as anyone can be after they've been accused of selling stolen goods and booked for a felony. It's probably not good for the DA to be seen with a common criminal."

"Screw that," Seth said. He tipped my chin up and studied me with his dark eyes before he kissed me. "You come first. I've been trying to tell you that for months. I hope someday you will believe me."

Being with Seth felt right and good. But doubts always swirled through my head. Was it too soon? Could anyone ever love me the way I wanted to be loved? If I couldn't make it work with CJ, could I make it work with anyone? While Seth's words made my heart beat faster, he had to be practical. "Face it. Your family wants your position as the DA to be a stepping-stone to a bigger political career. People have plans for you."

"You're my plan. None of the rest of it matters if you aren't there with me."

Seth had told me once last winter that he loved me. He *had* put me first during the last few months. Seth had let me guide how fast or slow our relationship went. And it had been slow. So hearing this, now, on such a rotten day, felt overwhelming. I leaned my head against his broad chest. "Thank you."

Seth tightened his grip on me. "Always."

CHAPTER SEVEN

Two hours later I sat at a high-top table at Gillganins, an Irish pub and restaurant close to one of the gates to Fitch Air Force Base. My friend Michelle Diaz sat across from me gripping the stem of her glass of cabernet so tightly I'm surprised it didn't snap. I took a sip of my Sam Adams lager, wondering why Michelle looked so stressed.

"Congratulations," I said loudly. The bar was noisy, lights were dim, booze flowed. It was filled with businesspeople and Air Force personnel. We were here to celebrate the fact that Michelle's name had been on the list of lieutenant colonels selected to be promoted to colonel. Once the list came out, it was forwarded to the Senate for approval. After that it was a waiting game for assignments and for the month that you'd actually pin on your new rank. But Michelle didn't seem like she was in the mood to celebrate.

"Are you okay?" I asked. We had met at Gillganins because her squadron had held a function here right after work. That and Gillganins was a fun place.

Michelle brushed her lush brown hair away from her face. It fell below her shoulders. During the day when she was in uniform, it was pinned up in a neat bun. Honestly, she had that whole "librarian by day, sexpot by night" look going on even though she was neither. Not that she tried to look that way. If anything she tried to downplay her beauty.

We'd met about ten years ago when my ex-husband and I'd been stationed at the same base as Michelle. She had traveled so much since she'd been assigned to Fitch that we hadn't seen much of each other. Plus until two months ago she'd been seeing another lieutenant colonel on base. After they broke up and her travel scheduled slowed, we'd gotten together a couple of times a week to go to a movie or lunch. We had taken up right where we'd left off ten years ago.

She scooted her barstool up closer to the table, glancing left and right before speaking. "Someone filed an IG complaint against me."

"What? Are you kidding me?" I asked. Michelle was a good officer with a good reputation. I was shocked.

"I wish," she said.

Complaints to the Inspector General were filed anonymously and they had to have something to do with fraud, waste, and abuse—or FWA, as it was called. That was bad enough, but even worse, it meant Michelle's name wouldn't be sent to the Senate and she couldn't be promoted until the allegations were cleared up. "I'm so sorry. That's just wrong."

Michelle drank some of her wine. "I think I need something stronger." She signaled a waitress and asked for two shots of tequila. When the waitress brought them, Michelle pushed one over to me. I hated doing shots but decided now wasn't the time to protest. So we clinked glasses and tossed them back.

The tequila burned down my throat and hit my almost empty stomach with a splat. But pretty soon its warmth spread through me. I realized that except for my few minutes with Seth, I'd felt numb all day since my arrest. I also knew alcohol was no way to solve a problem.

"You know how much I love being in the military," Michelle said. "I always tell my civilian counterparts that I've done more by ten a.m. than they'll do in a year."

"Maybe a lifetime," I said. It was true. Women in the military were afforded unique opportunities to have a lot of responsibility from a young age. And the good old boy barriers continued to come down, slowly, but steadily.

"I've traveled all over the world, interacted with people from other cultures that I never would have had the opportunity to meet otherwise. And now this."

"I'm sure it will be cleared up quickly," I said.

"Another?" Michelle asked, but she was signaling the waitress before I even had a chance to answer.

"Only if you give me your keys and we order some food. That last thing you need is more trouble." A DUI could tank a career in the military.

Michelle dug around in her purse and handed over her keys. I would have to order us a car from a ride-sharing app to get us home. She ordered two more shots. I ordered potato skins, mozzarella sticks, and wings for us to share. A nice healthy dinner. Plus two glasses of water.

I noticed a group of men at the bar watching us.

They weren't giving us come-hither looks. It was something creepier. Two of them leaned their backs against the bar and had their elbows resting on it. Three more stood on either side of them. They all held frothy mugs of beer. All had short haircuts, were clean-shaven, and wore Air Force uniforms.

"There are some guys over by the bar staring over here," I told Michelle.

She turned and looked their way. No subtle glance, but a steady stare until three of them turned their backs. One of the men leaning on the bar lifted his beer in her direction, but his expression was anything but pleasant.

"Who are they?" I asked.

"One is my boss."

"Which one is he?"

"The one who lifted his beer and has the lovely expression on his face. The butter bars work for me."

Butter bars are second lieutenants, so called because the pins indicating their rank are rectangles of gold that looked like two bars of butter. They now had their backs to us.

"The captain and major work for me, too. The major has his head so far up my colonel's rear end he can't see a thing. They are the assholes who filed the complaint."

I leaned back. Michelle rarely swore. "You know that for sure it's one of them?" I asked. "I thought IG complaints were anonymous."

"There's knowing and then there's knowing. I know."

"Do you have any idea why?"

"Some people resent women being in a position of power."

"And that's enough for someone to file a complaint?" I asked.

"It could be if it was worded correctly. They could say I hate men. And that I favored the women who worked for me."

"But you don't hate men." I'd seen Michelle interact with her troops before. She was firm, but fair. "You couldn't function in the Air Force if you did." There were approximately four men to every woman in the Air Force, and the odds were even more skewed in the other services. "Are you sure that's it?"

"No. They could say I was incompetent, wasting taxpayer money. The list is endless. And none of it's true."

The anger wafted off of Michelle like white-hot waves. It was catching and made me think of my arrest this morning. Those jerk fake hipsters had totally taken me in with their "We're from Indiana, oh shucks" routine. But I needed to shove all those feelings aside for the moment and try to help Michelle. The waitress brought our food, the water, and two more shots.

"Let's eat before we do the shots," I said. I was a lightweight when it came to tequila and didn't want to risk getting drunk when we were both on edge. I dug into the potato skins. Michelle grabbed a mozzarella stick. Not the best dinner in the world, but at least we'd have food in our stomachs. As Michelle was finishing the last wing, a male voice called out. "Suck it, baby."

We whipped our heads around. Her five co-workers

were still at the bar, but none were looking at us. In fact, it was conspicuous that they weren't since they had been all evening. The place was so crowded by now that it was impossible to know for sure who'd said it. It might have been her co-workers, but it just as easily could have been someone else. Michelle threw her napkin down and stood so quickly she knocked her stool over. I leaped up and blocked her in.

"You're not going over there." Michelle was bigger than me, stronger, too. I stood my ground, hoping I didn't have to wrestle her. It had been a few months since I'd had a self-defense lesson. When I'd taken them, I mostly ended up on my backside staring up at my trainer. I'm not sure how much they'd help me in this situation. "You don't know who said it or if it was even directed at you." I was convinced it was, but I wanted to defuse the situation.

"It was them. I recognized the major's voice. And it was directed at me."

Michelle snatched the barstool she'd knocked over and slammed it back into its original spot. I continued to stand near her. She sank onto her seat, fists clenched at her side. I was lucky she hadn't swung at me. I had no doubt if she had I'd be flat out on the floor.

"They aren't worth getting in trouble over." I jerked my head toward the men. "It's what they want you to do. They're deliberately provoking you. Why don't you tell me what's been going on?" When Michelle nodded, I scooted my barstool closer to hers and sat back down. Scooting closer served two purposes. I'd be able to hear her better and I could tackle her if I needed to. I hoped it wouldn't come to that. I rolled my shoulders to loosen up just in case.

Michelle tossed back the next tequila shot. I drank more water.

"The colonel's been setting me up to fail. He'll dump something on me last minute and then blame me in a meeting if whatever it was isn't finished. The major keeps not doing things I order him to do. And yes, it's come to ordering him instead of asking."

"That's awful."

"It is. I've always been good on teams and wanted to help my troops succeed. Up until a year ago my performance reports have always been impeccable."

"What happened a year ago?" I asked.

Michelle white-knuckled the edge of the table. "The colonel showed up. Everything was good at first. I thought we were working well together. We were until he shoved his hand down my uniform blouse and I tossed him across his office." She shook her head. "Some men think every single woman is dying to go to bed with him. Doesn't matter if he's married or not."

A lot of military women I knew had a harassment story to tell. They also had a lot of ways of dealing with it. Some decided they had to be just as tough as their male counterparts, some kept their heads down and tried to ignore the BS, and some took advantage of their feminine wiles. The last were in the minority, but they seemed to view the Air Force as one big smorgasbord of men.

"Did you report it?" I asked.

"No. I thought it would be okay."

"You should have."

"If I reported every man who'd touched me inappropriately or propositioned me, I'd do nothing but fill out reports. Sometimes I feel like I have an 'I'm easy' sign stamped on my forehead." She pointed at the tequila sitting in front of me. I pushed it over to her and watched her throw it back. She gave her shoulders a shake, then smiled.

"I didn't realize things were that bad," I said.

"It goes with the territory. Most of the time I just blow it off. I worry about the butter bars though. They're getting a terrible introduction to the Air Force and what being a good leader looks like. I've tried to help."

"So you don't know the specifics of the IG complaint? You were just speculating what it could be?"

"I don't. It's super-duper secret."

I worried about the depth of sarcasm in Michelle's voice. The resentment.

"I'm hoping they'll question one of my team who does stand by me," Michelle said. "If I hear what kind of questions they're asking it might give me a clue to what the complaint is about. That's the best way, the only way, to get any information."

"It sucks. Why don't you file a countercomplaint? This seems like it's gone too far."

She choked out a laugh. It wasn't a happy one. "I'd rather handle it myself. I'm a big girl and can take care of the likes of them." She swung her hair over her shoulder. "Let's forget about them and have fun."

CHAPTER EIGHT

I punched my alarm off and rolled out of bed at six Friday morning. My head ached from the beer and two shots of tequila I'd consumed last night. In the end I'd called my brother, Luke, instead of a car service. He had picked Michelle and me up and drove us home. We'd deposited Michelle at her house on base around one a.m. She'd flashed her ID to get us on. I even walked her to her room and tucked her in bed. At seven Luke was swinging by to pick me up and then Michelle to take us back to our cars—otherwise I'd still be snoozing. Then Luke was heading out of town for a day or two to cover some story for a local newspaper.

I moved about my small kitchen fixing coffee, which would have to do until I had time to get to Dunkin's. Their coffee was way better than mine even if I used their beans. My kitchen had just enough room for the usual appliances, a few cupboards, and a little table with two chairs. I drank a couple of sips of coffee as I stood by the table covered with a vintage tablecloth with pumpkins and leaves in oranges and yellows. But I decided to sit in the living room by the window that overlooked the town common.

I walked across the white-painted wide-planked wood floors of my living room. An old Oriental rug was soft under my feet. I skirted an old trunk I used as a coffee table. It sat in front of my garage-sale-find couch covered with white slipcovers my mom had made for me. The ceilings on one side of the room slanted down to a four-foot wall, adding to the charm of the room. My grandmother's rocking chair sat by a window that overlooked the town common with its towering white Congregational church. Since I was on the second floor, I had a spectacular view of the trees on the common that flamed bright reds, oranges, and yellows.

It was a good place to contemplate life. From the little pain in my stomach my subconscious must have been hard at the contemplating while I was sleeping last night. I had tried to block the anger and shock of my arrest yesterday by thinking about Michelle's problems and by drinking tequila, but another part of my brain had been obsessing about it. The part that made my head and stomach hurt. I drank some more coffee and rocked.

It was so great to have Luke living here in Ellington since we'd been apart for almost twenty years. He traveled a lot for his job as a reporter, but when he was home we saw each other as often as possible. I cringed thinking about him seeing me tipsy last night. I just shouldn't ever drink tequila. Michelle and I serenaded Luke all the way to her house. Then I'd told him how much I loved him and how happy I was that he lived here now. We'd been estranged for a long time until last spring. It was still hard for me to express my love for him, but apparently a couple of shots of tequila did the trick.

Pretty soon I managed to shove myself out of the rocker and went to get ready for the day. As I shampooed my hair in my big claw-foot tub, I decided after I retrieved my car I'd camp out at the Dunkin' Donuts on Great Road again for a bit and see if the Greens showed up. I went to Dunkin's almost every day anyway. It couldn't hurt. Then there was the neighbor who'd been standing on his porch and called the cops on me. Maybe he'd have some insight to share if the police hadn't told him not to talk to me. Pellner didn't want me talking to him, but Pellner didn't want me to talk to anyone. After a quick rinse, I got dressed in jeans and a T-shirt. Then I finished my morning routine by blow-drying my blond hair, which was down past my shoulders for the first time in a long time. A bit of eye shadow, some mascara, and a swipe of lipstick, and I was ready for whatever the day had in store for me. I just hoped it wasn't the police.

By eight thirty Luke, Michelle, and I were pulling into Gillganins' parking lot. All of us were armed with Dunkin's coffee and sharing a bag of donut holes. There were only two cars in the parking lot, my big white ten-year-old Suburban and Michelle's silver SUV. Luke parked equidistant between the two.

"Thanks for the ride," I said to Luke. "I'll miss you."

"No problem," he said. His tawny brown hair reached his collar. The lines around his blue-gray eyes made him look older than me even though he was a year younger. But he'd had some rough times in life after he gotten out of the Marines. Probably while he was in the Marines as well, not that he ever talked about it. Even though I was blond and blue-eyed, our faces were shaped the same and we made a lot of the same expressions.

"Thanks, Luke. It was nice to meet you and sorry about last night," Michelle said.

She'd been very sheepish when Luke and I arrived at her house. But considering everything, she looked pretty amazing in her BDU—battle dress uniform or what most civilians would call camouflage—and with her hair back in a bun. In fact, I think Luke had been flirting just a bit as he had glanced at her in the rearview mirror driving over here.

"No need to apologize. I'll miss you, too, Sarah."

"And you won't miss me?" Michelle teased.

Oh boy. This had to be the downside of having Luke around. He'd been popular in high school. The phone had always been ringing, girls dropping by. Some had even brought me gifts trying to butter me up. I hope we weren't going to relive that part of our lives.

"Of course I will." Luke winked at her.

Ugh, winking. I looked away. My eyes roaming the lot. What the heck? "Michelle, is someone in your car?"

Michelle turned away from Luke and we all got out of the car.

"Those jerks," Michelle said. "There have been plenty of practical jokes. I laughed at the whoopee cushion. The snake thing they rigged to spring out of my desk drawer. But a blowup doll? Breaking into my car? I've had it."

Luke and I followed her as she steamed across the lot. As we got near her car, I grabbed her arm.

"I don't think that's a blowup doll," I said. It looked like something far worse even through the dark tinted windows. The earlier gnawing in my stomach became an angry beast. Michelle snatched her arm out of my grasp. She stomped the last few feet and wrenched the door open.

Michelle screamed and jumped back. Luke and I rushed forward. The major from last night sat there. Dead. Very, very dead. He still wore his BDUs and there were marks around his neck like he'd been strangled. The major looked more like a mannequin than a person, and after an incident a couple of months ago, that didn't sit well with me. I backed away, bent over, and put my hands on my knees. Luke called 911. I was grateful that it wasn't me calling this time.

CHAPTER NINE

As much as I wanted to run as far away as possible from Michelle's car, I forced myself to walk around it, being careful not to touch or brush up against anything. Luke had taken Michelle over to his car, put her in the passenger seat, and blasted the heater. They were talking. It looked like Luke was holding her hand. I studied all the locks and didn't see any signs of scratches. None of the windows were broken. It didn't mean someone hadn't broken into the car, because tow truck drivers had those things, what did they call them—slim jims?—that allowed them to open the car without damaging the locks.

After my circuit around the car, I forced myself to stand near the dead major. I got close enough to get a good look but stood back far enough that none of my hair, which was whipping around in the wind, would land on him or the car. I confirmed my earlier impression that there was bruising around his neck. I didn't see any blood, and I was grateful his eyes were closed like he was just taking a quick nap.

I studied his hands. Lord help me, I couldn't believe I was standing here looking at a dead man's

hands for scratches. They looked sturdy with neatly
trimmed nails. There weren't any scratches on them,
and his uniform looked neat. It didn't look like he'd
been in a fight. There weren't any other bruises. It
seemed like he'd somehow willingly sat in Michelle's
car and that someone had surprised him from
behind. Sirens sounded in the distance.

I could be wrong. The police could probably figure
out a dozen different scenarios to fit this scene. Maybe
he'd been killed somewhere else and put here. But
why Michelle's car?

One hour later, Luke, Michelle, and I were still in
Gillganins' parking lot. Crime scene tape had been
strung around Michelle's car and strained against the
breeze to hold on. I felt the same way. Like forces
were pulling at me with unseen hands. The parking
lot was full of Ellington police cars, the medical ex-
aminers' vehicles, and military police. The OSI was
there, too. The Office of Special Investigations was
the Air Force's equivalent of the more famous Navy
NCIS. There would be a joint investigation since the
crime had occurred in Ellington and the victim was
a military officer. The Ellington police and the base
had memorandums of agreement, which meant they
cooperated when crimes crossed lines. So if a base
person committed a crime off base or if a civilian
committed a crime on base, both agencies would be
involved.

Michelle, Luke, and I had been separated right
after the first Ellington police officer had shown up.

I'd been trying to puzzle out how the major had ended up in Michelle's car. What the heck had happened after Luke and I had dropped Michelle off last night? I'd kept her keys after I tucked her in bed. I should have asked Michelle if she had a second set. She probably did. Didn't most people?

By now I'd already had to cancel an appointment with a client, had ignored a phone call from the Billerica police, and had tried to eavesdrop on conversations between the Ellington police and the OSI special agent who had shown up. I recognized him. Special Agent Frank Bristow. I'd met him when my ex-husband had been under a cloud, accused of murder. But even before that we'd known each other. Fitch was a small base, and we'd been seated beside each other at one of the many banquets that are part of military life.

He looked a little trimmer, a little grayer than the last time I'd seen him as he walked toward me. But no less rumpled. The collar on his shirt was frayed, and a small brown triangle left by an iron held too long in one spot marred a pocket. Grief had etched deep lines around his light brown eyes. His suit looked like he hadn't taken it to the cleaners in some time, or maybe he just dropped it on the floor when he got home.

While the base security forces were in charge of law enforcement and protecting the base, the OSI was in charge of serious offenses. They investigated terrorism, fraud, drug rings, as well as violent crimes and computer hacking. They wore suits instead of uniforms and were called special agents instead of by their military rank. Some were DoD employees instead of active duty. I knew that they worked closely with the base security forces.

"Mrs. Hooker, could we have a word?" Special Agent Bristow asked.

I could say no, but I was pretty sure we would have many words before the day was out. "It's Sarah. Winston." Right after CJ and I'd first split up, I'd never corrected anyone for calling me Mrs. Hooker. But I did now. That was the past. Winston was the present and the future.

"My apologies. I'd heard you and your husband were back together."

"No." He must not be plugged in to the rumor mill a small base could become. Or a big base for that matter. Secrets and base were as much an oxymoron as the overused military and intelligence jokes. "Things didn't work out."

"I'm sorry for that."

Special Agent Bristow's wife had died a couple of years ago. So he probably really meant what he said. He understood loss. Although loss by choice was different. If what had happened to me, to CJ and I, had been by choice.

"No worries. But I'm sure that's not what you want to talk to me about," I said.

"No. Of course not. It's this sad situation." He gestured toward Michelle's SUV. "How do you know Major Blade?"

"I don't know him. I didn't even know his name until just now."

Agent Bristow looked surprised.

"I know *of* him because I saw him here last night."

I explained how he'd been across the bar from Michelle and me but didn't add any context. "He was there with friends or maybe they were just colleagues." I thought about the taunting, the sneering, and how very angry Michelle had been. I didn't want to say any of that, and sparks of worry for Michelle, what the death of Major Blade meant for her, made me want to wring my hands. But I held them still. Okay, maybe they flinched a little and Agent Bristow noticed.

"But you recognized him this morning?"

"I did. He looked peaceful. How did he die? I saw the marks around his neck." When not wanting to throw a friend under the proverbial bus, try changing the subject. I hoped that Michelle wouldn't say anything without a lawyer. She could be in a lot of trouble. As soon as I could get free of Agent Bristow, I'd call Vincenzo myself.

Agent Bristow shook his head, which didn't surprise me. He wasn't one to share information, but I had to try.

"Was he married? Kids? Did he live on base?" I asked.

A shadow of a smile lifted the corners of Agent Bristow's face. "You should consider a career in law enforcement."

"No thanks. I'll stick with garage sales." I heard a car start up and saw Luke pulling away. My phone buzzed in my purse and I assumed it was him. I held my hand near my ear, thumb and pinky out, hoping he'd catch that I'd call him. Luke drove off slowly like he didn't want to leave but he'd been told to.

"Can I go?" I asked Agent Bristow.

"Not yet. You might as well get comfortable. It's

going to be a long day." Bristow gestured toward his car. "Let's talk in there."

I nodded. Gillganins was open because the crime scene was in the far corner of the parking lot. People had been walking by as they went in for breakfast with curious stares at the crime scene tape and all the vehicles. I'd be happy to be out of the limelight. Bristow held the door open for me, and I slid into the passenger seat. He noticed my shiver, so when he got in, he turned on his car and ran the heater. I settled into the corner, turning toward Bristow. The car was some kind of sedan, four doors, old upholstery now a dingy brown. But neat, no papers or coffee cups or evidence that it was driven often.

"So you didn't know Major Blade," Bristow said.

Since it was a statement I didn't answer.

"But you knew that Colonel Diaz did?"

Even though Michelle's rank was lieutenant colonel, when people spoke to or about a lieutenant colonel, they were called "colonel." "Yes." Maybe I should call Vincenzo for myself. But at least here, today, I didn't think I was in any trouble. I'd spent more time talking to the police the past two days than my friends.

Bristow remained calm. "Look, I've already talked to Colonel Diaz. I'm trying to confirm her story. Do you want to help her out or not?"

I hesitated. Over a year ago Bristow had worked on another case I'd become entangled in. He'd lied to me then, trying to get information. He could be doing that again. On the other hand, knowing Michelle, she'd have told him everything that happened last night already even if she shouldn't have. So I told him what I'd observed and put as much of the blame as possible on the group of officers who'd been taunting her.

"Did she mention that Major Blade was going to be frocked?" Blade asked.

"What?" In the Air Force that meant an officer could pin on the next higher rank before their official promotion date. It didn't happen very often. "So he's been selected to be a lieutenant colonel?"

"Yes."

Now it was Bristow's turn to give frustratingly short answers. "Why frock him?" If Bristow didn't answer, I would call one of my friends on base to try and find out. Someone would have heard something.

"He was going to take over for a colonel who deployed."

Oh, no. That was a big deal. In the military sometimes officers could do a job one rank above or below them. By being frocked it would give Blade the gravitas in meetings with people on either side of his rank. He would jump two ranks up the chain of command in power and prestige. "So he'd be over Michelle?"

"She wouldn't have directly reported to him, but yes."

Things were looking worse for Michelle instead of better.

"Who is taking the lead on this case? The Air Force or the locals?" It wouldn't exactly be the locals, because small departments in Massachusetts didn't have detectives who investigated homicides. The state troopers would be called in. I'm surprised they hadn't arrived yet.

"That's being discussed." Bristow waited. "You didn't answer my question."

"I didn't know he was being frocked or anything else about him until last night." I shrugged. "I think you should take a close look at the group he was with last night. They were all still at Gillganins when we left." I described them to him as best I could—two butter bars, a captain, and a colonel.

"Colonel Diaz was mad enough to try to storm over and you had to stop her?" Bristow asked.

Ugh, this all sounded so bad when it was repeated back to me. "I just tried to keep her from doing anything foolish."

"Like killing the major?"

"No. Don't twist my words. She might have thrown a drink in his face. One that he would have deserved, but she's not some raving lunatic. They kept baiting her. It was awful."

Bristow put his hands up. "I get that. The military can be pretty misogynistic, but there are lots of good decent men serving, too. I believe your ex-husband was one of them."

"I know that. What's going to happen to Michelle?"

"We'll follow the investigation through. She could be charged."

I opened my mouth to argue.

"We'll explore all evidence." Bristow looked around at the scene that continued to play out in front of us. Medical people moved around as did the police. Michelle stood with her arms wrapped around her waist. Her hair was coming out of her bun, and pieces draped onto her cheek. "It doesn't look good for her, though."

"I had her keys," I said.

"People usually have two sets."

I'd had that same thought earlier. The extra set of keys for my Suburban lived in a junk drawer in my kitchen. "She was in a good mood. I tucked her into bed myself." I wouldn't mention she had told me she loved me and that I was her best friend in the whole wide world. I doubted she remembered any of that this morning.

"She wasn't angry." Then it hit me. When Michelle had yanked open the door to her SUV the *bing, bing, bing* sounded that warns you your keys are still in the ignition. No matter. I still didn't believe she had gotten out of bed in the middle of the night and had come over here and killed Major Blade. She wouldn't have flirted with Luke on the way over here. Michelle's anger when she thought a blowup doll was in her car and surprise when she'd found Major Blade were real. I told Bristow just that.

He listened but didn't comment. I wanted to shake the man. To make him trust what I had told him was true.

"I need your contact information, and then you can go," Bristow said.

I recited it all and he typed it into his phone.

"She didn't kill Major Blade."

"Thanks for your help, Sarah. Don't talk about any of this to anyone." Bristow opened his car door, so I opened mine. The wind pushed back as I put my leg out. I caught the door just before it slammed onto it.

Some days everything was a struggle.

A shiny black sedan pulled into the parking lot and parked by the police tape. My blond hair blew in the wind, momentarily covering my eyes. I brushed it out of the way in time to see Seth and two of his assistants get out of the car. For a moment I was surprised, but then realized that of course, as DA, he would be at the scene of a murder. He took a moment, surveying the scene before he spotted me. I wanted to run over and throw myself in his arms, but of course I couldn't do that. He gazed at me for a moment until his assistant said something and a police officer held up the crime scene tape for him to duck under.

After watching Seth for a minute, I looked around for Michelle but didn't see her. I knew Michelle didn't kill Major Blade, but who did?

CHAPTER TEN

I turned onto my street at ten thirty. It's never a good thing to see a police car sitting in front of your house. It's even worse when you realize they are there for you. But I couldn't think of any other reason a Billerica police car would be parked at the curb. I'd been ignoring their calls all morning with good reason. I was already stressed after having found a body. Blade's murder, the implication that Michelle did it, and being grilled by the OSI had added a staggering stack of teetering trouble to my life this morning. I parked my Suburban and decided to ignore the car. Maybe there was some slight chance I was wrong.

I made it all the way to the second step of the porch before a car door slammed and a voice called out, "Sarah Winston."

I stopped and sighed, berating myself for not having tried to just drive on by when I had the chance. But being chased down the street and pulled over was even less appealing than this. I turned toward the voice. Officer Jones stood feet away from me. Glowering.

"What can I do for you?" I asked. I hoped I sounded helpful and cooperative instead of annoyed.

"Where did you keep the stolen goods before the garage sale?"

Since I stood on the porch and Officer Jones was a couple of steps down, we were almost eye to eye. I don't think he liked that. I'm pretty sure he used his size to intimidate people. Why wouldn't he?

"The Greens," I emphasized *Greens*, "rented a storage unit at that place on the west side of Billerica. But I told you that yesterday."

Jones folded his big, brawny arms over his chest and studied me. I kept eye contact with him as long as I could.

"What's this about?" I asked.

"Why was the storage unit you mentioned and the place you had the sale rented in your name?" Jones asked.

What? That wasn't possible. My whole body wavered for a second like it had been hit with the first jolt of an earthquake. I hoped Jones didn't notice. "It couldn't have been. You can check my credit history. If they rented these places, it wasn't with my credit cards. I would have known." I kept on top of what I placed on my cards and always paid it off at the end of the month. Had I checked my account in the past week or two? Maybe not. However, I certainly wasn't going to let Officer Jones know that.

"Like I said. There's no record of the Greens renting a unit out there. But there was one rented to a Sarah Winston."

I wanted to collapse on the steps but tried to hold myself steady. "That can't be." He must be lying. Trying to rattle me. It was working, all too well.

"It is." Officer Jones turned and went back to his car.

I waited until he started it and took off before I actually did collapse onto the top step. I knew people had devices that could steal your credit card information when you walked by them. It seemed like people like the Greens would certainly be the types to have such a thing. I quickly checked my credit card account using the app on my phone.

Oh, no. There were the two charges. I stared down at them for a few seconds, willing them to go away. But of course they didn't. I called my bank to report the two fraudulent charges.

"I don't know how this happened," I told the customer service representative.

"Between you and me, all those credit cards with the chips? They are incredibly easy to steal the information from. Someone has to have a radio frequency identification reader, what you might know as an RFID reader, and they can just suck out the information when you walk by if your cards aren't protected."

This wasn't what I wanted to hear. I'd heard about all of this before but didn't think it would ever happen to me. I gave the customer service representative all the information about the two charges, thanked him, and hung up. I don't know if the Greens had something that fancy. They could have just looked in my purse the first time we met when I'd gone to the bathroom. Hook. Line. Sinker. They had me at hello with their "we can watch your purse" routine.

I followed up my call to the bank with one to Vincenzo. I told him about Officer Jones's visit and the credit card charges. His voice calmed me a little as he assured me this was nothing to worry about. I wasn't sure I believed him, but sitting here worrying wouldn't resolve anything.

I went up to my apartment and made another pot of coffee before I called Luke. He'd left more than one message on my phone.

"Are you okay?" he asked.

"As okay as one can be after seeing a dead body. A victim of a crime," I added. "I thought you were leaving town."

"Not now. I rescheduled. Did you get a sense of how he died?" Luke asked.

I thought about what I'd seen in the car. About Bristow's warning not to talk about it. "Not really. Did you?"

Luke as a trained reporter might have seen something I didn't. That and his background as a Marine had given him excellent observational skills.

"I didn't get a very good look at the body, because I was worried about Michelle." He paused. "But my brief glimpse? He looked peaceful. Did you know him?"

I explained that I'd only seen him for the first time last night and that I didn't even know his name until this morning. "I wish I'd paid more attention last night to his interactions with other people in the bar. But I was trying to distract Michelle. Shift her focus from Blade and his obnoxious friends to having a bit of fun. I'm kicking myself now."

"Don't blame yourself. It's the last thing anyone expected."

"Anyone but his murderer," I said.

* * *

Fifteen minutes later I parked in front of the storage unit the Greens had used—my storage unit according to Officer Jones and my credit card. The lock dangled on the big garage-type metal door. When I got out and examined it, it looked like some-one had taken bolt cutters to it. Probably Officer Jones. I yanked the door up anyway. It rattled in the track like a skeleton in a scary movie. It didn't sur-prise me to find the unit empty. After all, the stuff had been moved to the garage sale site. I flipped on the light and walked in anyway, standing in the middle and turning full circle.

Alas, there were no scraps of paper, no messages scrawled on the wall, just a spot of old oil on the con-crete floor. It there had been anything, Officer Jones would have gotten to it before me anyway. I pulled the door closed, returned to my Suburban, and drove over to the rental office. A woman with springy gray hair sat behind the scratched counter watching a soap opera on a flat-screen TV that took up half the wall. The actors were almost life size.

She glanced back and forth between the TV and me. Clearly not delighted with my presence.

"I can wait until a commercial," I told her. I'd rather wait a few minutes and have her full attention than have her be impatient because of the interrup-tion. The place smelled of tuna fish and burned popcorn. There were lots of notices pinned to a cork bulletin board. I walked over to take a closer look. There were coupons for Tony's, a terrible Italian restaurant in Billerica that made truly awful lasagna, an ad for a cheap oil change, and calendars of community events that dated back five years. Nothing helpful here, either. The volume of the TV went down, so I headed back over to the counter.

"You need a storage unit?" the woman asked.

"No. I need information about the people who rented unit 1761." I figured being blunt would get to the point faster and the woman back to her soap opera.

She squinted at me. "You're Sarah Winston."

"Yes. How did you know?"

"Cops brought in a photo of you and asked me if I'd ever seen you before."

"What did you tell them?" I asked.

"That I hadn't."

That was good news. Maybe now Officer Jones would believe me.

"But that doesn't get you off the hook. I'm not here twenty-four/seven, and we have a system where you can fill out the information online and get a code for the gate." She looked at the TV. An ad for antacid was playing. I might need one.

"Is that what happened when 1761 was rented?"

"No, a guy came in and filled out the paperwork. Paid cash."

"Cash? There's a charge on my credit card for the unit."

"He paid cash for the first month and then added the credit card information later."

"How long did they have the unit?"

"Just a couple of months," she said, checking the TV again. Another commercial.

"Didn't you think it was odd that a man was named 'Sarah'?" I asked.

She shrugged. "I've heard a lot of odd names."

"What did he look like?"

She shrugged again. "Brown hair, beard, thinnish."

That pretty much described Alex Green. "What about security camera video?"

"It's on a forty-eight-hour loop. If nothing goes wrong, we don't save it." The soap came back on. She went over and turned the sound up. I headed for the door.

"You got a brother, honey?" the woman asked.

"Yes. Why?"

"The police asked me about that."

CHAPTER ELEVEN

That pretty much described my brother as well as Alex Green, I thought as I drove over to Kitty Thompson's house. If the police thought I was making the Greens up, my brother and I pretty much fit the bill, too. Great. Combine that with what Officer Jones had told me and things were looking worse. Although Alex had a birthmark and Luke didn't.

Seth called as I parked in front of Kitty's house at eleven forty-five.

"I'm sorry I couldn't talk to you at Gillganins this morning."

"I understand. I wanted to run over and throw myself at you."

"Hmm, I like the sound of that. Want to do that tonight?"

I smiled. "Your place or mine?"

"Yours?" Seth asked.

"Yes." At least this lousy day would have a happy ending.

"How are you?" Seth asked.

I loved that he didn't ask, *"Are you okay?"* That he

knew I couldn't be completely okay after what I'd seen this morning. I didn't know how he did his job. He dealt with bad people and crime scenes day in and out.

"I'm staying busy. It keeps my mind off things. In fact, I'm parked in front of a new client's house. I need to get going."

"Okay. See you tonight."

I forced myself to get out and knock on the door. At least talking to Seth had left a smile on my face.

Kitty answered the door. Today she wore a long-sleeve dress with a print of kittens playing with balls all over it. Somehow it worked for her. "Come in." Kitty bounced a bit as she said it. "Where do you want to start?"

I always tried to do the task I hated the most first when working. I probably needed to apply that philosophy to my personal life, too. "The basement."

"Okay. I took down a comfy chair and a table to make the place a little more bearable. There's also a space heater down there, too. But best of all, I talked to Toulouse, and he's promised to keep you company." Kitty beamed at me.

Oh boy. "That is very generous of Toulouse, but if he has other things to do . . ." I let the statement trail off because I was beginning to wonder if Kitty was sane and if I should be going down in her basement.

"He took a liking to you last time you were here. I don't think I could separate the two of you if I wanted to."

As we headed through the kitchen to the basement, I noted that there wasn't a lock on the door that would keep me down there. That made me feel a tiny bit better. Toulouse appeared and followed us down the stairs, where Kitty had placed a pink upholstered chair with a back that was shaped like a cat's head. It sat near a table that would be great for sorting and pricing. Kitty had also brought down a couple of bright standing lamps.

Kitty turned on the space heater, and in a few minutes it chased away some of the damp and musty smell. Toulouse curled up on a cushion shaped like a cat next to the chair.

"I'll be up working in my office if you need anything," Kitty said. "There's a kettle on the stove and a variety of tea bags if you want some."

My fears of being kidnapped faded. But as a precaution I would send a group text to my two closest friends, Stella and Carol, letting them know where I was.

"Great. I'll get started then."

Kitty climbed the stairs and she didn't close the door between the basement and the kitchen. Whew. I lifted the closest box off its stack and set it on the table. A little tingle of excitement went through me. The anticipation of the search never left me no matter how many sales I did. Although most yielded nothing too exciting, there was always hope. Going to garage sales was like finding a good partner. You had to kiss a lot of frogs before you found a treasure.

I opened the lid and started unwrapping cat figurines in every shape and color. Some looked like they might be from the sixties. None of them were signed, which would have added value. The sheer amount was almost overwhelming. I did some quick research on cat figurines. Most of these had been mass produced and wouldn't sell for more than a couple of dollars, if that. After I priced each one, I rewrapped them and put them back in the box. I put a big red X on the front of the box and moved it to the other side of the basement. I went up and made myself a cup of tea.

The kettle of course looked like a cat. The water poured out of its mouth and the handle was its tail. And while I'd rather have a cup of Dunkin's coffee, English breakfast tea would hold me over for now. I went back and opened another box. I unwrapped a tiny bronze cat that sat on a pedestal and another and another until there were a set of nine. Could these be Burmese opium weights? I wasn't sure, so I did a quick online search—they were.

If these were all original, they were probably worth more than the two other boxes I'd sorted through combined. The term "opium weights" was a bit of a misnomer. They had an actual practical use—to weigh things like vegetables or spices that were being sold at markets. And while they might have also been used in the opium trade, it wasn't their main purpose. I liked how the heaviness of them felt in my hand. They weren't intricately carved, but the whiskers stood out. Their faces looked a bit evil with their wide eyes and grins. I set them aside to do some more research before pricing them.

After an hour and a half my stomach growled, which startled Toulouse. "I'm sorry," I told him as I stood and stretched my arms above my head. I turned off the space heater and lights and climbed the stairs with Toulouse by my side.

Kitty stood in the kitchen with a large butcher knife in her hand. I stood stock-still.

"I'm making a salad," she said, pointing at a head of romaine with the knife. "Would you like to stay for lunch?"

Yeesh, my imagination was on overdrive. "No thanks. I have another appointment." I squatted down and patted Toulouse. "You were excellent company."

Kitty and Toulouse walked me to the door.

"I found a set of Burmese opium weights in one of your boxes. Do you think they are originals?" I asked Kitty.

"I had an aunt who was a world traveler and loved cats. I think they must be," Kitty said. "I remember the set you mentioned. I always thought the cats looked a bit wicked. I like happy cats."

Me too, I thought as I left. Me too.

At two I yanked open the door of DiNapoli's Roast Beef and Pizza, like I was ripping a stubborn bandage off a wound. I worried that if I avoided public places in Ellington it might make me look guilty. And starting here was safe because the owners, Angelo and Rosalie DiNapoli, were dear friends, almost family. They wouldn't let anyone give me any grief, especially not Angelo. His name meant messenger of God. And woe to you if you crossed him unjustly. Rosalie stood behind the counter taking orders. A menu board hung over her head. The open kitchen was behind her. Angelo had his back to the counter while he let a round of pizza dough fly up into the air before catching it and sending it back up.

DiNapoli's was divided into two sections. The left side was where you ordered, and beyond it the kitchen. The right side was a long, narrow space filled with unmatched tables and chairs, some of which I found for them at garage sales. A low wall separated the kitchen from the dining area.

When it was my turn to order Rosalie smiled. "Sarah, it's good to see you." Her dark brown eyes sparkled. Her brown hair curled around her ears, and her clothes were neat and practical.

It warmed my heart just to come in here.

"We have a special today." Rosalie said it loud enough so the whole place could hear her. "It's for people who have been falsely accused. A bowl of New England clam chowder and a half a sandwich for fifty percent off."

This was Rosalie's way of telling the locals she believed me. I'd only lived in Ellington a couple of years and was about as far from a local as possible. When things went wrong in this town, people assumed it was someone who was new to town who did it.

A man behind me piped up. "My ex-wife accused me of having an affair. Do I get the special?"

"I said falsely accused," Rosalie said. Everyone laughed and the man shrugged.

"Gotta try," he said.

"Maybe that's your problem," Rosalie answered. But her smile took the sting out of her words.

"I'll have the clam chowder and half a sandwich," I said.

"Try the pesto, fresh mozzarella, and tomato panini," Rosalie said. "Angelo used a new recipe for the clam chowder."

"It's *bellisimo*," Angelo called without turning around.

"I assume he didn't use tomatoes," I joked.

Rosalie made the sign of the cross, and Angelo whipped toward me still managing to catch the pizza dough. His hair was thinning, but he didn't try anything fancy to disguise the fact.

"I'm kidding. I know there's a law against putting tomatoes in New England clam chowder." The law was archaic but still on the books in Massachusetts.

"Tomatoes have no place in chowder." Angelo pronounced it *chowdah*. One of the reasons I loved Massachusetts was the charming accents. "It's one of the many things wrong with New York. Who puts tomatoes in chowder?" Out of the corner of my eye I saw people nodding in agreement.

"I'm a believer," I said. I wouldn't admit to anyone here that I liked the tomato-based Manhattan-style chowder, too.

"Go sit," Rosalie said. "I'll be over when things calm down. What do you want to drink?"

"Just water, please," I said. Rosalie filled a glass and handed it to me.

I sat at a table and thought about what a day it had been so far. The weight of Major Blade's death settled on me. Five minutes later a server brought me my food, a large plate with a bowl of clam chowder, the half sandwich, and a side of homemade potato chips. Steam rose off the chowder. It was thick with plump clams and potatoes and spiced with just the right amount of pepper. It didn't take long until I was scraping the last bits from the bottom of the bowl.

I cleansed my palate with some water and chips. They crunched nicely. Then I attacked my sandwich. By the time I finished eating, the line was gone and Rosalie came to sit across from me.

"Do you need something stronger than water?" she asked. They had gotten a license to serve wine and beer a few months ago. I kind of missed the days when they snuck wine to me in a kiddie cup with a lid and a bendy straw.

"No thanks. I have more work to do this afternoon." I left off that the work was trying to track down the Greens. "So what have the good folks of Ellington been saying about me?" Running a business in a small town depended on the goodwill of its inhabitants.

"They're backing you. Officer Jones is a known hothead. People aren't happy. A petition is circulating for you."

That warmed me way more than any glass of wine could. "Unknowingly I *was* in possession of stolen goods."

"They set you up." Angelo joined us at the table. He had a rolling pin in his hand and waved it around. "When I get my hands on them." He grasped the rolling pin more tightly.

"Angelo, you can't do anything to jeopardize your business. Where would I eat? Think how skinny I'd get."

"But—"

"You don't want me to eat at Tony's." Tony's was the Italian restaurant in Billerica that I'd seen the coupons for earlier. Angelo always went on about their fake cheese and poor-quality ingredients. I'd eaten there once and didn't plan on going back again, not that I'd be welcome after an incident when Angelo was in a lasagna bake-off up against Tony himself.

Angelo shrugged. "You're right. Have you talked to Mike 'the Big Cheese' Titone? Maybe he can help."

I shook my head no. Mike was connected to the Mob, and I wasn't ever sure if he was the good guy he proclaimed he was or a great liar. He had helped me once too often, and I didn't want to owe him any more favors than I already did. I'm pretty sure he had a running tally sheet in his head about who owed him what. "I'll figure it out."

"What about Seth?" Angelo asked. "He should be doing something."

"He had to recuse himself," I said.

"That's not right." Angelo shook the rolling pin.

"He's running for office. Dropping charges would put him in an awkward position," I said.

More customers came in, so Rosalie and Angelo stood.

"It's fine," I said. "We all know that I didn't do this. It will resolve itself soon enough." I hoped that was true. But I worried that Officer Jones wasn't even looking for the Greens. Why would he when he thought I was guilty?

CHAPTER TWELVE

A youngish man wearing a skinny-legged suit with a plaid shirt and red bow tie was adjusting a dull painting of rectangles on the wall of a rental office in the north part of Ellington when I walked in at three-fifteen. This was my third stop after I left DiNapoli's on my quest to find the apartment complex where the Greens had told me they lived.

"Hi, I'm looking for a new apartment."

The man smiled. "Then you've come to the right place. We have everything from studios to three-bedroom units. And we are pet-friendly. What did you have in mind?"

"My friends Kate and Alex Green loved their unit. Something like that would be perfect." I had no idea how big or small their place was. They'd told me it was small, but they'd told me a lot of things. Hopefully, they had some connection to this place because I was running out of options. There were only so many apartment complexes in Ellington. Although maybe they lied about that along with everything else. I'd tried the line twice to no avail.

"Oh, I love the Greens," the man said.

Finally. "Me too." Make that I'd love to get my hands on the Greens. "Do you have a unit near theirs?"

"Theirs is available," he said.

"They moved out?" My voice sounded shaky. I didn't want him to catch on that I was a fraud. "I mean they moved out already? I thought it was going to be a couple of more months."

"Their house was done sooner than they thought."

"That's fantastic for them."

"Would you like to look at their old unit? The light in it is wonderful."

"Yes, please."

"I'm just going to give you the key because I'm expecting someone else."

Darn. That must mean the place was completely empty or he wouldn't let me go up there alone. If some of their stuff was still there I might have had a chance to find a clue as to who they really were and where they'd gone. However, without him along it would be easier to snoop. He'd probably wonder why I was looking in the toilet tank. I took the key, found the apartment, and let myself in. Since it was a corner unit it did have nice light, but other than that it was a square beige box with no soul. Beige flooring, beige walls, beige appliances. It overlooked the parking lot and pool. Just in case, I did a quick search. Freezer empty. Refrigerator, a bottle of crusty-looking ketchup. I gave it a shake to make sure there wasn't anything hidden in the bit of ketchup left. There wasn't. Dishwasher, stove, and microwave clear. Although from the bits of dirt clinging to everything, I didn't think they'd be getting their deposit back.

I went through the kitchen cupboards. Under the

sink was a bottle of vodka with one swig left. It said something about how desperate I was feeling that I actually considered knocking it back. Wanting to day drink was never a good thing for me. The coat closet had a couple of wire hangers in it. I walked into the bedroom. It was obvious where all the furniture had been because of indentations in the carpet. Bed, nightstand, bureau, all frustratingly gone. I opened the closet and spotted a scrap of paper on the floor.

It was a small rectangle with numbers on it and a safety pin through it. I picked it up. It was probably from a dry cleaner, but which one? I stuffed it in my purse just in case I could think of some way to turn it into concrete information. And yes, I really did look in the toilet tank and felt behind it. The bathroom yielded nothing but some moldy grout in the shower and toothpaste stains in the sink.

I locked the apartment and knocked on the door of the apartment next to the Greens. No one answered. Back in the office I returned the key. A couple sat on chairs against one wall filling out an application.

"What did you think?" the man asked me.

"I'm just not sure," I said.

He gestured to the couple. "If you're not going to take it, they probably will. End units are at a premium."

The couple looked up at me hopefully. At least I was going to make someone's day. "I just can't commit today. But thank you for letting me look."

I called Michelle a little before four to check in and see how she was doing. We decided to meet at a Dunkin' Donuts in Lexington. Just far enough from

base that we might have some privacy and wouldn't
run in to anyone we knew. I walked in twenty minutes
later. The smell of coffee and sweet scent of donuts
always made me happy. Michelle was still in her uniform when I joined her with a large iced coffee, cream
and sugar required.

"How are you doing?" I asked as I slid into the
booth.

Fortunately, Dunkin's was quiet in the afternoon.
There was a man across the way working on a cross-
word puzzle. He didn't even look up when I came in.
Michelle's face was understandably pale. Lines
around her eyes showed her tension, as did the set of
her jaw. She stirred her coffee so hard some slopped
over the top.

"I haven't been arrested. Yet."

That made one of us. "Do you have friends who
are supporting you? Co-workers?" I asked.

"I went to the office after Bristow finally let me go.
It was obvious everyone knew. They divided themselves into two groups. One group stared at me like
I had two heads. The other made excuses to come
into my office like I was some kind of display at a
museum." Michelle fidgeted with a ring on her right
hand. "They asked the stupidest questions. Stuff they
already knew the answers to, trying to get me to talk
about what happened."

"I'm sorry."

Michelle lifted and dropped her shoulders. "Actually, there was another group. A few people were
concerned about me. Concerned about Blade."

"What's next?" I asked.

"I'll get through the weekend and go to work on

Monday. If I'm not in jail. But I'm pretty sure I'll be persona non grata there."

"That's not right."

"Probably not, but it's to be expected."

"I don't like to think of you being so alone. Do you want to stay with me for a while? I can sleep on my couch."

"Now if your brother Luke made that offer, I might take him up on it." Michelle managed a slight smile. Her smile broadened when I made a disgusted face.

"What about other friends?"

"There's a certain social isolation that comes with being a female in the military. Even more so as you move up in rank. I have a friend who served in the Navy. Back in the day she was the only female on a ship of twenty-five hundred."

"I have a few single friends who might trade places with her," I said.

"Some people considered her an intruder. She was a JAG investigating a drug ring. I know she was happy when she got back home."

"I'll bet." I didn't envy the job of judge advocate general.

"Although even that was a bit of a goat rope. Her brother had agreed to stay with her kids. But her ex-husband decided her place was better for throwing parties than his, so he kind of took over."

"Are you kidding me?" I asked.

"I wish I was. Some days I wonder why I chose this life."

"Because you are smart and capable. The military needs more people like you," I said. "But that still isn't helping you sort through all of this."

"There's a secret group on a social media site. Female officers from all the branches. We share everything from inspirational quotes to what men to never be alone with. We bitch about the military community, which isn't always welcoming to women to the point sometimes we're shunned. We complain about the unfairness of the weight standards. No one takes pregnancy into consideration. Even our uniforms are less forgiving than men's."

"It must be hard to retain women then," I said.

"They leave mid-career twice as often as men," Michelle said. "I've been doing a study. On my own time. Maybe that's another reason for the IG complaint. Sorry for the whining. I'm just feeling a little down about everything today."

"It's understandable. Did you talk to Vincenzo?" I asked. I'd referred so much business to him, I should be getting a finder's fee.

"Yes."

"And?"

"He said not to talk to anyone."

"That's excellent advice."

"But Sarah, you know I wouldn't kill Blade. I might have hated the guy, but I would have dealt with it more head-on."

It seemed to me murdering someone is about as head-on as you could get. "Did you leave your house last night? After I dropped you off?" I held up a hand. "Wait. Don't answer that. I could be forced to testify against you."

"There's nothing for you to testify about." She sipped her coffee. "Do you remember seeing a pair of my running shoes at the top of the steps when you took me home last night?"

"Which steps? The ones to your front door?"

"No, the ones inside. Near my bedroom."

"I don't think so. But I wasn't paying that close of attention."

"You would have seen them. I almost fell over them this morning when I went downstairs. At the time I figured you'd stuck them there for some reason."

"I didn't." I rethought last night. "I know they weren't there when I left."

"They were muddy and had bits of grass clinging to them. The mud was still soft like I'd been out for a run in them recently."

We stared at each other.

"What if I did do it?"

CHAPTER THIRTEEN

"You didn't do it." I wouldn't admit that her question scared me. "It's not how you handle things."

"I've had some pretty dark thoughts lately," Michelle said.

"Everyone has them. Dark thoughts are a lot different than taking action."

Michelle just stared down at the coffee cup she was squeezing. "It's not like I have anyone to provide me an alibi."

"What do you remember about last night?"

"Ugh, it's so embarrassing." Michelle stared down at the table. It looked like she wished she could disappear.

"Everyone does something stupid once in a while. Don't be too hard on yourself." I'd drunk-texted someone once right after CJ and I broke up the first time. Not my finest moment.

"I remember you tucking me into my bed. And you saying you'd put a glass of water by the bed in case I got thirsty. I chugged it this morning." Michelle paused.

"You were in no condition to go out running when I left you." Michelle was an avid runner. Under normal circumstances she could easily make it to Gillganins and back. She ran marathons for fun. "Have you ever drunk-run before? Or do you sleepwalk?"

"I was a sleepwalker when I was a kid, but that was years and years ago."

"What else do you remember?"

"Not much. This morning I found your note saying you and Luke would pick me up this morning."

"What time was that?"

"Around six. Have you ever thought about being an interrogator? You're good at it," Michelle said.

"Absolutely. I'm going to give up the fun of the garage sale business so I can spend my days scaring people." I took a sip of my iced coffee. "That means you would have had to go out between say one thirty and five if you were back in bed to wake up again at six." I thought for a moment. "Realistically the window is probably even smaller than that. What did you do next?"

"I went downstairs to make some coffee and almost tripped over the shoes. I came very close to tumbling down the stairs."

A chill that had nothing to do with my iced coffee rattled me. "What if someone wanted you to tumble down the stairs? Two birds with one pair of shoes."

"What are you talking about?"

"Someone kills the major, stuffs his body in your car, uses your shoes, and then plants them hoping you'd fall down the stairs. You'd could have been seriously injured or killed. Then everyone assumes it was you and the case is closed."

If possible, Michelle paled even more. Maybe I shouldn't have been so blunt.

"Who knew you were going to be at Gillganins last night?" I asked.

"It was a squadron party, so everyone in the squadron."

"How many people is that?"

"One hundred and twenty."

"That's a lot of suspects," I said.

"Plus their families and other squadrons were invited."

"Can you give me a list of all the people in your squadron?" I asked.

Michelle shook her head. "No. It wouldn't be ethical."

While her answer frustrated me, it's why I knew that Michelle didn't kill Blade. I hoped Bristow would see it that way, too.

I reached across the table and grabbed her hand. "You didn't do it. We'll find out who did."

I realized after I left Michelle that there must be security cameras around the base that may or may not have captured her leaving between the hours of one thirty and five a.m. So instead of going home I called James to see if he could meet me. James used to work for CJ when CJ was the commander of the base security police force. Thinking of CJ always left a little pang in my heart. I wondered if the pang would ever completely go away.

James had to sponsor me on base because I no longer had an ID that would get me on. But I still went through all of the rigmarole to get a pass, which included showing my driver's license and proof of insurance. We met in the parking lot behind the Shoppette on Fitch. The Shoppette was a combination 7-Eleven-type store and liquor store. In the military the liquor store was called the Class Six. I had no idea why.

Even when CJ had been the commander, I didn't know all of the security measures that safeguarded the base. I did know a few ways to sneak on, although not that any of them were foolproof. There was always a risk of being caught. I knew there were cameras around the buildings. At least one at the skate park because kids liked to hang out there. There had to be some around the perimeter, but I didn't know how many or where they were.

James pulled up in his personal truck instead of one of the base police cars and wasn't in uniform. He was a few years younger than I was and older than most of his peers because he'd enlisted later in life, not right out of high school. I hopped out of my Suburban and into his truck.

"Off duty?" I asked. James looked better every time I saw him, more relaxed and confident. He'd gone through a rough patch after a deployment, and at the time I'd been scared for him.

"For now. We're all working long hours because of Major Blade's death."

"Even though it happened off base?"

James nodded. "There's plenty of angles to follow up on."

That news gave me hope. "So Michelle—Colonel Diaz—isn't the only suspect?"

"That's not what I said."

I waited for a moment, but he didn't add anything.

"So can I watch the tapes from the gate last night?" I knew the gates had security cameras. They made no attempt to camouflage them. Logic told me that Michelle would have had to run out the Travis Gate because it was the closest to Gillganins. I couldn't imagine her trying to scale the perimeter fence with the razor wire on top of it when she was drunk.

"No. You can't see them. Everyone's all over it right now. And it's a murder investigation."

His tone said you should know better than to ask. I did, but I had to anyway. "Did you watch them?"

James nodded.

"And?" I asked.

"And nothing. I'm sorry but I can't tell you anything. And I don't want you to get in trouble."

"That's why you met me?"

"Yes."

I was disappointed, but understood. "I get that you can't let me watch them for myself, but what did you see?"

James looked out through the windshield for a moment. There was a good chance he wouldn't tell me so when he started talking it took me by surprise.

"A figure in a hoodie and sweats ran off base toward Gillganins at two thirty this morning. Someone about the size of Colonel Diaz. But it's not conclusive. It's not like there is a clear shot of the person's face."

I thought about the muddy shoes Michelle had found in her house. She'd have to tell someone about them. "Thanks, James. Does the medical examiner have a time of death?"

James nodded. "An approximate. A range anyway." With any luck it would be while I was still with

Michelle. Blade's body could have been moved or it could have been in the car. Luke had picked us up at the front of Gillganins. We hadn't been anyplace near her car. "Is it within the range of the person running off base?"

James nodded.

Darn it. So much for luck. "It seems like someone carefully planned Blade's murder."

"Why do you think that?" James asked.

"Because they left his body in Michelle's car. They must have been watching her for an opportunity. Then they broke into her house and took her keys. Lured Blade to the car. Pretended to be her running." I almost mentioned the shoes but managed to bite that statement back.

"Or Colonel Diaz did it and it was a crime of passion."

"She didn't," I said.

"Someone killed Major Blade," James said. "I don't think it was Colonel Diaz. If that's true it means a murderer is on the loose. Be careful."

As I drove off base toward Gillganins I glanced at my clock. It was five thirty, but it seemed more like midnight. I thought about the runner James had seen on the security footage. Part of this area was wooded. But there were a smattering of apartment and office buildings. I might as well stop and see if I could find anything out, if these places had cameras that might have caught a picture of the runner. Chances were the police had already been by, but maybe I'd get lucky.

At the first office building the stony-faced security guard wouldn't let me in or answer any questions. I made it into the second building and the security office, but the woman in charge escorted me right back out. I'm guessing someone was going to get a talking-to about letting me in, in the first place.

I drove across the street to an apartment complex. The management office didn't face the road. But there were security cameras on the street side of the building. A woman who looked to be in her fifties greeted me from behind a desk when I walked in. She had a streak of purple running through her long graying hair. A door was open to an office behind her. I explained what I wanted and why. As I talked she kept glancing behind her toward the open office.

She tilted her head to the office and I stopped. A twentysomething man hustled out of the office. He straightened his tie and looked down his nose at me. I wasn't sure if it was because he was quite tall or he just enjoyed looking down on people. In this moment I wished I was taller than average or at least had on heels instead of flats.

"The police have been here and instructed us not to share any information we may or may not have regarding this case." He looked at the woman I'd been speaking with. "You knew that and should have told her that immediately."

"But I wasn't sure what she wanted when she came in," the woman protested.

"It became very apparent after the first couple of sentences."

"But it isn't polite to cut someone off when they are speaking."

"We've had this discussion before," the man said. "You need to step it up if you want to succeed here."

Ugh, I hated bosses who reprimanded employees in front of other people. I'd like to tweak his nose and explain good management techniques.

I looked at the woman. "Thank you." *And good luck*, I thought, glancing back at her boss as I left. I was unlocking the door to my Suburban when the woman called out. "Wait."

CHAPTER FOURTEEN

"Excuse me," she said when she walked over to me. "Sorry about that."

"Not your fault."

"And I'm sorry about your friend."

"Thank you," I said.

"My boss is a jerk, but I live here. Working for him provides a salary and it reduces my rent."

This area was expensive. I'd been lucky to find my apartment and so understood the need to find a cheap place to live. I smiled at her. "Hey, we all do what we have to." I thought of my upcoming Cat-tastic Garage Sale.

"I'm Patty Sanchez." She held out her hand and we shook. "I can't show you the apartment complex security footage because the police took it. But I have my own security camera and it points toward the street."

I introduced myself. "You need to give that to the police, too." I hated saying that but felt obligated.

"I did. But it backs up to my computer, so I still

have a copy. If you can wait fifteen minutes, I'll get a break and I can show it to you."

"Thanks. Sounds good."

Fifteen minutes later Patty led me to her apartment. It was on the first floor of the four-story building, and there was a break in the trees that allowed her a glimpse of the road. It wasn't much but maybe it would provide some hint.

"Someone broke into my apartment a couple of months ago, so I got my own security camera. Plus one of those doorbells that have a motion detector so I can see who's at the door."

The apartment was small with few furnishings. There was a gas fireplace on one wall that probably made the place seem homier. We sat at the round dining room table. She powered up her computer, typed in a few things, and swiveled the laptop to me.

"Just hit play," she said. "The picture quality isn't great because it's dark out. And with the porch light on it's even worse."

At first there were just the trees and a view of the empty road. A couple of cars went by. Then a runner appeared. I hit pause. Like James said, the person had a build similar to Michelle's, but it was too blurry to tell who it was. I also couldn't see the shoes clearly, either.

"You can speed it forward now," the woman said.

I did and at the forty-five-minute mark the person ran back by, heading toward base.

"Is there any way to enhance this?" I asked.

The woman laughed. "I'm not the CIA, honey. But

I can send you the clip. Maybe you know someone that can help out."

Did I? It didn't seem like anyone I knew had that great of computer skills. "I'm not sure I know anyone, but please send it anyway."

The woman clicked a few more buttons and it swooshed away. She stood so I did, too.

"I have to get back to the office," she said.

"Thank you so much for your help." I dug around in my purse, found a business card, and handed it to her. "If you think of anything else, please let me know."

"And if you hear of any decent office jobs, let me know."

"I will."

Even though it had been a long day, I didn't want to go up to my empty apartment, so I walked over to my friend Carol Carson's shop, Paint and Wine. Although I usually called it Paint and Whine because I was over there to cry on her shoulder often enough. She had a class going on when I arrived, but from the progress of their paintings and the number of empty wine bottles, it looked like it was almost over.

They were painting what looked like the Old North Bridge in Concord. Some of the paintings were amazing and others looked like the owners had spent more time drinking than painting. That was the fun thing about these classes. There wasn't any pressure. Carol gave me the once-over as she walked toward me.

"Why don't you go in the back and pour yourself a glass of wine?" Carol asked. "I'll be done in a half hour or so." Carol was tall and even taller with her high-heeled boots on, slender, and her clothes never seemed to have a drop of paint on them. Even when she worked with little kids.

Carol's store was divided into thirds. The biggest space was the art studio where she taught groups of people to paint. It was full of tables, stools, and small easels. The back third was where Carol painted and stored supplies. I admired her current piece. An almost finished seascape with a Victorian house topped by a widow's walk. It might be a commissioned piece. She did those sometimes.

I rummaged through her wine and found an open bottle of Mélange from Paradise Springs, a winery in Virginia, according to the label on the bottle. After pouring myself a glass, I settled on a fainting couch and pulled up the news on my phone. There was no new news on the murder of Major Blade. Or if there was no one was sharing it. I refused to Google my own name. If there were stories about my arrest, I didn't want to read them when I was alone.

I sent the tape of the person running—I refused to believe it was Michelle—to Luke. Maybe one of his reporter friends would know someone who could work some magic on it and make a face appear. One that wasn't Michelle's. As I waited, I put together a plan for tomorrow morning. I was running a yard sale at ten. But it was all set up and ready to go except for pulling a couple of tables out of the garage and putting up a few signs. That would give me a couple of hours to go to garage sales on my own first.

People who threw garage sales usually enjoyed going to them, too. I still had the one slightly fuzzy picture of the Greens. Maybe if I showed the picture around, someone would recognize them. Maybe the garage sale I had run for the Greens wasn't the first time they'd sold stolen goods. It was a long shot, but my only other clue was the dry-cleaning ticket from their former apartment. And it wasn't much of a clue at all.

When Carol's class finished at seven, I helped her clean up. As we worked, she filled me in on her kids, twin boys and a daughter, and her husband, Brad, who worked at the Veterans Administration hospital nearby. I'd met Carol almost twenty years ago around the time I'd met CJ. Brad had been active duty, too, and we'd all been friends ever since. Four years ago both CJ and Brad were stationed here. Carol and Brad liked the area so much when he retired from the military they stayed here.

After all the supplies were put away and tables were free of paint, we went to her back room and poured more wine. Thankfully, I was walking instead of driving. Carol filled a plate with cheese and crackers.

"How are you?" Carol asked after I wolfed down a few crackers.

"Other than hungry?" I brushed some crumbs off my shirt into my hand and carried them over to the trash.

"Sit and tell me what's going on," Carol said.

I filled her in on finding Major Blade's body. "Did you know him?"

Carol took a big swallow of her wine. "He's a complete creep. We were at a dining out once and he hit on me. I've avoided him ever since."

A dining out was big formal dinner and dance. They were held a few times a year. The military members wore their mess dress, formal uniform, and the civilians wore gowns and tuxes. "I'm sorry. Does Brad know?"

Carol looked down for a moment. "I never told him. He would have killed him."

We both stared at each other.

"Maybe we have a motive. Major Blade may have messed with the wrong woman," I said. "Have you ever heard anything else about him?"

"No, but he was one of those guys every woman I know tried to avoid being alone with."

I'd have to go on base and see what else I could find out. I hadn't volunteered at the thrift shop for a while. It was actually a pretty good source of gossip now that I couldn't be a member of the Spouses' Club and didn't live on base. We sat quietly sipping our wine for a few minutes.

"With anyone else I'd think that was the only thing bothering them. But with you I get the feeling there's something else," Carol said.

I sat on my hands, which suddenly felt cold. "I was arrested."

"What?" Carol jumped up, came over to sit by me, and put her arms around me. "What happened?"

I sobbed it all out on her shoulder. Frankly, I'm not sure she caught what had happened because my voice was so shaky. I finally quieted. Then I used her bathroom to clean my face up.

"They let me out on my own recognizance," I said when I came back out.

"Seth must be all over this," Carol said.

"He can't be." I held up a hand when Carol started to protest. "He had to recuse himself. It only makes sense." Her reaction wasn't any better than Angelo's. I put my head in my hands for a minute. "This could mess up his chance of getting reelected."

"If that's all he cares about, he's not worth anything anyway."

"He came over as soon as he found out. And told me I was more important than the campaign when I was worrying about it in front of him." Carol had only met Seth a few times and didn't have a good feel for what he was like yet. Brad and CJ were good friends, and while I wished things were different for now, the four of us hanging out would be awkward. It was just too soon—for all of us.

"I'm glad to hear that. But I bet behind the scenes he's doing everything he can."

That made me feel a little bit better. I hoped Carol was right. "In the morning I'm going to hit some garage sales and see if anyone else has run into the Greens."

"You have a picture of them?"

I nodded.

"Let me see it."

I took out my phone and swiped through until I found the one picture I had of them. The photo I'd shown to Officer Jones. I took a minute to edit the photo, cropping around their faces as closely as possible. The photo was still pretty blurry. Darn it. I handed the phone to Carol. "Recognize them?"

She studied the photo. "Nothing. Sorry. It's not a great shot."

"Yeah. I don't usually have photos of my clients." I stood. "Thanks for listening."

"Why don't I go with you to the sales in the morning? The kids need new clothes. They always need new clothes."

"That would be great. I'll pick you up at six thirty," I said.

"Ugh. Okay. Six thirty it is."

CHAPTER FIFTEEN

I met Luke at eight for a late dinner at DiNapoli's. All that watching Angelo toss pizza dough around at lunch had given me a craving, so I'd convinced Luke to come here. A large white pizza with artichokes, kalamata olives, and red peppers sat between us along with a pitcher of Sam Adams beer. I lifted a piece to put on my plate. Steam puffed off it and strings of cheese tried to keep it attached to the mother ship. But I won in the end.

Luke took a piece. "I don't think the DiNapolis like me."

Inwardly, I smiled. They were so loyal to me. I tried to keep it hidden from Luke. "New Englanders are reserved. Suspicious of newcomers. Top that with what happened last spring and they are afraid you'll hurt me again." I sprinkled some hot peppers on my pizza. "You'll win them over. It just might take some time."

"You are lucky to have such loyal friends."

"I am. I'm also lucky you moved here. It's nice to have family close by." We'd grown up in Pacific Grove, California, the town next to Monterey. Our parents and the rest of our family still lived out there. We munched our pizza for a while.

"How's Michelle?" Luke asked.

I didn't know quite what to say. I didn't want to tell him about the muddy shoes or Michelle's own concerns about what happened last night. I guess it boiled down to I didn't quite trust when I was talking to my brother and when I was talking to a reporter.

"Reporter or brother?" I asked.

"Brother. Guy that got in the middle of a murder when helping out his sister and her friend."

"I'm sorry about that. I should have ordered a car."

"I'm teasing. I was glad to be there with you."

"Glad?"

"It gave me a chance to be the overprotective younger brother for once."

"In that case I'm glad you were there, too." I rubbed my temples.

"Any thoughts on who killed the guy?" Luke asked.

I filled him in on what Carol had just told me. "What about the men with him the night at the bar? Major Blade was with a colonel, a captain, and two butter bars. They all were drinking a lot. Maybe something happened after we left. I need to get their names from Michelle." Maybe I should go back to Gillganins and talk to the bartenders. They could have seen something.

"Is there any chance Michelle did it?" Luke asked.

"No. Why are you even asking that?" Luke didn't even know about the shoes or video of the Michelle-like person running by.

"Just playing devil's advocate."

"Don't. It makes you sound like a reporter not a

brother. The good news is she hasn't been arrested. Did you get the footage from the security camera I sent you?"

"I did. I gave it to a guy, who knows a guy who supposedly is going to take a look at it."

"Thank you. It means a lot that you would take the time to do this for me."

"Who said this was for you? Have you seen your friend Michelle?" Luke asked with a jaunty grin.

I made a face at him. One of the many of the repertoire of faces I'd used on him when we were growing up. This one, part disgust and part disapproval. "Leave her alone. She's vulnerable right now. Not to mention she'd probably eat you up and spit you out."

Luke grinned again.

"Stop it," I warned.

Luke nodded. "What about you? Any word on your situation?"

"Nothing. Yet," I said. My appetite went away, and I stared down at my piece of pizza.

Luke reached over and covered my hand for a moment. "I didn't mean to upset you. But I brought some research with me. Maybe between us we can figure something out."

"What kind of research?"

"I looked into things that had been stolen from SuiteSwapz. But let's eat this great pizza first." Luke glanced over to where Angelo was frowning at us from the kitchen. "He's going to think I'm being mean to you if you don't eat. Then I'll never get on his good side."

I laughed. "Okay. I want them to like you, too. CJ used to worry they were going to spit in his food."

Luke glanced at the pizza.

I laughed again. "Don't worry. It's safe. You're with me."

We ate as much as we could. When there were only two pieces left, Luke reached into his backpack and pulled out his laptop. I went around the table and sat beside him. After a few keystrokes he brought up a map of New England. It had little red dots in about fifteen different locations.

"This is all the SuiteSwapzs that have been robbed from the past two years."

"It's not that many. And they seemed to be scattered around randomly." I didn't add "so not very helpful."

"That's what I thought, too."

"But?" I asked.

"But nothing. I couldn't find any connection. Let me zoom the map out. This one is of the whole country, and I did it for the past ten years. I used a different-colored dot for each year. Then I broke down the total number of robberies per year at the bottom."

I studied the chart. "We have to assume that not all SuiteSwapz robberies were reported as that. So the numbers each year could be higher."

"I was thinking the same thing. Some of them could get recorded as just a plain old robbery that had nothing to do with being a SuiteSwapz," Luke said.

"Thanks for putting this together." I appreciated his effort but didn't see how it helped.

Luke zoomed back in to just the New England states. "Nothing strikes you?"

I studied the different locales. Some were touristy areas, but that figured because why else would there be SuiteSwapzs around? "Sorry. I appreciate you taking the time. Will you send it to me? Maybe something will come to me."

Luke looked disappointed. "I was hoping that it would be a clue for you."

"Do you know which ones were solved? That the robbers were caught?"

"Great question. I didn't think of that. I'll do some more research and then send you the updated map."

"Do you want to take the extra pizza home?" I asked.

Luke stood and rubbed his stomach. "Absolutely."

I took the leftover pizza over to the counter to be boxed up. I gave Luke a quick hug and then handed him the pizza. "Thanks," I said.

He nodded and waved at Rosalie and Angelo, who just gave him the stink eye. That was progress. At least they didn't turn their backs to him.

I settled on my couch. I loved my little space. Downstairs I could hear Stella singing something, but I couldn't make out the words. She used to travel Europe with an opera company and now taught voice at Berklee College of Music in Boston. I propped my feet up on my trunk and started searching for garage sales that started early or ran late tomorrow.

I mapped them out on my phone. I had a project I was working on for my mom. She had always raved about my aunt's Christmas wreath made with vintage ornaments. I'd started collecting them and planned to make Mom one for Christmas this year. Not obsessing about my problems was always a good thing.

The computer *bing*ed telling me an e-mail had arrived. It was from Luke with the map he'd created attached. Luke sent a note that he'd send an updated version once he had information about which robberies had been solved. Unfortunately, he thought it would take a couple of days to figure it all out.

There was a knock on my door. I set my computer aside and hurried down the hall to my door. I looked through the peephole. Seth stood there in a light blue V-neck sweater and jeans. My heart accelerated as I opened the door. I'd been so focused I'd forgotten he was coming over. I hoped I looked okay and that I didn't have pizza in my teeth.

I smoothed my hair. "I forgot you were coming."

"Do you want me to go?" he asked.

I pulled him in, slammed the door, and pushed him against it. We kissed. When I pulled back, Seth grinned.

"Does this mean you want me to stay?" he asked.

"Yes, please."

CHAPTER SIXTEEN

Carol and I pulled up to our third garage sale at 7:30 a.m. So far we hadn't had much luck, but that's how garage sales were. Some days you hit the jackpot and some days you went home empty-handed. I'd shown my fuzzy picture of the Greens at the first two, but no one had recognized them. We climbed out of my Suburban and went our separate ways. Carol headed over to tables full of children's clothes, toys, and sports equipment. I headed over to the furniture.

Seth had asked me to finish decorating his bedroom. I'd done most of his house soon after he'd moved in, but then things had gotten complicated between us and I'd never finished. There was an empty space off to one side of the converted attic. Since I'd first seen the space, I'd envisioned it with bookshelves filled with books and maybe some art, a couple of comfy chairs or a love seat, end tables, and lamps. But I'd yet to find anything that fit that picture or at a price I was willing to pay. It was kind of silly because I could take Seth to any antiques store, and he could buy whatever I chose. But the thrill of the hunt is what made it all so satisfying. It was so much fun spending someone else's money.

I found a slim end table that was about a foot and a half long and a half a foot wide. There was a partially raised Japanese scene on top complete with trees and tiny geisha girls. It wasn't something I'd normally be attracted to, but for some reason it intrigued me. It had one lower bottom shelf that was big enough to hold a plant or some books. I gave it a shake and the sniff test. It was sturdy and didn't smell. It was light enough that I could carry it with me as I continued to look. The table wasn't priced, which might work to my advantage.

I spotted two sets of glass-fronted barrister shelves. The real things, not reproductions. I hurried over and saw that they still had the paper label reading THE GLOBE-WERNICKE CO. LTD., an Ohio company that was probably the most famous for these kinds of shelves. The shelves came in stackable units with a glass front that lifted and slid back. And these looked like they were mahogany.

I couldn't believe they hadn't been snapped up already. I whipped my measuring tape out of my purse and did some quick measurements. Then I double-checked the notes section in my phone to make sure they'd work in Seth's bedroom. Since it was a converted attic, the ceilings sloped down to five-foot walls. But these would be a perfect fit. The table I'd found would work with them, too. I didn't think everything had to be a perfect match. In fact, I liked it better when things complemented each other.

"Excuse me," I called to a woman who looked like she was running the sale. I didn't dare leave the shelves unattended. More people had arrived, and a couple was steaming toward me. The shelves were pricey for something selling at a garage sale, which might be why they were still here. But even at three hundred dollars apiece they were a bargain.

"I'll take these." I pointed to the shelves. I didn't even try to negotiate a better price. I knew they were worth it, and besides the couple heading this way had determined looks on their faces. I didn't want to be mid-negotiation and have them swoop in with a better offer.

"Okay," the woman said. "I hate to part with them, but I'm downsizing."

"I know how hard that is." When CJ and I had first split up, I'd moved from a four-bedroom house on base to my one-bedroom apartment. It had been gut wrenching at the time. Everything had been. "If it makes you feel any better, they are going to a great home and will be well loved." Loving furniture sounded kind of crazy, but there was something special about a piece with some history to it.

"Thank you. That does help. They were my grandfather's. From his law practice. Can you believe my kids don't want anything to do with them? It made me sad."

"The friend I'm buying them for is a lawyer, too. And a very good one." I didn't want to mention Seth's name. She'd probably recognize it because he'd done a lot of good for the county this past year and had frequently been in the news. The other couple showed up. They were both nicely dressed. "We'd like those," the woman said, pointing at the shelves.

"I'm sorry, but you're too late. They just sold," the owner said.

The woman looked at the price. "We'll double what's she's paying."

Rats. That would tempt anyone.

The owner shook her head. "They're sold. You'll have to talk to her." She gestured to me.

The woman looked at me.

"Sorry. They aren't for sale," I said. The woman looked so crestfallen I almost caved. I could double my money right there, but that didn't seem fair to the owner. And they were perfect for Seth's room.

After the couple walked off, I gestured toward the table I'd found. "There's no price on this."

The woman turned the table over, but she didn't find a price, either. "I'll throw it in with the shelves since you didn't hassle me about the price."

"Thank you. You don't have any vintage Christmas ornaments by chance?" I said.

"Sorry. The few I have are going with me."

I stayed by the shelves until Carol was done shopping. She had an armful of clothes and a couple of movies.

"Look, I found an old version of *A Christmas Carol.* The kids are just the right age to love it this year."

Carol negotiated with the owner for the clothes and movies. I felt like a proud mom watching her. I'd taken her to her first garage sale about a year and a half ago. At the time she didn't want to ask anyone for a better price, but now she bargained like a pro. After Carol put her stuff in my Suburban, she helped me carry the shelves over and get them in the back.

"Did you ask the woman if she recognized the Greens?" Carol asked.

"I was so excited about the shelves and table I forgot. Hang on. I'll be right back."

I trotted across the lawn where the woman stood talking to someone. After they finished up, I showed her the picture. "Any chance you recognize either of these people? I know it's hard to see, but the man has a small birthmark like a comma on his right cheek."

She studied the picture. "I'm not sure. Why are you looking for them?"

Ah, the awkward question. "They stole something from me at a garage sale." It was true. They'd stolen my reputation.

"I think I saw them at the flea market in Ellington about a month ago."

A buzz slid through me. I tried to keep calm so I wouldn't scare the woman.

"They had a booth." She looked at the picture again. "But the picture is so fuzzy I can't be sure. Sorry."

"Thank you," I said. I dug one of my cards out of my purse. "If you ever see them again, will you please call me?"

The woman nodded and shoved my card in her pocket. My hand trembled by the time I got back to the car. I quickly told Carol what the woman had said. "If they had a booth, the flea market might have some record of them." I looked at the time. "But I can't go now. I need to drop you off and get to the garage sale I'm running. Thanks for coming with me."

"I hope that helps you track them down. Or better yet, tell the police or Seth. Let them do the tracking."

"Maybe I will."

"That's a no," Carol said.

I shrugged. "I'll let Vincenzo know so his investigator can look into it." I didn't add that I would also check it out myself.

After I dropped off Carol, I hastily put up signs for the garage sale I was running this morning. I got to the house around nine fifteen. The sale was uneventful, but we had a great turnout. It had run long because of a late influx of bargainers, so we'd stayed open far longer than we planned. It made my client happy and made more money for me, so I couldn't complain. As soon as it wrapped up, I drove over to the flea market on the west side of Ellington. It was closed by the time I arrived at five. Chains were draped across the entrance, so I couldn't get in to see if anyone was still around. Rats. I finally had a lead and couldn't do anything about it. Fortunately, the flea was open again tomorrow. I'd just have to come back in the morning.

Instead of heading home I drove over to Seth's house. I could drop off the bookcases. When he'd left last night, he said he'd be home in the late afternoon and it was already early evening, so he should be there. That put a smile back on my face.

CHAPTER SEVENTEEN

I spotted a sleek silver car in Seth's driveway and knew Nichole More was there. Ugh. I thought about driving on by. She was one of the few people in my life who intimidated me. Maybe it was because she'd known Seth all her life, and their mothers had planned for them to get married. My showing up had ruined that plan for all three of them. Seth had always assured me he wasn't interested in Nichole, but she was definitely interested in him. Maybe I was jealous because she was a rich successful defense lawyer and I wasn't. I parked across the street and gave myself another talking-to. I was smart and I ran my own business. I would never want to be Nichole. But I would love her car.

I knocked on the door. Seth had insisted on giving me a key, but up to this point I hadn't ever used it. And it would be a long time before I would. Nichole answered with a glass of some kind of sparkling wine in her hand. She was tall and slender—"willowy" came to mind. Her hair always seemed to shine, and she was a couple of inches taller than Seth. The kind of woman I had always seen him with in photos on the society pages of the newspaper.

She called over her shoulder. "Seth, we have company."

Oh, she was an expert at getting under my skin. *Don't let it show.* I smiled. "Hi, Nichole," I said, opening the door, which forced her to take a step back. She gestured for me to follow her.

Seth came down the hall, all handsome and manly. "Sarah."

There was no mistaking the joy in his voice or in his expression. Why did I let Nichole get to me?

"Would you like some prosecco? Or a glass of red wine?" he asked.

"Some prosecco would be great. Thanks."

He gave me a quick kiss on the cheek. "Go sit in the living room. We're celebrating."

I headed to the living room, wondering what they were celebrating. Since Nichole was a defense attorney and Seth a prosecuting attorney, it didn't seem likely that it was a case. They were always on opposite sides in a courtroom. Nichole draped herself on the couch, so I sat in the chair I'd found for Seth earlier in the year. I forced myself to relax back into the leather upholstery that I'd picked out when I'd had it reupholstered.

"What are you celebrating?" I asked.

Nichole actually blushed.

Seth returned with two glasses of prosecco. "She's engaged."

What? I took one of the glasses from Seth and lifted it. "Congratulations." I managed not to say, "wow, that was fast," because she'd been vigorously pursuing

Seth only a few months ago. I notice a flash of a ring on her hand. "Oh, can I see your ring?"

Nichole blushed again but held out her hand. What woman didn't want to show off her ring? It was a beautiful emerald surrounded by diamonds.

"It's lovely, Nichole. I wish you every happiness."

"Thank you. And to you, too." She looked back and forth between Seth and me.

That caused me to blush. We were early days still.

"Chip is a lucky guy," Seth said. "He's been in love with Nichole since the day she knocked him down on the playground in kindergarten."

Nichole blushed for a third time. "He took my ball." She looked at me. "I couldn't let him get away with that."

I laughed. "Good for you. It seems like that attitude has served you well."

Nichole smiled at me. A genuine smile. "It has. I almost always get what I want." She glanced at Seth, but he didn't even notice.

After we finished our prosecco and Nichole left, Seth dipped me into a big deep kiss.

"What are you doing here?" Seth asked when he'd straightened me back up. "It's an unexpected and very pleasant surprise. I've noticed you aren't one to just drop in."

He was right. Seth was a smart, handsome man. He'd been named Massachusetts's Most Eligible Bachelor three years in a row, the third time being only a few short weeks ago. The man had dated a string of model types before me. Not that I didn't think I was a catch, but it did bring out all my insecurities. I was just a regular woman, a little flabby in spots, loved to eat, self-conscious in swimwear, and always hoping I would lose five pounds. "I found some shelves for the sitting area of your master bedroom."

"It's going to have a sitting area?" he asked in mock surprise.

I slapped his arm. "You know it is. Help me carry them in. I'm so excited to see how they look."

Thirty minutes later I had them positioned just where I wanted them. I'd polished the wood to a soft glow and cleaned the old, wavy glass. I stepped back, right into Seth.

He put his arms around me. "You look sexy when you polish."

I leaned back against him, admiring my work. "You're a nut. They're perfect."

Seth kissed my neck. "You're perfect."

"Hardly."

"Perfect for me."

I sighed with happiness.

"Stay." He pulled me closer. "Please."

Seth made me feel like a teenager again, a mass of nerves with her crush. "Okay." It came out soft, low.

Seth scooped me up and tossed me on his bed.

I walked into the office at the flea market at ten on Sunday morning. An old coot smoked away under a NO SMOKING sign. He stubbed out his cigarette.

"Help ya?" His face had a stubble of gray hair. Bright blue eyes, alert eyes, belied my first impression of him.

"I'm looking for someone," I said.

"I hope it's me."

I laughed. "Sorry. It's a young couple who had a booth here around a month ago."

"I'm going to need more to go on than that," he said, scratching his jawline. "Probably had a hundred booths over the past month or so."

"That many?"

"Transient group, flea marketers. They take their things where they think they'll sell best. Or they pick their markets based on the day of the week."

That was disappointing. "Their last name is Green. Kate and Alex Green?" At least that's what they'd said their last name was. Although a search under those names had yielded nothing. The only good side of any of this was that I realized I needed to be more businesslike. My business had started as a whim. Something to keep me busy and a way to make money after my first split with CJ almost two years ago. Now it was a real business. A verbal agreement wasn't going to be good enough anymore. I was going to have to do a formal contract, check IDs, contact references if I had any suspicions. And from now on I was going to have a lot of suspicions.

He got up slowly like his knees were stiff and hobbled over to an ancient file cabinet. It was more dents and scratches than smooth metal. He fought to get a drawer open. It screeched and complained as he pulled it out. I wanted to do the same. After he rummaged around in the drawer, he turned toward me. "Nothing under Green. Sorry."

"Would you mind taking a look at a picture and see if you recognize them?"

"Don't mind at all."

I handed him my phone, cued to the picture.

"Alex has a small birthmark in the shape of a comma on his right cheek. It's hard to see in the photo."

He studied it for a couple of moments before shaking his head. "Sorry. They don't stand out." He handed the phone back to me.

I was lucky he'd done this much for me. "Is there anyone else that helps out in the office?"

"Just me."

I handed him my business card and turned toward the door.

"You might ask the vendors in the food court. They have as much or more contact than I do with the people who set up their booths here."

"Okay. Thanks for your time."

"I'm not usually so free with my information. But I'm a sucker for that lost puppy look you have."

Lost puppy? I was no lost puppy. But then again if it got someone to help me, I would use it to my advantage.

The hot dog and cotton candy people didn't recognize the name or the people in the photograph. I left my card with them anyway. I followed my nose to the popcorn lady. She had cynical eyes and hair that looked like a piece of just-popped popcorn. I stood to the side of the booth until there was no line. I ordered a medium bag of regular popcorn with plenty of salt and extra butter. Resisting popcorn was futile.

After money was exchanged for popcorn, I gave the lady my spiel—complete with what I hoped was a lost puppy dog look.

She laughed. "That look ain't going to work on

me, honey. But I'll look at your picture." I handed her my phone and mentioned the birthmark. "Oh yeah, I remember him."

Finally. Someone remembered them. "Do you know them?"

"All I know is their order. He was plain popcorn no salt, no butter. She was caramel corn."

Hmmm, maybe that's how I should remember my clients, by the stuff they had. One person could be old sheets, another lovely antiques. Or cats. "Have they been here recently?"

"Only remember seeing them the one time. I never forget the plain popcorn people. Can't trust them."

"Do you know their names?"

She pursed her lips and gazed up at the ceiling. "Maybe Young. Maybe not. Plain popcorn. That I won't forget."

CHAPTER EIGHTEEN

I gave her my card, thanked her, and hurried back down to the office with the new information. Like the last time, he got up slowly and wrestled with the drawer. The man flipped through files with excruciating care. I was about to start bouncing around like Kitty had the first day I had met her. *Breathe, this is probably another dead end.*

The man pulled a raggedy manila folder out of the file cabinet. He hobbled back to the desk, pulled out a pair of reading glasses, opened the folder, and perused it.

"May I see it?"

He shut the folder and looked at me over his readers. "Why do you want to find them so badly? Not for some nefarious purpose, I hope."

"No." I explained what had happened to me.

He scratched his jaw while I talked. "I can't have people selling stolen goods here. That would ruin my reputation."

I totally got that.

"Might shut me down even."

"I hear you," I said, nodding empathetically.

"But I can't let you see the folder. It's private." He set the folder on the desk. "I have to step away for a minute. Don't be here when I get back."

"Thank you," I said. The minute he was out of sight I snatched up the folder. It was a two-page contract. They'd signed it Jane and Neil Young. Yeesh. The address they gave him was the same one I'd tracked them down to at the apartment complex, so it was no help. *The phone number.* It was different from the one I had for them. The one they called me from. A new lead. I snapped a picture of it with my phone. I checked to make sure the number was clear in the photo. It was. I left the office and almost ran out of the flea market. With any luck this would somehow help me out of the mess I was in. I dialed the number as I hurried back to my car.

"Burke's Dry Cleaners. How can I help you?" The woman's voice sounded bored and not interested in helping me at all.

Dry cleaners? I'd found a tag from the dry cleaners in the Greens'/Youngs'/whoever's apartment. This didn't sound like Kate Green, but maybe they were related or maybe she worked there.

"May I speak to Jane Young?" I figured that name might be more real than Green. Surely, the flea market guy asked for some form of ID.

"No one here by that name."

"How about Kate Green?" Maybe she switched back and forth between the two names.

"No Kates. No Janes. No Greens. No Youngs. Do you need anything dry-cleaned?"

"Not today. Thanks." Darn. Another freaking dead end. I slumped into my car. Apparently, the flea market wasn't any more careful about checking up on people than I had been. I didn't think I was ever going to catch a break. Even though it wasn't much to go on, I called Vincenzo and relayed this latest information. I climbed in my car not ready to give up yet. Surely there was something else I could do.

The faint smell of sweet-and-sour chicken greeted me when I went in the back entrance of the thrift shop at eleven. Ten years ago this space had been a Chinese restaurant. How the smell clung after all these years was a mystery. I slipped one of the blue bib aprons over my head so people would know I was a volunteer. I went out to the front where the merchandise was out on display. My friend Eleanor was behind the cash register ringing up a line of people and smiling her bright smile. She had sponsored me on base. We'd known each other for a couple of years but didn't hang out all that often.

While the line was good for the thrift shop, it wasn't good for my chances of talking to Eleanor. One of the other volunteers signaled to me.

"Hey, can you help me shelve books? We got a huge donation of books."

"Oh, I'd love to," I said. Maybe I'd find something good to read that would distract me from my own drama.

First, we carted the boxes from the back to the front. Fortunately, there was plenty of shelving available. Then we started organizing the books. We separated the kids' mysteries from the adult ones, although I knew there were plenty of adult collectors who would want the Nancy Drew, Hardy Boys, and Trixie Belden books.

"Did you hear what Becky Cane and her cohorts did?" my volunteer partner asked.

"I—"

"They asked Erin Imhoff to run the charity auction."

"Oh. Erin is an excellent choice." Erin and I had lived near each other back when CJ was still active duty. She was a hard worker and a hoot.

"She was. Erin set everything up. She gathered all the donations, she organized the event space. Erin even bought all the decorations, did all the advertising, and sold all the tickets."

"That sounds like Erin," I said.

"Yeah. Then Becky and her clan invited her out to lunch. They told her they didn't need her anymore. They didn't give her any credit for all of her hard work."

"That's not good." Ugh. I hated this kind of drama that popped up in the Spouses' Club from time to time. The Spouses' Club was for people who were married to active-duty or retired military members. They sponsored all kinds of activities and outings, and held fund-raisers. The Spouses' Club did such good work ninety percent of the time by raising money for scholarships and other worthy causes. But it was this type of thing that made people not want to join.

"They asked Erin to tell people she stepped back."

"I'm guessing that didn't go over well," I said.

"Oh, no. I'm surprised Erin didn't take an ad out in the base paper. But she let everyone know."

"Good for her."

"Erin told them where to go."

That made me smile. Erin wasn't one to mince words.

"But nobody wants to stand up to Becky because of who her husband is."

Becky's husband was a colonel and second-in-command on the base. He had a bit of reputation of being a jerk. His position could make or break someone's career. Becky seemed to be very aware of that and, as far as I could tell, used it to her advantage.

I'd known Becky for almost fifteen years. We'd gotten off to a rocky start. A general's wife asked me to fill a position on the Spouses' Club board. It was a position usually filled by a colonel's spouse. At the time CJ had been a lowly captain.

After I said yes, the general's wife told me she'd call Becky and let her know. Becky had been the president of the club at the time. Later in the day Becky had called me. She'd said she had a great idea and suggested I take the board position the general's wife had already talked to me about. I was new enough to the military at the time that I just went along with Becky and I didn't let on that I knew it wasn't her idea.

After that initial incident we'd always gotten along, although I was always careful what I said around her. Becky, despite her flaws, was a hard worker and a go-getter. That had been one active Spouses' Club. She pulled off a great combination of fun activities and charitable events. It had been one of the best clubs I'd been associated with. Over the years I'd heard chat about Becky on and off. Since she'd always been friendly to me, I ignored it. But this troubled me. Maybe the power was going to Becky's head.

"Becky and Erin are friends of mine. I'd rather not

talk about this," I said. In reality, even though Becky had been stationed here for a couple of years, since my divorce we hadn't seen much of each other. I chalked it up to us both being busy, but maybe since I was no longer in a position to be helpful, she didn't want to waste her time. *Stop it.* That wasn't ever who she'd been to me. Except that first time.

The other woman shrugged but frowned at me. Whatever. We finished our work quickly. By that time I was starving. Fortunately, one of the workers had brought in a slow cooker full of chili. After I ate I spent the rest of the afternoon helping customers and dusting. That seemed like a never-ending task. When it was closing time, I asked Eleanor if she had time for coffee at the Dunkin' Donuts on base. We agreed to meet there in ten minutes.

Eleanor and I sat at a table in an open area between the BX or base exchange, a small version of a department store, and the commissary, the military version of a grocery store. There were some stalls along one wall where vendors sold local souvenirs, sweatshirts with military logos, and sports team clothing and hats. On the other side there was the Dunkin's, a Burger King, and a pizza place. A few people browsed around, but there weren't a lot of people around at four. We both had iced coffee.

"Did you know Major Blade?" I asked.

Eleanor crossed herself. Her light blond hair hung loose around her face. She had those apple cheeks that would make her look young forever. "I've met him, and my husband worked with him."

"What did you think? What's his reputation?"

Eleanor crumbled some of the donut in front of her. "I didn't care for him. My husband said he was a hard worker. A fast burner with a penchant for sucking up."

A fast burner was someone who got promoted below the zone, before the normal time for them to be promoted. Most of the time that happened when a superior saw something that separated a military member from their peers.

"What about your personal opinion?"

"I wouldn't turn my back to him without fear of being stabbed. He was skeevy."

"That's pretty much what I've heard," I said. "I can't believe I'm going to ask you this because I'm going to sound like dialogue from a bad movie. Can you think of anyone that had it in for him? Hated him?"

Eleanor drank some of her coffee. "Not beyond anything I've already said."

Maybe it was love gone wrong if it wasn't hate. "What about friends? Did he have a girlfriend?"

"I'm not sure who he hangs out with. I heard he had a girlfriend, but she doesn't live here. They met when he was stationed somewhere else."

"Do you know her name?" I asked.

"I don't, but I can try to find out."

"Thanks. I feel so bad for Michelle. She didn't kill him."

"How's Michelle doing?" Eleanor asked.

"Mad at the world. Did you know there was an IG complaint against her?"

Eleanor shook her head. "Good grief. She's as

straightforward as they come. I can't imagine her breaking a rule."

"Yeah, me neither." We chitchatted while we finished our coffee and then we walked out to our cars.

"Are you coming to the charity auction?" Eleanor asked.

"I wasn't planning to. I heard there was some drama."

"I like Becky," Eleanor said. "But sometimes she gets power hungry and doesn't think through her actions."

"Have you talked to Erin? Is she okay?"

Eleanor laughed. "Erin always comes out on top. The woman is fierce."

I smiled. "She is."

CHAPTER NINETEEN

I knocked on my landlady and friend Stella's door when I got home at five. I had spotted her boyfriend's car outside when I parked, and I wanted to talk to him. My apartment was right above hers, although hers was a little bigger than mine because hers had what they called a "bump out" in the back. It added an extra room.

Stella let me in. Her black-and-white tuxedo cat Tux ran over and rubbed around my ankles until I picked him up. "Who's the best-looking cat in Ellington?" I asked him. I'd gotten him a bow-tie collar to show off his Hollywood looks. "You should be on TV." I kissed the top of his head, set him back down, and said hello to Stella's boyfriend, Nathan Bossum. He was an Ellington police officer who I accidentally nicknamed Awesome last winter.

"Glass of wine?" Stella asked. She looked at me closely. "Shot of scotch? You may need that more."

"A glass of wine would be great," I said. I wasn't a fan of scotch.

"Coming up," said Awesome. He went into the kitchen. A cork popped.

Stella came over and gave me a hug. "Are you okay?"

"Do you realize how many times you've asked me that since I moved in here?" I'd found this place just over a year and a half ago. In an area that was full of expensive homes and apartments, it had been perfect. And meeting Stella had been icing on the proverbial cake.

Awesome came back with three glasses of wine, which he distributed. He sat on the couch. Stella snuggled against him and he put his arm around her. They were so cute together. I took the chair across from them.

"I guess you heard what happened to me?"

"I can't believe you were arrested." Stella waved her hands around. "What was that guy thinking? Who does he think he is?"

"It will be all right, Stella," I said. "Vincenzo has an investigator looking for the Greens." I hoped the investigator would have good news soon. Each day, each hour, that passed with no news upped my anxiety.

Awesome looked between us and wisely stayed silent. The man was learning.

"Awesome," I said, "I have the phone number that may be connected to the people who stuck me with the stolen goods."

Awesome set his wineglass down and removed his arm from around Stella's shoulders.

"How did you get the number?" he asked.

"It's the number they called me on all of the time." He didn't look amused. "I know you don't think I should be poking around, but I'm pretty sure that Officer Jones isn't motivated to find the Greens. He thinks I'm making them up." Awesome twirled a finger like I should go on. "Face it. I pretty much got caught red-handed with a bunch of stolen goods. What reason is there for him to believe me or look for anyone else?" I choked up a little when I said, *believe me.*

I took a sip of wine and realized how on edge I was. The running around the past couple of days and three restless nights were taking a toll. One that I couldn't afford. I needed to stay sharp, on top of things. "It's the phone number the Greens *used* to call me. Couldn't you just look into it? Track their calls?"

"Do the Billerica police have the number?" Awesome asked.

"Yes. Of course. I gave it to them the morning of my arrest. But like I said, I don't think they are that motivated to find anyone else. They have me."

"I'll see what I can do," Awesome finally said. "It's not my case or even the Ellington PD's case."

"Thanks," I said. I sent him a quick text with the number. "Stella, how is play practice going?" Stella had a part in *The Phantom of the Opera*, which was opening in Boston in a couple of weeks. It was her first big production since she'd sung opera in Europe awhile back.

"About the shot of scotch," she said.

I couldn't decide if she was joking or not.

"It's going well. Maybe too well," she said.

"Theater people are so superstitious," I said.

"We are. We're doing a full dress rehearsal next Friday. Hopefully, it will be a disaster."

I stood. "Break a leg. Thanks for the wine. I'm going to bed early tonight." I walked to the door with Tux trotting along beside me. I bent down and rubbed his ears. "And thanks, Awesome."

"Don't thank me yet," he said. "There might not be anything I can do."

"I get that, and I appreciate that you didn't just tell me no." It's what I'd expected.

Up in my apartment, I fixed and ate a salad. I slouched on my couch and flipped on the local news. Two seconds later I sat bolt upright and scrambled for the remote to turn the volume up. Seth's rival who was a fellow prosecutor was on. He was talking about me. I grabbed my phone and did a quick Internet search. My being arrested was big news, but more for the trouble it was going to cause Seth and his campaign than any real interest in the crime. No mention was made of the Greens.

Seth's campaign manager had released a brief statement explaining that Seth for obvious reasons had recused himself and that his rival should, too. Then he was put in the awkward position of defending me. The news switched to Seth, who stood charmingly in front of his office building. A reporter asked him if he'd stand by me.

"Of course. Sarah has obviously been set up. Her arrest was hasty."

He shouldn't have said that. What are you doing, Seth? I was equal parts warmed and chilled. His campaign staff and, good grief, even worse, his parents, must hate me for causing problems for Seth. I flipped off the TV. I was going to have to talk to Seth, make him understand that we shouldn't see each other for the sake of his campaign. I know he said he didn't care about it, but I did.

After sitting for a few minutes, I dialed his number.

"You saw the news, didn't you?" Seth asked.

"I did."

"I know what you are going to say, so just don't. Please."

"We don't see each other every day as it is." How could I explain the quagmire of emotions stirring in me? "You might not care, but I would feel terrible if this tanked your campaign. You're a good man. A good DA. People other than me need you, too."

"I don't want to abandon you when you need me."

"You aren't. Let's just take it a day at a time. Okay? Please?"

"A day at a time," he agreed.

I hoped that this way he could huddle with his staff and come up with a solution for dealing with the situation. I sent a text to Carol in case she'd seen the news, letting her know I was okay before I turned off my phone. I was determined to find the Greens, by whatever means necessary.

A knock sounded on my door. It was senseless to try and pretend I wasn't here since the lights were blazing. I hoped it was Stella and she was coming to check on me. I peeked out my peephole, then stood back. Apparently, *by whatever means necessary* had just arrived.

CHAPTER TWENTY

Mike "the Big Cheese" Titone was not a guy you wanted to owe a favor to. But I did. More than one. Mike had Mob connections, but he also had a good side. I was just never sure which Mike Titone would show up—the charmer or the snake. But tonight it didn't matter because if the devil himself had shown up and said he'd help, I would have said let's do this. I wasn't sure that Mike showing up was much better. Mike owned a legitimate, as far as I could tell, cheese shop in the North End of Boston.

I opened my door. "Come in."

He not only came in but walked past me into the living room like he owned the place. We sat on opposite ends of the couch. I wasn't getting much of a read from his icy blue eyes. Sometimes he scared me to death and other times he was Mr. Fix-it.

"You're in trouble and you've created trouble for Seth. I don't want that trouble to blow back on me," Mike said. He put his feet up on my trunk. "Seth needs to win this election for a number of reasons."

Ah, self-serving Mike was here. Mike and Seth had

an interesting relationship where Mike sometimes helped Seth out by providing information on crimes. That coming out would be very bad for a lot of people, especially Mike. I could whine and say it wasn't like I wanted to be arrested, but what good would that do? I thought about stalling him until I was more comfortable by offering something to drink. Best to get him out of here as quickly as possible, though.

"Why are you here?" I asked.

Mike tapped his fingers on the arm of the couch. "To find the people who set you up. So tell me about the Greens."

I spilled everything I could think of. Mike had fingers in a lot of wheels of cheese. His network knew a dark underbelly of the world I didn't. Maybe that world included the Greens.

I showed him the fuzzy picture on my phone. "This is the only photo I have of them." I showed him the blur on Alex's face that was the comma-shaped birthmark.

He frowned at it. "It's not much. But send it to me just in case."

"We need them alive so they will spill what they did. Cement boots in the river might be satisfying"— boy would it—"but it won't help Seth or me." I couldn't believe I actually had to say that to someone.

Mike gave a little shake of his head that seemed to indicate I was an idiot.

He stood. "No one does cement boots anymore. Such a cliché." Then he left.

What did they do instead?

* * *

Monday morning I sat in the courtroom waiting for my turn to be arraigned. It was just after eight. Vincenzo had somehow whisked me in a back entrance when we spotted the media gathered in the front.

Seth wasn't there for obvious reasons, but we had talked on the phone earlier. *Talked* was a stretch. Argued about how to proceed from here was more like it. Seth pushed for ignoring what was going on, but I couldn't for either of our sakes. Since I had court, we put off making any final decisions.

A bit of commotion broke out behind where Vincenzo and I were sitting. I turned around to see Seth's opponent stride in. His silver hair shined in the harsh lighting.

Vincenzo leaned over to me. "Ignore him. Turn back around."

I did as I was told. "Why's he here?"

"Only for political gain, trying to use the situation for votes."

"Is he going to be the prosecutor on my case?"

"I can't imagine anyone would allow that."

Great. I noticed the judge and the clerks, who'd looked a bit bored minutes ago, had perked up. A few minutes later my name was called. I went and stood in front of a microphone just as Vincenzo had instructed me. I listened to the clerk reading the charges against me. It didn't sound good, and my lip started to quiver. Vincenzo had told me to try and hold my emotions in check. I pressed my lips firmly together.

Our best outcome would be a dismissal, but that

didn't happen. The judge set a pretrial conference date for next week. Minutes later Vincenzo had whisked me out of the courtroom and back home.

"That was all routine," Vincenzo said. "We're fine."

"Did your investigator find anything out about the Greens?" I asked.

Small wrinkles formed around Vincenzo's mouth. Not a good sign.

"Not yet, although she said the information you've been providing has given her some leads."

"That's good." A little flutter of hope filled my chest. Or maybe it was gas or the onset of a heart attack.

"You have nothing to worry about. Even if we don't find the Greens, we have a good case."

Good didn't sound great to me.

"Just go about your routine. Don't talk to the press. Maybe you and Seth should go out to dinner someplace showy in Boston to prove to people you didn't do anything wrong."

"I'm not dragging Seth into this any more than he already has been. And that's not negotiable."

I didn't tell Vincenzo about my conversation with Mike last night. I didn't want him to say Mike needed to butt out. I needed all hands on deck, to use every resource possible. That might sound a little damsel-in-distress after trying to prove to myself that I was a strong, independent woman. But sometimes even the hero of a story needs a little help.

After the arraignment I changed clothes and headed straight over to Kitty's house. I'd told her that

I'd be there by ten and would only be a little bit late. There were a million things I'd rather be doing right now—tracking down the Greens, helping Michelle, taking a nap—especially taking a nap. However, it didn't take long to get into a rhythm of pricing and checking prices once I arrived. I set a few things aside to consult with an antiques dealer friend. Toulouse kept me company again. He alternated between purrs and gentle snores. It was soothing.

I unwrapped two ceramic and porcelain bowls. Both of them were shaped like cats' heads but hollowed out like a bowl. They were about four inches tall and it looked like a bit of wax was in the bottom of each, which puzzled me. They had whimsical faces that reminded me of the illustrations from a book my grandmother read to me when I was a kid. Those had been happy times, snuggled under her down comforter in a cast-iron bed with my grandmother beside me. It was our special girls' time as she called it.

I wanted to hug the bowls to me. After some quick research I realized they were fairy lamps. Very popular in the late 1800s, they were used as night-lights when a new smaller better burning candle was invented by Samuel Clarke. His lamps often had a fairy on the bottom and the term stuck. One was chipped, but even with the chips they were cute and would probably bring in around fifty dollars each.

Next, I pulled out a large quilt. "Look, Toulouse, it's a cat quilt." Toulouse lifted his head and seemed to peer at the quilt. It had a white background and backing. But the appliqués were little yellow cats sitting on what looked like pussy willow branches. Just looking at the cats made me happy. I almost laughed out loud when I realized Kitty and all of her things were converting me into more of a cat lover than I'd ever been.

The quilt was obviously hand-stitched. The batting was thin, but it was in good condition. It would make a great wall hanging or throw on a bed or couch. I guessed it was from the thirties considering the design and soft cotton material. I priced it at two hundred dollars but made a note to myself to do some more research.

The fairy lamps and quilt were the best two finds of the day. Everything else seemed to be fairly modern and mundane. I had doubts that Kitty was going to finance all she wanted done on the house with what I'd found so far. Then again, I had doubts about almost everything right now, including my ability to find the Greens and clear Michelle's name. The evidence was mounting against me. There were the charges on my credit card. The fact that Alex and Luke looked a bit alike. The way the Greens had covered their tracks so well.

I had to shake all those doubts off and try to find my normal positive attitude, if not about my personal problems then at least about this sale. Maybe the sheer volume of items, if it was a well-attended sale, would make up for the difference. I was going to have to be creative in how I marketed this sale so I could find cat lovers to attend.

When I was in the foyer by the front door, I hollered to Kitty that I was heading out.

She came to the top of the stairs. "How did it go?"

"You have so many cute things," I said as she trotted down the stairs.

"But nothing of great value?" She sounded so disappointed.

"I'm finding gems here and there." I told her excitedly about the quilt and fairy lamps.

"I've found most of it at garage sales and flea markets. So at least I won't lose money on them."

"That's excellent news." I paused. "Can I show you a picture of someone and see if you recognize them from any garage sales?" I took out my phone and found the picture of the Greens. "Here."

"Why are you looking for them?"

I figured I might as well tell her the whole story. I probably should have sooner. Frankly, I was surprised she hadn't heard the news. I filled her in on what happened. "If you don't want me to continue here, I understand."

Kitty looked at the floor for a minute and then over at Toulouse. "Toulouse is an excellent judge of character. If he's okay with you, then so am I."

Thank heavens for Toulouse. Kitty looked at the picture again. She enlarged it.

"I think that's the Youngs," she said.

My heart leaped. "You know them?"

"I met them at the flea market in Ellington. I bought a cute signed cat print from them." She looked at me in horror. "Do you think it's stolen?"

"It might be. I can have one of the Ellington police officers check."

Kitty ran up the stairs and returned with a cute print of three brightly painted cats. "Will you just take it with you? If it's not stolen, bring it back. But I don't want a tainted cat in my house. It will create negative energy."

"Sure," I said. "Do you know the Youngs from anywhere else? Or have any contact information for them?"

"I don't." Kitty paused. "They seemed so lovely. But selling stolen cat goods. What awful, awful people." Kitty picked up Toulouse and gave him a kiss. "I should have listened to him. I showed him the print and he just walked off with his tail in the air."

I thought about making a crack about cat burglars but didn't think Kitty would appreciate it. "Do you belong to any cat-related groups that I could send flyers to about your garage sale?"

"You mean my Cat-tastic Garage Sale? I do. Why don't I e-mail you a list?"

"Great." I hustled out with the weight of other things on my mind.

CHAPTER TWENTY-ONE

I swung by the police station to see Pellner. He was out on patrol, so I met him at a Dunkin's on Great Road just after one. I'd been spending a lot of time in Dunkin's lately. Pellner stood by his patrol car with a giant coffee cup in his hand.

"Rough night?" I asked.

"Picking up extra duties as much as possible. I keep thinking about the five kids I have to put through college."

Pellner's oldest daughter was in high school. Stella gave her private voice lessons. She'd sung the national anthem before a Celtics game last winter. His oldest son was in high school too.

"I heard about the arraignment," Pellner said. "How are you holding up?"

"Fine." I didn't want to elaborate nor did Pellner really want to hear about the emotional black hole in my soul that grew larger every day.

He studied me for a minute. He didn't need his cop sense to know my "fine" was a lie. "What's up?" Pellner asked.

I was grateful he chose to move on. "Did the phone number I gave Awesome yield any information?"

"He mentioned the phone number to me this morning." Pellner crossed his arms over his chest.

"Pellner, this isn't just about me anymore. It's about Seth. His opponent is trying to use the situation against him. Seth doesn't deserve that. He's a good DA. A better one than that guy would ever be."

Pellner nodded. "That's true. But we have to go through channels to get the information on someone's phone. Legal channels." He emphasized the word *legal*. "It takes time."

Of course it did. "I have some new information since I talked to him and a possible stolen print."

Pellner frowned, his dimples deep. "You have more stolen goods? With you? In your car?"

"Whoa. A client of mine gave it to me." I quickly told him how Kitty came to have the print. I got it out of the back of my Suburban and gave it to him.

"I'll see what I can find out," Pellner said. "But from now on you might want to call me or Awesome if you have something you think is stolen instead of hauling it around in your car. You are in enough trouble as it is."

I got a text from Michelle asking if I'd meet with a Chief Master Sergeant Rooney. He worked with Michelle, according to the text, and had spoken with the Inspector General team. I told her sure and arranged to meet him at DiNapoli's for a late lunch. My stomach was rumbling.

Fifteen minutes later, the chief and I both had

DiNapoli's famous roast beef sandwiches sitting in front of us. One sandwich was enough for three meals. Sometimes I wondered how the DiNapolis made any money with their generous portions, but the place was always packed.

"Michelle said you'd already been interviewed by the IG?" I asked. CJ had always said that the master sergeants were the ones who really ran the Air Force. And that if you needed something done, they could do it or figure out who could. This was just the kind of person who might know enough about Blade and his background to help Michelle's case.

The chief nodded as he chewed and swallowed. He took a big drink of his iced tea. "They did. Late yesterday afternoon." His light hair was in a military precision crew cut, which highlighted his broad face.

"Did their questions give you any indication of what the charges were in the complaint?"

"Damn—sorry ma'am—straight they did."

"It's Sarah, not ma'am." While CJ was active duty, I'd been nearly ma'am-ed to death. But there wasn't any need for it now. I watched the chief eat. He was broad shouldered and slim waisted. He must work out a ton the way he was powering down his sandwich. I tried to be patient, but my right leg started to jiggle.

After the chief swigged about half of his iced tea, he finally seemed ready to talk. I only picked at my sandwich.

"Their questions were bull sh—uh, bull. Sorry."

I waved my hand to indicate I didn't care.

"They asked me if I'd been treated fairly by Colonel Diaz. If she favored the women troops. If I'd seen anything 'untoward'—their words—between Colonel Diaz and Major Blade."

"So, in other words, someone did accuse her of sexual harassment." Up to this point it had been all speculation. I didn't add I thought it was Blade, because that seemed obvious and now he was dead. This wasn't good news. "Did you ever see any of that kind of behavior?"

"Only from Major Blade. He was a real pr—sorry, jerk."

"How so?" I asked.

"He'd talk about women sometimes while they were in earshot. Who looked hot. Who wanted him bad. It was ridiculous. Trust me, none of those women were interested. They kept their heads down and did their jobs."

"Do you think Blade is the one who filed the complaint?" I asked.

"Probably. But he poisoned a lot of the younger troops against Colonel Diaz."

"So maybe he convinced someone else to file the complaint?"

"Who knows? But Blade manipulating someone wouldn't be a big surprise. He had a certain charm about him." His face got pink. "Don't tell anyone I said that. They'll take away my man card."

I laughed and crossed my heart. But it was interesting that he'd called Blade charming. "Was there anything specific that happened that would make him file an IG complaint?"

"It didn't take long for Colonel Diaz to find out what Blade was saying about the women troops. She shut him down, publicly in front of the whole squadron.

Told him his behavior was unacceptable and made him apologize. To the group not just the individuals."

"When did all of this happen?" I asked.

"About six months ago. Blade went along with it. Gave the most insincere apology I'd ever heard. But I watched him when he sat back down. The man wasn't happy. He had it in for her."

"Did she know?"

"She's not stupid."

"Do you think Michelle could have killed him?" I wanted to make sure Rooney was as loyal as Michelle thought. That she had at least some people in her squadron who had her back.

"Was she capable? Yes. Would she do it? Maybe in self-defense, but otherwise she'd use the chain of command."

"Thanks for meeting with me."

"You're welcome, ma'am."

"Sarah."

He just grinned at me. I'd never be Sarah to him. But that wasn't my biggest worry. Michelle knew the chain of command, in this case the colonel above her, wasn't going to support her. If her commander didn't have her back, who would? Rooney wasn't convinced that Blade had filed the complaint. Maybe I needed to focus on the other men who were with Blade at the bar that night, too.

I pulled up in front of the ranch house where Luke lived at 2:30. It had green siding and a large picture window where the old woman he rented from often sat. Luke lived in the basement apartment. A large maple flamed orange in the front yard. The afternoon was warm. The blue sky dazzled. I could see the tall white spire of a church pointing upward in the distance. Its bells chimed on the hour. Fall in New England was hard to beat. I had brought the leftover roast beef sandwich with me. I waved toward the picture window as I walked to a side entrance and knocked. Luke yelled, "Come in."

I stepped into the small foyer. There was a plain white door to the left that led to the owner's apartment, but I trotted down the steps into Luke's living room. It was paneled in knotty pine wood, had old avocado shag carpeting and tiny windows that let little light in.

Luke came out of the kitchen. I held up a bag with the roast beef sandwich from DiNapoli's.

"Hey, Luke, do you want—" I stopped abruptly when Michelle walked out of Luke's bedroom, buttoning up the jacket of her uniform.

CHAPTER TWENTY-TWO

Oh boy. I remembered what Michelle said about not minding sleeping on Luke's couch if he offered it. But from the looks on their rosy faces, I was pretty sure that wasn't where she was sleeping. I couldn't have popped over at a worse time. "You two aren't seeing each other, are you?" I asked.

Luke looked to Michelle. *Always the gentleman.*

"Sort of," Michelle said, smiling over at Luke.

"This is a terrible idea," I said. "He's a reporter. You're a suspect. He"—I jabbed a finger at Luke—"thinks you're a source." Under different circumstances I might not feel this way. I wouldn't feel this way. Under different circumstances I'd be happy for them.

I flung myself down on a low-slung couch with a nubby fabric. It looked like it had been here as long as the house had, which was probably sometime in the fifties. I set the bag with the sandwich on the floor along with my purse.

Luke walked over and stood by Michelle. "She's not a source."

"Then what do you two talk about?" I asked.

They grinned at each other.

"We haven't done all that much talking," Michelle said.

"Oh, ick." I grabbed a throw pillow, one I'd bought at a garage sale to try to cheer Luke's apartment up, and held it over my face. Why had I come by now? This was not something you wanted to hear about your younger brother.

Luke pried the throw pillow out of my hands and swatted my arm with it. "Grow up," he said.

"I have to get back to work," Michelle said. She picked up her purse and the hat for her uniform off a scratched-up old end table. "I'll call you when I'm done. See you later, Sarah."

I waved my hand.

"I'll walk you to the door," Luke said to Michelle.

He hummed as he trotted back down the stairs. *Hummed.* Luke wasn't a hummer. At least he hadn't been growing up. It's not that I didn't want him to be happy or Michelle for that matter. It just seemed like their timing was lousy.

"Luke, Michelle is a murder suspect. Bristow thinks she had an accomplice. Who better than an overprotective boyfriend to kill Blade? This seems dangerous for both of you."

Luke sat by me and picked up my hand, holding it between his. "No one knows."

"I know. Your nosy landlady probably knows. How did this happen?"

"I called her after you and I had dinner at DiNapoli's. She was lonely. I'm lonely. I invited her over for a beer, and we hit it off."

"You're lonely?" I had no idea. Maybe I hadn't been spending enough time with him.

"It's been a long time since I'd stayed in one place long enough to even have a relationship. One that lasted longer than a week or two." He let go of my hand.

After Luke had finished his enlistment with the Marines, he'd had a tough time. Done things he shouldn't have. Ones that he regretted and made amends for. We were still getting to know each other again. From the time I'd married CJ and moved away from Pacific Grove twenty years ago to last spring, Luke and I had only talked on the phone twice. They hadn't been pleasant conversations. There were still remnants of the hurt he'd caused our family with his disappearing act that lingered even though I had tried to wish them away.

"Besides I didn't meet her until—"

I cut Luke off. "The night Blade died. That makes it look even worse. Or the police will think you're lying about that, too." It sickened me to think of all the ways this could cause trouble for the two of them.

"It's going to be okay," Luke said.

It was obvious I wasn't going to talk any sense into him. I'd have to try Michelle. "Just proceed with caution. Please," I said.

"Does that mean we have your blessing?" Luke asked with a grin.

I whacked him with the throw pillow.

"I'll take that as a yes. Now what are you doing here anyway?"

"I came to see if you had any updates on the

SuiteSwapz burglaries." I'd been so surprised to see Michelle I almost forgot why I was here.

"Let me get my laptop. Do you want anything to drink?" Luke asked.

"Just some water. I'll get it."

"Grab me one, too."

A few moments later we settled back on the couch.

"What's in the bag?" Luke asked.

"Are you hungry? I have a roast beef sandwich from DiNapoli's."

"Of course I'm hungry."

I laughed. When Luke was in high school, he could have a snack, eat a meal, and have another snack. I'd envied it back then and I still did now. I went to his even-smaller-than-mine kitchen and put half of the sandwich on a plate and the quarter I hadn't eaten on another one. I'd brought a bag of chips, took it to the living room, and set it all between us. "I need to find you a coffee table."

"That would be great," Luke said. Then he dug into his sandwich.

In between bites he fiddled with his laptop. "I had better luck than I thought I would separating the solved cases from the ones that weren't," Luke said.

"My smart little brother."

"Naw, another reporter I know had been tracking SuiteSwapz robberies and had already done a boat-load of research."

"Smart enough to find out someone had already done the work." I patted his knee. Luke fired up his laptop and brought up a map of the United States. "Take a look at this and tell me what you see."

Luke turned the computer to me. I studied the map while we ate. "The red dots are unsolved?"

Luke nodded. "And if you click on the red dot, you'll see the year the burglary occurred."

I clicked away for a few minutes. "Holy crap."

"You saw what I did?" Luke asked, leaning forward.

"The biggest clusters are around towns with Air Force bases, not vacation spots like I thought the first time I looked at this. And they happened in clumps of consecutive years. So the same person could be stationed at different bases over the span of their career."

"Exactly what I thought."

"So the Greens or Youngs or whoever they actually are might be stationed at Fitch." I couldn't believe it. "Someone else must know."

"Not if the Greens are as clever as they seem to be. They've been doing this for almost ten years."

"I need to tell Pellner about this," I said. "Will you forward that to me?"

"I kind of hate helping the police," Luke said.

"Oh, stop being a reporter for just a few minutes. Why can't you all just get along?" I shook my head. "Besides, you'll be helping me."

"In that case, here you go."

My phone *bing*ed with the arrival of the file.

We finished our sandwiches in silence. Luke cleaned up.

"I hate to make you leave, but I have to get going. Let me know if you need anything."

What I needed was answers.

* * *

When I got home, I sent Pellner the map Luke had forwarded to me with a brief explanation of what was going on and our thought process. Then I sent a similar message to Special Agent Bristow. Normally, the OSI wouldn't deal with a simple burglary, but this looked like a multistate event. Maybe carried out by one person or persons who'd moved multiple times. However, I'd also realized it could be a group of people doing the same thing across the country. I also mentioned to Bristow that he might try to see if the Greens/Youngs were in the military. I wished I had a better picture of them to send him.

I needed to go to Gillganins but didn't think driving over there and trying to give someone the third degree would work. I had to assume the police had questioned them and told them not to talk to anyone. I'd have to be wilier than that. I checked their events calendar and grimaced. Then I shot off a text to Stella asking her if she wanted to go to karaoke tonight. She'd probably be suspicious because she knew that karaoke wasn't my favorite thing.

Seconds later the phone rang. Stella.

"Why do you want to go to karaoke?" Stella asked.

"To sing?"

Stella snorted. "Yeah, right. Does this have something to do with the dead guy in your friend's car or your arrest?"

Darn it all. "Hey, I realize that Awesome probably warned you off this, but I need to talk to the bartenders. I figured a few drinks and some good tips might soften them up. But I totally get that you don't want to go."

"Who said I didn't want to go? Of course I'm in. I just wanted advance warning of what I was getting myself into." I heard something thud in the background. "I've got to run," Stella said. "I think some of the backdrops for *Phantom* set just fell over. That's great."

"It's great that the backdrop fell over? Or great that you're going to see me?"

"Both. But if the backdrop fell over things are starting to go wrong. Which is good. See you tonight."

She hung up before I had a chance to say anything. I smiled at the phone. It had been a lucky day when I found this apartment and Stella. My phone rang again. I didn't recognize the number but answered anyway.

"Sarah, this is Becky Cane. Do you have a minute?"

Becky's voice was brisk as always. "Sure. What's up?" Becky and I didn't talk that often. In fact it had been several months. Becky sniffed and then cleared her throat.

"You always seem so sensible, and I need your advice."

I couldn't have been more surprised. "Okay." I drew the word *okay* out so long I almost sounded Southern. And I definitely sounded hesitant.

"People are spreading terrible rumors about me. They are saying that I let Erin Imhoff do all of the work on the charity auction, kicked her off the committee, and then took credit for everything. It's just not true."

I didn't want to get in the middle of this. "I'm sorry to hear that." I also didn't want her to know I'd already heard the story.

"What happened is Erin said she'd take charge and then she completely dropped the ball. I knew she had some family issues, but if she'd just come to me we would have worked around it. Instead she did nothing and I had to scramble like I've never scrambled before to save the event."

"That's not good." I hoped that was neutral enough.

"I kept her name in the program as a committee member. Made sure she knew she was still welcome. But she somehow blamed me."

I couldn't decide if this was a load of bologna or if she was telling the truth. That just didn't sound like Erin unless she'd become completely depressed. I didn't want what I'd heard at the thrift shop to color my opinion too much. "I'm so sorry to hear this." And I was in more ways than Becky could possibly know.

"What do you think I should do?" Becky asked.

"Stand up for yourself." If Becky was telling the truth, it was good advice. And if not?

It couldn't hurt to air things out.

"It's just that everyone loves Erin so much. She's sweet and warm." Becky's voice cracked. It sounded like she was ready to cry. "I realize I come off as aloof. But it's born of shyness that I've tried to overcome. I'd rather stay home and read than go to all the functions I have to. I do my best."

Wow, that was a shocker to me. Maybe I'd rushed to judgment with Becky, too. It was true that a lot was expected of a military spouse, especially when their partner was in a leadership position. "Maybe you should let people see that vulnerable side of you once in a while. And maybe you should try to talk to Erin."

"Do you think I should?" Becky asked.

I wasn't sure which suggestion she was responding to. Maybe both. "Yes. It wouldn't hurt." While I had her on the phone I wanted to ask her what she'd heard about Major Blade.

"Thank you, Sarah," Becky said. "How have you been? I know you've had a lot to deal with this past couple of years."

Way more than I was willing to share. "I'm doing good. Thanks." I paused. "Did you know Major Blade?" I might as well just say it.

"I knew of him. But of course since his murder, everyone knows who he was."

"I've heard widely varying things about him." Not quite true, but maybe that would make Becky speak more freely.

"Like I said, I didn't know him well. But you know who did? Erin Imhoff and her husband. I wouldn't say this to anyone but you, but there were some stories going around about the three of them."

I wasn't sure I believed her, but I shrugged it off because I wanted to hear what she might reveal. "What kind of stories?"

"Sexual improprieties."

Whoa. That wasn't what I was expecting to hear, and I had a hard time believing it.

"Really?"

"Yes. But I think it's nonsense. They were all good friends. That's all it was. People just like to blow things out of proportion around here when they're bored."

"That's certainly true."

"Thanks for listening to me. I have to run. Another committee meeting to attend."

It was nice of Becky to defend Erin after all that had gone on between them. But part of me wondered about Becky's sincerity. Maybe I needed to arrange to talk to Erin. Since she knew Major Blade, and I hoped not in the biblical sense, maybe Erin would know something that would help Michelle.

CHAPTER TWENTY-THREE

I checked in on my online garage sale business. Things had been running smoothly. But I'd had a worrisome thought. What if someone was using my site to move stolen goods? If they'd set me up in person, why not online, where anonymity was even easier? People had to know someone to join the group, but some people were careless in their recommendations. I had another administrator, and we usually were good at spotting fake accounts. It wouldn't hurt to do a run-through now, though.

An hour later my eyes hurt from staring at the screen, but I was fairly certain all the members were actual people and not spammers. The stolen goods thing was much harder to figure out. As far as I could tell, things looked legitimate. I checked my email, found the list of cat organizations from Kitty, and sent emails to them about the upcoming Cat-tastic Garage Sale.

After that was done, I tilted my head back against the sofa and closed my eyes for a minute, which turned into a couple of hours. After my nap I did some cleaning and fixed a quick fluffernutter sandwich. The sandwich was perfect for soaking up the alcohol I'd drink later this evening. It also gave me enough of a lift to shower and get ready to go to Gillganins.

Stella and I took seats at the bar. Almost exactly where Major Blade had stood the other night. If only these barstools could talk. But the two bartenders who'd been working the other night were here, so maybe my plan would work. Peppy Irish jig music played through speakers. The bar was a large rectangle with seating on all four sides. Most of the barstools were already full even though it was only eight thirty. I looked over the crowd hoping I wouldn't recognize anyone. It would be terrible to find that the police were celebrating a promotion or retirement here. Or if the base police were here for the same reason. I had an agenda tonight and didn't need any distractions. So far the coast seemed actually clear.

"How was your play practice this afternoon?" I asked Stella.

"Terrible." She signaled to the bartender.

"That's great," I said.

"It is, isn't it?" Stella said.

"How can I help you ladies?" the bartender asked. He had a pouf of hair that stood three inches high. His smile seemed practiced, like someone who'd been in the hospitality industry a long time.

I ordered a Cape Cod—cranberry juice and vodka—and Stella ordered a scotch on the rocks.

Stella stood up.

"Where are you going?" I asked.

"To pick out a song."

"I was just using the whole karaoke thing as a guise. I didn't mean we actually needed to sing." My voice sounded a little desperate.

"I told Awesome I was bringing you to karaoke to get your mind off everything that's going on. You don't want to make a liar of me, do you?" She grinned and waltzed off.

"Ugh."

"Troubles?" It was the bartender with our drinks.

I took a sip of my Cape Cod. "Not more than usual." Way more than usual but he didn't really care.

"How about you?" I asked.

"Can't complain. I could, but what good would it do, right?" he said.

"You must see and hear a lot of crazy stuff in here." I hoped I was leading the witness. I took another drink. "This is great."

He smiled. "Thanks. Yeah, it can be pretty nuts some nights. An Air Force dude who was in here the other night was found dead in a car. The woman who killed him was in here that night, too."

Oh, no. He thinks Michelle is guilty. "I heard a body was found in the parking lot." I had to admit that to him. He'd know everyone around here would have heard that. "But I didn't realize they'd actually been in here. Did you serve them?"

"I served the dead guy." He crossed himself. "No disrespect to him."

"I'm sorry. That must seem creepy."

"Not as creepy as he was."

Carol had said he was creepy, too. "Really?"

The bartender nodded.

"How so?"

"Hey, whadda you have to do to get a drink around here?" It was a man on the other side of the bar.

"Oops. Duty calls." The bartender winked as he hustled off.

Stella slipped onto the stool next to me. "Did you find anything out? I saw you were deep in conversation, so I lingered over by the music lists."

"Not much. He just told me the major was creepy then some jerk wanted a drink and he took off."

"Imagine wanting a drink at a bar. The nerve," Stella said.

I laughed. "Did you pick out a song?"

"A song? I had to linger over there so long that I picked out several. We are going to have fun tonight." Stella knocked her glass against mine.

"Why me?" I asked the ceiling.

"Because you're lucky," Stella said bumping her shoulder against mine.

A man got up on the small stage and launched into "Danny Boy." It brought the mood of the room down, but everyone joined in. The next two singers, a young couple, caterwauled their way through what might have been a Beyoncé song.

"We're up next," Stella said. She grabbed my hand and dragged me up to the stage.

Stella had picked "I Gotta Feeling" by The Black Eyed Peas. It was a fun song and in a key I could sing. Pretty soon the whole crowd was on their feet singing about tonight being a good night. I smiled when I spotted Carol edging her way across the room. She joined us onstage. By the time we finished everyone was dancing. Stella, Carol, and I took an exaggerated bow at the end of the song.

"What are you doing here?" I asked Carol when we settled back at the bar.

"Stella sent me a text. I decided I could use a girls' night out."

"I'm happy you're here," I said.

"So, what are we trying to find out?" Carol asked.

I must be way more transparent than I realized. "Anything we can about Major Blade. The bartender said he was creepy, too. But then he had to go back to work, so I didn't find out why he thought that."

A different bartender came by. We ordered another round of drinks. We chatted, laughed, and I kept an eye out for any of the other men who had been with Major Blade the night I'd been here with Michelle. I noticed the first bartender was chopping limes near us and turned to Carol.

"So why didn't you like Major Blade?" I asked her, already knowing the answer.

"The creep hit on me at a party," Carol said.

The bartender looked up and gave Carol the once-over. "You're his type."

"Tall and blond?" I asked. I left out the part about stacked.

He pointed to Carol's left hand. "No. Married." He looked at Stella and me. "He wouldn't have been interested in you two at all."

Stella, Carol, and I exchanged glances eyes wide.

"Really?" I asked. "Married women?"

The bartender nodded. "I've seen him doing it all the time, but he even bragged about it to me. Said women whose husbands were deployed were desperate for action. Easy targets."

Holy crap. The bartender went back to chopping his limes. Carol, Stella, and I huddled together.

"If that's true, and it seems like it is, then the list of suspects is miles long," I said.

"There's more married people on base than single people," Carol added.

I swirled the tiny black straw in my drink around, mixing the cranberry juice and vodka. "I need to find out if the men who were with Blade that night were married. Maybe Blade had been overly friendly with one of their wives. And something horrible happened while they were all here. Something worth killing someone over."

Stella jerked her head toward the bartender. "He might know more or might have overheard something."

The guy in charge of karaoke called out. "Stella, you're up next."

"Oh boy," Stella said, "you're never going to believe what song I picked for us."

"Us?" I said. "I've already been up there once."

But Carol and Stella poked and prodded me up to the stage. And then we all sang "Your Cheatin' Heart" by Hank Williams. We couldn't even look at each other. By the time the song was over I knew what I had to do next.

CHAPTER TWENTY-FOUR

I sat across from Michelle Tuesday morning in her office. It was nine fifteen and she'd sponsored me on base. Her face looked paler than it had yesterday when she was at Luke's house. Maybe he was good for her. I wished I'd stopped at Dunkin's to get coffee and donuts. Something, anything to try and perk her up.

Her office was spacious with a round conference table that sat four on one end and her large, impressive-looking desk with two guest chairs on the other. Dark drapes hung on either side of a window that overlooked the parade field and track. The office was an anomaly for the usual Air Force office. Most offices were much smaller. I never understood how spaces were allocated in the Air Force. "How are you holding up?" I asked.

Michelle wiggled her hand back and forth, indicating so-so. "They had me in for another round of questioning yesterday afternoon after I saw you at Luke's house." She colored slightly. "I think they are hoping I'll crack and confess so they can all go home. I don't plan to make their lives that easy."

"Did you have a lawyer with you?" I asked.

"Yes. Vincenzo DiNapoli. He's amazing. Thank you for recommending him."

"You're welcome." I hesitated before bringing up an uncomfortable subject. "Did you tell them about your running shoes?"

"No." Michelle picked up a pen and tapped it furiously against the edge of her desk.

"Did you at least tell Vincenzo?"

Michelle looked down at her pen and set it down.

"What if they get a search warrant?" I asked.

"They won't find them. I threw them in a dumpster over by the TLF."

The temporary lodging facility was basically a hotel for military people on base. Military families could stay there when they were moving, if they were here vacationing, or here on business. I wanted to thunk my head on the edge of her desk. Michelle must not know about the video the police had. I filled her in.

"Michelle, we have to figure this out. Someone is trying to set you up. They were desperate enough to break into your house, steal your shoes, and who knows what else, in an attempt to impersonate you on a late-night run."

"I've added some new locks and bolts to my doors and lower windows."

"Tossing the shoes means you don't have DNA evidence the person might have left behind," I said.

Michelle rubbed her temples. "I'm an idiot."

"We can't undo what's done." I struggled to find any further words of comfort and decided to tackle the issue of why I was here. "So tell me about the men who were at the bar the night we were there. Are any of them married?"

"The colonel is. So is the captain and one of the butter bars."

"Have any of them been deployed recently?"

"The captain just got back from a hundred-and-seventy-nine-day tour in Afghanistan."

They sent people back after 179 days because at 180 days they had to start paying them extra and it could be considered a PCS—permanent change of station.

"What about the colonel?" I asked.

"He was gone about a year ago for a while."

"And the butter bar?"

"He's been TDY a lot down to the Pentagon but not on a deployment. Why are you asking about this?"

TDY stood for temporary duty, which was more or less like a business trip in the civilian world. I told her what the bartender told me last night.

"That leaves most of the base as possible suspects," Michelle said.

"It does. But it seems more likely to me that something happened that night to make someone lash out. Maybe those guys weren't as buddy-buddy as they seemed. Did they hang out together before that night?" It seemed unlikely to me. A colonel hanging out with butter bars could be risky. It could create chain-of-command issues. The military had a traditional hierarchy set up long ago, which at times even I didn't understand.

Michelle looked over my head at something behind me for a few moments, then back at me. "I think Major Blade golfed with the colonel sometimes.

Maybe with the captain on occasion. But the colonel is a rule follower. He'd be very careful about who he spent time with and where. Office functions were one thing, but off duty was another."

"Do you know their wives?"

"Not that well. I've seen them at social functions, but it's not like I'm friends with any of them."

"Do you know their names?" If I had that information, I could check them out through the spouses' network.

"I'll text them to you." Michelle got out her phone, jotted some notes, and seconds later my phone *bing*ed, letting me know she'd hit send.

I looked at the text. "I don't know any of them. Although the colonel's wife's name sounds familiar." The base was small as Air Force bases went. But it was big enough that I didn't know everyone. My social circle had included our neighbors, people who volunteered at the thrift shop, who were in the Spouses' Club, and the people in the squadron CJ had been in charge of. And since I'd moved off base almost two years ago, there'd been lots of personnel changes. So it wasn't surprising that I didn't know any of them.

"Thanks for the information." Now for the hard part. "I love my brother, but you have to remember he's a freaking reporter."

Michelle laughed. I was flabbergasted. This was serious. Her career. Even worse, if things went badly, it could be her life.

"It's not funny," I said. I sounded so prissy and uptight that I almost didn't recognize myself.

"I'm sorry. It's just the expression you made."

"And please don't tell me again about the 'talking' business. I can only take so much."

"When we realized we liked each other, beyond being buddies, we laid some ground rules."

I didn't want to think about what they had laid.

"We don't talk about the murder. But I trust Luke. Even if we did talk about it, he wouldn't ever do anything to hurt me."

Yeesh. She had it bad. "You barely know each other. I'm not sure *I* trust him completely, and he's my brother." Last spring I'd been afraid he'd committed a murder.

"He's a good man at heart. And he's been through a lot."

"He told you about his past?" I asked. *So early in their relationship?*

"Yes. I was joking when I said we hadn't talked that much." She smiled again. "I wish you could have seen your face. We've talked for hours."

"But what about the police? If they think two people had to be working together, they might think it was you and Luke."

"Luke told me you were concerned about that. We don't think it will be a problem."

Part of me wanted to grab Michelle and shake some sense into her. What could I say? They were both adults and knew the risks they were facing. "I guess that makes it none of my business."

"That's where you are wrong. You care about us both. So it is your business."

That reminded me I had more questions than answers about Major Blade. I stood.

"Thanks for stopping by." Michelle tried a smile, but it looked more like a wince.

"We'll figure this out," I said as I walked to her office door. I realized I had two more stops to make before I left base.

Special Agent Bristow's office was a stark contrast to Michelle's. Small, dark, filled with files and books. He had to move things so there was a chair clear for me to sit in. Battered venetian blinds blocked most of the sunlight from coming in.

"How did you get on base?" he asked.

"Michelle Diaz sponsored me on." No sense in lying. He could easily call the visitors' center to see who had.

"And the pass included time to come over and see me?"

"Yes." The pass allowed me to be on base for two hours. Although it didn't say I could wander around wherever I wanted to.

Bristow let it go and didn't press me on the topic anymore. In fact, he just leaned back in his chair and looked over his readers at me. I was used to this technique since CJ had been in law enforcement for years. It didn't bother me, but I didn't want to waste time, either.

"I wondered if anything came of the message I sent you about the Greens possibly being in the military."

"You don't have any proof that this would come under the OSI purview."

"I looked it up. I know you concentrate on felonies and terrorism—"

"Among other things," Bristow said.

"But I read that you also investigate major burglaries. And if the Greens are military and moving from base to base stealing from SuiteSwapzs, then that surely would qualify."

"That's a couple of big ifs. I'd like to help you out but with the murder of Major Blade and a few other ongoing cases, I don't have time."

I stared at him with what I hoped was the lost puppy dog eyes the guy at the flea market said I had.

"Do you have something in your eye? I have some drops," Bristow said.

So much for the lost puppy eyes. "I was at Gillganins last night, and the bartender told me something I thought you should know."

Bristow looked up toward the ceiling, more like the heavens, as if he could find some patience there. "We've interviewed the staff at Gillganins."

"So you know that Major Blade had a thing for married women? Especially women whose husbands were deployed?"

Bristow didn't say anything. I took that to mean that he didn't know. "And of the four other men he was with at the bar that night, three were married and had been either deployed or traveling a lot." I paused. "Now that is a motive for you."

Bristow stood up. "So is having an IG complaint filed against you."

I stood up, too. "Killing someone doesn't make an IG complaint go away. It would only make it worse. Why would Michelle do that?"

Bristow walked over and opened the door to his office.

"Have you interviewed the wives of those men?" I asked.

"We haven't. Thanks for coming by." He paused. "And for the information."

I was pretty sure he wanted to tell me to butt out, but he was too polite. And probably having me feed him some of what I knew was better than not talking to me at all. At least that's what I told myself. I knew I should leave base, but I had one more stop to make.

CHAPTER TWENTY-FIVE

I parked my Suburban behind the thrift shop. Eleanor's Mini Cooper was there. I thought she'd be a good starting point to find out about the wives of the officers at the bar Thursday night. The thrift shop wasn't open to the public today, but there was always work to be done. I let myself in through the back door and found Eleanor with a dustrag in her hand by the section of glasses and dishware. Her hair was pulled back in a low ponytail.

"Do you have another dustcloth?" I asked. "I can help."

"There's a whole bucketful right there." Eleanor pointed to a bucket near the book section. It also held a spray bottle of glass cleaner.

The shelves were a jumble of dishes, all different types of glasses from water to champagne to kids' juice cups. Usually it looked more organized. "What happened?"

"We had such a crowd yesterday. The whole place looks like it was hit by a tornado."

I grabbed a dustcloth. "Then I'm glad I stopped by."

"Why did you stop by?"

"This has to stay between us." Eleanor nodded. I filled her in on what I'd heard from the bartender at Gillganins and described the men who were with Blade. "So I wanted to know if you knew any of their wives." I separated out a section of glasses, dusted the shelf and the glasses as needed.

"I know the colonel's wife. She's quiet. Doesn't belong to the Spouses' Club or volunteer here at the thrift shop. Both of their kids are off at college."

That sounded like a recipe for loneliness. "Maybe she volunteers someplace else on base." There were plenty of other opportunities like the base chapel or the Airman's Attic that provided furniture and house-hold goods to enlisted troops who needed them. The Red Cross or base schools. There were more oppor-tunities than not.

"She works out a lot. And I think she works for an accounting firm in Ellington part-time."

So maybe she wasn't so lonely. But I couldn't rule her out completely. We continued to clean and reor-ganize. "What about the captain's wife?"

"Don't you know Joy?"

I thought for a moment. "I don't think so."

"Wow. I thought everyone knew her or of her," Eleanor said. "Maybe they moved here after you left base."

"How come?"

"She's just . . ." Eleanor paused. "She's just fun."

"Fun?" That's not what I'd been expecting.

"Joy has more energy than ten cats hyped up on catnip. She volunteers for everything and no job is beneath her, so she's very popular. Not to mention she's gorgeous. Luscious red hair, clear blue eyes, and a figure that would make a Kardashian jealous. Men adore her, too."

"Know anything about her marriage?"

"She seems to love her husband," Eleanor said. "Talks about him in glowing terms and wears a locket with his picture and one of his dog tags around her neck every single day. She says it's her good-luck charm. It's so lively when she volunteers here. I'm surprised you haven't run into her."

"She doesn't sound familiar." Hmmm, she didn't seem like a woman who would be vulnerable to a man like Major Blade. Maybe she's overcompensating for something that was lacking in her marriage. I moved around another set of glasses. "What about the butter bar's wife?"

"She seems nice, but maybe a little on the nervous side."

"How so?" I asked.

"She just seems like she wants to do the right thing. I always see her watching the higher ranking wives at events and then imitating them."

"How?"

"She'll show up at the next thing in similar clothes or jewelry or makeup."

"She must not have a lot of confidence."

"No, and I think she's pretty young. The butter bar is just out of college, and I think she's still working on her degree."

"That means she could still be in her early twenties." A time when people were still trying to figure out who they were. Yeesh. I still hadn't figured out who I was, but it was different than how I felt in my twenties. She sounded like the kind of woman Major Blade might home in on. "I can totally relate to that. I felt the same way when CJ and I were first married. Military life was so different, and I was always afraid I'd offend someone and hurt his career."

"It can be a lot of pressure." Eleanor stepped back from the glasses and looked over our work. "Thanks for helping clean up. This looks fantastic."

"You're welcome." We tossed our dustcloths back into the bucket. Eleanor picked it up and carried it to the back of the shop.

"Did any of this help you?" she asked.

"I'm not sure," I said. "But thanks for the information."

As I drove home, I thought about the three very different women. Joy seemed the least likely to be susceptible to someone like Major Blade. And maybe I was wrong about all of this anyway. There was a whole bar full of people there that night. Lots of military but lots of civilians, too. It was a very popular place. And who said Major Blade only hit on military wives? Civilians traveled, too, and their wives could be lonely. There were just too many suspects. And how was I going to get close to any of the wives Eleanor and I had talked about?

Ugh. I was never going to figure this out before Michelle was arrested. But I couldn't give up. As good a man as Special Agent Bristow is, I couldn't count on him not to go for the easy answer. He said it himself: He has a lot of cases open. He's busy. So a simple solution would probably seem very appealing.

Unfortunately, it felt like Officer Jones took much the same approach, which is why Michelle wasn't the only one I was worried about. Going back and forth between her case and mine was exhausting. I hoped I didn't overlook some detail that could be important to either case. Other than getting convicted, it was my biggest fear.

Thirty minutes later I opened the door to Burke's Dry Cleaners. I'd run home and found a dress in the back of my closet that the label was marked DRY CLEANING ONLY. It wasn't dirty, but I figured out that I'd have a lot better chance of getting questions answered if I was a paying customer. I had wadded it into a ball so at least it was wrinkled.

A buzzer buzzed noisily when I walked in. It was warm in here and there was a slight chemical smell, even though a sign on the front window said they were an organic cleaner. It wasn't an entirely unpleasant smell.

An energetic woman bustled to the counter from the back. "Help you?" she asked.

It sounded like the same woman I'd talked to when I'd called. Only today she was a lot more energetic.

"I need to dry-clean this dress."

"Any stains?" she asked. She took a pen out that was stuck over her ear. Her hair looked a bit damp. It must be a hard place to work.

Since it was clean, no. "No. Not this time." I smiled as she filled out a form on one of those old-fashioned pads with carbon paper in between two thin pieces of paper.

"We will have this done in two days unless you need it earlier. There's a small fee for twenty-four-hour service."

"Two days is fine." It was now or never. "I have a question for you," I said. "Is there any way you could look up a phone number and see if the person is a customer?" I didn't hold out a lot of hope since the woman was writing things down on a pad of paper instead of using a computer.

"Of course, we can. I just use the pad as backup. The whole system crashed one day a couple of weeks ago, and it was a disaster for the next forty-eight hours. We couldn't find a thing."

"Would you look up a number for me?"

"No."

I wasn't going to try the lost puppy eye thing after my experience with Bristow. Instead, I was just going to throw myself on her mercy. I poured out the story of what happened at the garage sale. How the phone number the Greens had used to call me and the dry-cleaning tag I'd found at the apartment were my only connection to the Greens/Youngs. "I've been hand-cuffed, had a mug shot taken, tossed in a holding cell, and arraigned," I said. "There's a pretrial conference set up for next week. I'm scared about what might happen."

"I heard about you over at DiNapoli's," she said. "If you're good in Rosalie's eyes you are okay by me. Let me see the phone number."

"Thank you." *Thank you, Rosalie.* I read it off to her

and she typed it into a computer. She mumbled a bit while she did it like she was debating what to do with me. "The phone number is for a customer with the last name of Fitzwater."

That was a new one. I didn't hold out a lot of hope that it was a real name, either. "Is there an address listed?"

"We only keep an address for people who want their dry cleaning delivered," she said.

I took the tag out of my pocket and handed it to her. "Is there any chance this is one of yours?" I asked.

She squinted at the tag. "It is."

"Do the numbers have any significance?" I asked. I tried not to get my hopes up because up to this point everything had been an abysmal failure.

"They do," she said.

"Would you explain it to me? Please?" I tried to keep any hint of desperation from my voice.

The woman gave me a sympathetic look. "The first two numbers tell me it's from this store. We own three dry cleaners in the area. The second two," she pointed to a 07, "mean they brought it in on a Saturday. The seventh day of the week."

That at least I could have figured out. I nodded.

"And the last two numbers tell me it's a military uniform."

Finally, something concrete. A solid connection between the Greens and the military.

"Can you tell if the uniform was for a male or female?" I asked.

"No. We charge the same no matter whose uniform it is."

"Thank you." I turned to go but whipped back around. "Is there any chance they have something left that they are supposed to pick up?" If they did, I could contact Pellner or Awesome and let them know. Maybe the Greens would finally be caught.

She typed some more into the computer. "No. Sorry. They don't have anything here."

CHAPTER TWENTY-SIX

I sat in the dry cleaners' parking lot. I used my phone to do a quick search of the name Fitzwater. Nothing came up in Ellington or on the base. I broadened my search to the greater Boston metropolitan area. Nothing. I called Eleanor to see if she knew anyone by that name. That was a bust, too. I sent a quick e-mail to Bristow and one to Pellner with the new information. Maybe one of them would be able to find a connection now that I was fairly certain that one or the other of the Greens was in the military. Why else would they be dry-cleaning a uniform? With the beard Alex Green had, it must be Kate. Unless he did some kind of undercover work or had been on leave long enough to grow a beard like that.

Maybe I was all wrong about this, too. I'd been questioning myself a lot since they'd fooled me so completely with their "aw, shucks" Midwestern act. They could have purchased uniforms at a military supply place and just pretended to be in the military. People wanted to help out those who served, and around here it would be a heck of a way to blend in.

My phone rang as I drove home. It showed that the

call was from the Billerica police. They should be calling Vincenzo, not me. I tossed it back in my purse. My heart thumped at a frantic pace. What did they want? I figured if it was any good news I'd hear it from Seth or Vincenzo. I was trying to remain calm, but the ragged edges of panic chewed at me.

I thought again that Michelle wasn't the only one who had to worry about her situation. Maybe I needed to worry more about my case than hers. I would love to talk to Pellner about the Greens, his thoughts on the map Luke had put together, and the information I'd just sent him. But he might know the Billerica police wanted to talk to me, so I decided to avoid him, too.

I pulled over, dug my phone back out of my purse, and called Vincenzo. All these calls to him were going to cost me a fortune. I left a voice mail saying I'd gotten a call from the Billerica police, but that I hadn't answered it. It didn't seem right that they were calling me, and I didn't want them to do it again.

All the stress of everything made me feel like I was going to break. If only I could run away just for a few hours without any consequences. *Why not?* I hadn't gotten any of those dire warnings you see on TV about not leaving town. It was a lovely fall afternoon. No one would miss me. The more I thought about it the more I liked the idea of a mini-break. There were a bunch of very cute antiques stores in Essex, Massachusetts. They even called themselves America's antiques capital. Essex was only thirty-five miles away and sat on the Essex River in the middle of a beautiful salt marsh. It would be peaceful.

If I took the back roads, it would be a pleasant fall

drive. I could look for chairs for the sitting room at Seth's house. I could shop for vintage ornaments for the wreath I wanted to make. The glory of a few hours to myself sang to me like a siren song. I could head over to Ipswich and eat at one of their famous clam shacks. A little self-care and procrastination never hurt anyone, did it? Maybe a short getaway would clear my head and open it to new possibilities.

Two hours later I had a bag full of vintage ornaments in my trunk. But chair shopping was discouraging. I'd seen lots of wingbacks, ladder, and Rocco chairs. Too traditional, uncomfortable, and fancy—just in that order—for Seth's sitting room. I wasn't even sure what kind of chairs I wanted when I walked into the next shop. Only that they weren't anything I'd already seen.

I'd been here before and knew the owner had a huge barn full of furniture behind the store. She'd let me look through it a couple of times in the past. Usually, her things were way out of my price range, which was more like twenty-five to one hundred dollars. Who was I kidding? My price range was more like zero. Dumpster-diving and hand-me-downs were more my style. Or an "at the end of a garage sale" bargain when the person was desperate to get rid of things. I always had to watch my pennies and whatever other money I earned. Three things saved me from poverty. The money I made from the now annual New England's Largest Garage Sale, my savings, and I still got half of CJ's retirement pay as part of our divorce settlement.

The store was beautifully arranged with bright lights and high-quality furnishings. I preferred shops that were jumbled with things to dig through. Then it was like going on a scavenger hunt as a kid. I would never know what I'd find. I spotted the owner at the back of the store and wended my way past Hollywood Regency chairs, stunning but not comfortable enough, sideboards, and settees.

"Hi," I said when I reached her, "I'm looking for some comfortable reading chairs for a sitting room off a bedroom. I'm not sure what I want. I only know what I don't want." I ran my list by her as she nodded.

"It's nice to see you again. Thanks for stopping back by." She smiled like she was happy I was there. "We just got a big shipment in from an estate in Andover. It's all in the barn and was more or less just dumped back there. I haven't had time to sort through everything. If you want to take a chance, you're welcome to go have a look around."

"Thank you. That would be fantastic."

She retrieved a key and handed it to me. "It's at the back of the barn in the far-left corner. The light switch is to the right of the door."

"Great. I'll be back in a bit." I walked out her back door, crossed an alley, and unlocked the barn. I felt for the light switch and flipped the lights on. It was cool in here. Even with the lights on, it was a bit dim. I felt invigorated as I made my way to the back. Maybe I'd find something wonderful. The place was cavernous. Who knew what treasures were waiting for me? There were two mission-style oak chairs with thick leather cushions on the backs and seats near the middle of the barn. Very masculine and I loved the clean lines. But still not what I was looking for. I waded in deeper. The farther I went the dimmer it was. Frankly, it was all too quiet and a little creepy. But I was on a mission and wasn't going to let that stop me.

I made it to the far-left corner. There was a jumble of furnishings. Some things were stacked on top of others. It's good thing I'd built up a lot of muscle over the past year and a half or so, hauling stuff around. Coffee tables were on top of couches, nightstands on beds. I spotted something across the way and edged by, over, and around furniture. I pulled a standing lamp off a mahogany magazine rack. Then I stood back. This was them.

The two chairs were art deco club chairs. Possibly French. Probably from the 1930s. The light-colored upholstery looked like silk. I ran my hand across the seat. It felt like silk, too. The chairs had a great curved design with high-gloss-lacquered wood arms. I ran my hand over the curve of the furniture, too. The wood looked good with just a few nicks. The upholstery had a pull here and there, but no rips. I sat down in one. Amazing. They were even comfortable.

I wondered how much they were. The problem with antiques is they didn't have any intrinsic value. Take midcentury modern pieces. Ten years ago no one cared for things from the fifties, so they were cheap. But now they were all the rage and prices had skyrocketed for grandma's old mixing bowls or that cool laminated kidney-shaped table on wire legs. The interest in the art deco era came and went. But I feared because of the construction and materials along with the interest in all things are deco right now, these two chairs would be expensive.

These were perfect and I wanted them bad. I

snapped a couple of photos with my phone and then made my way back to the front of the barn. I turned off the lights and locked back up.

"Any luck?" the owner asked when I went back into the store.

"I found a couple of old art deco chairs that might work." I accented the *old* and *might* while trying to keep my voice nonchalant. I didn't want to sound too excited even though inside I was doing a happy dance. "I took a couple of pictures, so you don't have to trek out there." I showed her the photos and mentally crossed my fingers.

"Oh, I remember those. They are stunning."

Darn. "How much do you want for them?"

"I was thinking three thousand, and that's a deal."

Three thousand? Yikes. "There are some chips in the wood on the arms and snags in the upholstery."

She narrowed her eyes. "I'm going to kill my movers. They were perfect when I saw them at the estate."

I'd taken pictures of the chips and snags, so I showed those to her.

"Maddening."

"How about one thousand since they're damaged?" I accented the damaged. Five hundred apiece for them was a bargain.

"No way. You're not even close. Two thousand."

At least she was willing to bargain. That was a good sign. "Fifteen hundred. That's the best I can do."

She tapped her hand against her thigh. "Oh, all right. But you have to load them yourself."

"Done." I handed her my credit card before she could change her mind. I was lucky to have caught her on a slow day with a new shipment.

* * *

At three thirty I was back on the road, a sweaty mess, but the two chairs were loaded in the back of my Suburban. I swung through Ipswich and bought an order of clams to go. I ate them as I drove home. When I got back to Ellington, I couldn't decide whether to just go over to Seth's house in Bedford to drop the chairs off or stop at home to clean up first.

I used my rearview mirror and ran my fingers through my hair. As long as no one got close enough to smell me, I'd be okay. Seth should still be at work because he worked crazy long hours. I worried a little bit about even going over to Seth's because of my impending pretrial conference. But I didn't have anywhere else to put the chairs.

I pulled into Seth's driveway. I didn't have his garage door opener, so I would have to use my key to his house for the first time. I'd walked about three steps down the hall when I heard a woman laughing and Seth's voice.

CHAPTER TWENTY-SEVEN

Oh, no. I reversed course and headed back to the door as quietly as possible. Seth must have parked in his garage and who knows where the woman had parked. I'd been so focused I hadn't noticed any stray cars around.

"Sarah?"

Seth. I turned. "I didn't think you were home. I should have knocked or rung the bell." Or better yet not have come at all. Why did I have to decide to try this today of all days. When he was home. With a woman.

"No. That's fine. I'm glad you're here. Come in."

"You have company. I'm not fit for company."

"You look gorgeous. You could do a mud run and be fit for anything."

Seth melted my heart. Nichole peeked around the corner.

"Besides," Seth added, "it's just Nichole."

A distressed look passed over Nichole's face for just a moment.

"Hi, Nichole," I said before Seth could say anything else. I wondered if there was any possibility that Nichole had made up her fiancé to make Seth jealous. But Seth knew her fiancé, so unless the guy decided to help Nichole out . . . *stop it.* I had to get over my insecurity when it came to Nichole. "I found some chairs for you."

"Sarah's creating a sitting room upstairs for me, in a corner of the master bedroom," Seth said to Nichole. "She found some beautiful antique barristers' bookcases for the space."

"I planned to put the chairs in your garage until you were home to help me carry them up." I looked back and forth between Seth and Nichole. "But here you are."

"I decided to work from home this afternoon. The phones were going crazy at the office," Seth said. "Let's bring the chairs in." He shrugged out of his suit jacket and undid his tie. If Nichole weren't here . . .

"I can help," Nichole said. But she was wearing a beautiful dress that must have cost her hundreds of dollars and shoes with four-inch heels.

"No," I said. "Your dress is gorgeous. I don't want you to damage it hauling furniture."

"You like it?" Nichole smiled.

"Purple looks great on you," I said. Way better than envy green did on me.

"Thanks," Nichole said. "I'll just wait in the living room then."

"Hey, Nicky, will you take this and toss it on the back of one of the dining room chairs?"

Seth gave his suit coat and tie to Nichole. He didn't notice her grimace when he used the nickname. One I'd never heard him use before. Once we were outside, Seth pulled me to him and kissed the heck out of me.

"Your neighbors," I said. "They'll see us."

"So? They'll know what a lucky man I am."

We walked toward my car. "I hope you like the chairs. They are a bit different." I opened the back. The backs of the chairs faced us, and it was hard to see what they looked like.

"I love them," Seth said.

"Oh, stop. You can't even see them yet."

Seth hugged me. "The fabric looks nice."

We pulled the first one out and set it on the driveway. "What do you think? And for goodness' sake be honest. You have to live with them. Besides, if you don't like them I can sell them for more than I bought them for."

He walked around the chair and then sat in it. "Very comfortable. And they look great. Thank you."

We carried the chairs inside one at a time. Nichole met us in the hallway again.

"What do you think?" Seth asked her.

"They're gorgeous," Nichole said. "Well done."

"There's a nice shop up in Essex," I said.

"Sounds interesting," Nichole said.

She didn't sound very interested at all. I knew from past experience that she liked modern things more than antiques. Go figure.

"I need to get going," Nichole said. "Thanks for your help, Seth."

Even though I was curious about what help Seth had given her, I kept my mouth shut. None of my business. After Nichole left Seth pulled me into another hug.

"I love it when you get jealous," he said.

I blustered a bit. "Why would you think that?"

He kissed the tip of my nose. "That very expressive face of yours."

Rats. I wondered if there were classes that taught you how to have a poker face.

"It means you care about me. The only thing there ever was between Nichole and me was wishful thinking on our mothers' parts. We've always been pals."

I wasn't about to point out that may have only been on his side of things.

"And if you are wondering what I helped Nichole with, it was a suggestion of a gift for the groom-to-be."

"I—" Oh, what the heck. Why deny it when my face probably said otherwise.

We carried the chairs upstairs. I shifted them one way and then another until I got them just where I wanted them. The slender Japanese table I'd bought on Saturday was perfect between them. I stepped back to admire all of it. Seth came up beside me and pulled me to him. I sunk into his arms.

"You need a good reading lamp," I said.

He nuzzled my neck. "Let's worry about that later."

Since I was almost melting, I thought that sounded like a very smart idea.

My phone rang at 6:07 Wednesday morning. I rolled over to my nightstand and felt around for it. By the time I had my phone in my hand, it had stopped ringing. The call had been from Pellner. I'd had a late night and was hoping to sleep in. I closed my eyes, but worrying about what Pellner wanted kept me awake, so I called him back.

"What?" I said when he answered.

"You sound bright and cheery this morning."

"It's barely after six."

"You're Miss Garage Sale. I thought you were a morning person."

"Only when I have to be," I said. I needed coffee. "So did you call because you were bored? Lonely?" Although with a wife and five kids I could probably rule out bored. Probably looking for some time alone would be more like it for Pellner.

Pellner *hummph*ed. "I'm calling to tell you the print you brought me of the cats was stolen."

I sat up, finally awake. "Really? From where? Someplace local?"

"Beavercreek, Ohio."

Beavercreek was a suburb of Dayton, Ohio. And Wright-Patterson Air Force Base was in Dayton. CJ and I had stayed with friends who lived in Beaver Creek when we were moving across country once.

"There's an Air Force base there," I said. Not that this bit of information helped identify who the Greens are.

"I'm aware," Pellner said.

Mr. Full of Information. "This couldn't have waited until a more reasonable time? Say eight or nine."

"I'll be off duty and home with my family by then."

"Okay, then. Thanks for letting me know."

"You might want to tell your client that she won't be getting her print back."

"I will."

As I went through my morning routine, which

started with making coffee and ended with a shower, I thought over my day. I planned to call Bristow, meet with a new client, and go to see Erin Imhoff. Next on the list was to avoid seeing Seth in public so he'd stay out of the limelight with his political rival. And then making another effort to find the Greens. The first few things on my list should be fairly easy. Seth had a trial starting next Monday and that would keep him busy. We had talked for a few minutes after my shower. I'd had to assure him I was okay and that I wasn't worrying too much about the pretrial conference. It was much easier to fake it on a phone call than in person. I'd never mentioned Vincenzo's idea that we go out somewhere fancy for dinner to be seen. And I hoped Seth wouldn't run into Vincenzo in court.

The Greens/Youngs/Fitzwaters—whatever their name really was—they were the ones who stumped me. If Vincenzo's investigator and Mike Titone couldn't find them, how could I? And for all I knew they'd left the area by now and were on the run. That made the most sense although desertion had major consequences. I didn't want to believe they had run because that left me in the crosshairs of the legal system. The crosshairs of Seth's political opponent. With one stupid action I seemed to have managed to ruin my life and maybe Seth's, too. *No pity parties, Sarah.* They were counterproductive and wouldn't find answers for me or Michelle.

If one of the Greens was in the military, maybe they were still in town because they didn't want to desert. If one or both of them was enlisted, maybe their reenlistment was almost over. Or if one of them was an officer they could be close to separating— leaving before retiring. They seemed too young to be retiring. You had to serve twenty years. Either option was much better so they could get an honorable discharge. And face it, up to this point they'd never been caught, so why panic and draw attention to themselves now?

At 8:00 a.m. I called Special Agent Bristow and was surprised when he answered. "Any chance anyone fitting the description of the Greens has gone AWOL?" I asked.

"Do you think we wouldn't have thought of that?" Bristow asked.

"And?" I prayed he would tell me what he had learned.

"Do you think I can answer that?"

Darn it. "I hope so, but from your question I'm guessing not."

"Bingo."

"I have a court appearance next week. I'm feeling a bit desperate. A lot desperate. And don't tell me to trust the system. Seth Anderson's political opponent would like nothing more than to dangle him out in the wind with this. Seth is a good man and doesn't deserve this." I'd been saying that a lot this week. I worried I was starting to sound unhinged.

"I get that," Bristow said. "No one has gone AWOL this week."

Maybe unhinged was the way to go when I wanted information. "Thank you. Any luck finding people who were stationed at the same bases at the same

time as Major Blade?" I was thinking maybe someone
had an old grudge. Maybe they were stationed here
now, too.

"It will take thousands of man-hours to sort through
all that."

I guess unhinged only got one so far.

"I'm not saying someone isn't working on it,
though."

"Thanks, Bristow. I was also wondering—"

"I have to go, Sarah," Bristow said.

After that all I had was dead air.

CHAPTER TWENTY-EIGHT

An hour later I drove away from my new client's house. A normal-looking woman, not that I'd count on appearances anymore since the Greens had looked normal, too. I took along a contract, one that Vincenzo had a friend draw up for me. She'd signed it without protest. And seemed to enjoy talking about where her antiques came from. That was my subtle way of trying to make sure she owned them and hadn't stolen them. My questions about her lovely neighbors and how long had she lived here came off as friendly and not as an interrogation, which is what it was. I'd satisfied myself that she was legitimate but would look her up on social media later today.

I arranged to "bump" into Erin at the Ellington Library at 10:30. The Spouses' Club had a book group that met there once a month in the meeting room. Erin led the group. I used to attend back when CJ was still active duty. The Ellington Library was catty-corner from the police station, which I'd rather avoid, but I thought bumping into Erin might work better than calling her.

I browsed the mystery section as I waited, thinking about the irony of that. I looked through the movies, too, but nothing appealed to me. I finally heard chattering voices coming down the hall and peeked out behind a shelf. Erin wasn't with the group. I hoped it meant she was still in the room and not that she didn't attend today. A few moments later I heard footsteps clattering down the hall. I came around the corner.

"Erin. I haven't seen you in ages," I said. We hugged. Erin was a tiny thing with big loose brown curls and lovely pale skin. Her smile didn't seem as bright as normal, and I wondered if that was because Major Blade had been murdered.

"What are you doing here?" Erin asked.

"Looking for something to read," I said. "What about you?"

"We just finished book group."

My status with anything to do with base and Spouses' Club activities was always awkward. I couldn't be a member of the Spouses' Club anymore, because I was no longer a spouse of an active-duty or retired military member. They didn't care at the thrift shop because they always needed volunteers.

"I could send you the list of books we've been reading."

"That would be great."

"You know you could come even if you aren't technically affiliated with the base anymore," Erin said.

Tears sprang to my eyes. It had to be stress. I wasn't normally a crier. "Thank you," I said, hoping she wouldn't notice the tears.

"Hey, do you have time for coffee?" Erin asked. The sympathy in her voice almost did me in.

"Sure. The Dunkin's on Great Road?" That way I could keep an eye out for the Greens. Although I was beginning to think their meeting me there had been a one-off for them. It made sense that they wouldn't be with a patsy at a place where they regularly went.

"I'll be there in five," she said.

We settled in with coffee and glazed donut holes. I gazed over the other people. No sign of the Greens.

"How are you doing?" Erin asked. She leaned in and dropped her voice.

I figured I was a huge topic on base right now what with the arrest and finding Major Blade dead. I could brush it off or use it to my advantage. I gave myself a mental shake. What was I becoming through all of this? Some kind of manipulator or whiner? Being arrested had rocked my world and not in a good way, but I couldn't let it change who I was.

"It hasn't been the best week of my life. I guess you heard about my being arrested."

"Totally unfair. I've told anyone who mentioned it just that. No one who knows you would ever believe you'd sell stolen goods." She leaned forward. "There are a lot of new people on base since you moved off. But trust me, anyone who knows you sticks up for you."

I sat back. Wow. The talk on base must be out of control.

"I'm being thoughtless," Erin said. "I've been the subject of some unwanted gossip myself as of late."

"Oh, I'm sorry to hear that." I was. I didn't add anything, hoping she'd elaborate. With the stuff going on between her and Becky, and what Becky had said about the gossip about Erin, her husband, and Blade, Erin must be getting a lot of unwanted attention, too.

"Becky threw me under the bus and ran me over a couple of times because of the fund-raiser."

I murmured something sympathetic. Then I broke off a piece of donut hole and shoved it into my mouth so I'd keep quiet.

"I have to admit I dropped the ball on a couple of things. My dad was ill, and I had to fly home in the middle of arrangements. But Becky made it sound like I didn't do anything. And that I should be grateful she left me in the program." Erin crumbled one of the donut holes.

"How's your dad?" I asked.

"He's doing fine. It was just a little health scare, and my mother doesn't handle stress well."

"I'm sorry about the situation with you and Becky."

"I know she's a friend of yours," Erin said. "But I've been trying to own up to my part and keep the facts out there."

The woman at the thrift store had told me a different story than either Becky's or Erin's. She made it sound like she'd heard it all from Erin, which contradicted what she just said. But that isn't what I wanted to talk about. "That's not always easy," I said. "Did you hear that I was there when Major Blade was found dead?"

Now tears showed up in Erin's eyes. "I did."

"Oh dear. Were you friends with him?"

"My husband was at the academy with him. He

was the best man at our wedding." She picked up a napkin and dabbed at her eyes.

"That's tough then."

"My husband is going to be one of the pallbearers. And I've heard there are some nasty rumors going around about the three of us."

"Really?" I kept my tone as neutral as possible. "That's awful." I didn't want her to know that people—Becky—had been gossiping about her.

"Blade was a flirt. There's no doubt about that. But a harmless one," Erin said. "He was at the Protestant church service on base every Sunday."

Maybe repenting I thought, but I managed to keep that to myself. It was interesting how people could only see certain sides of their friends.

"He volunteered at the Youth Center and tutored kids, too," Erin said.

This was a side of Major Blade I hadn't heard of. "Did he have a girlfriend?" I asked. An upset girlfriend might have a reason to kill him.

"No one serious," Erin said.

"Eleanor thought he had one who lived somewhere else."

Erin shook her head. "He did for a while, but they broke up." She paused. "There are a lot of rumors about Blade, but he wasn't a bad man. You believe me, don't you?" Erin asked.

Was there a little too much desperation in her voice? Or did I just want a bunch of square clues to fit into a round hole to get Michelle off the hook? "Of course. I know what being the focus of attention on base is like. Not fun."

Erin left a few minutes later after we both promised

we'd stay in better touch. I stayed to finish my coffee and to try and think things through. People killed other people for a lot of reasons. Could Erin's husband have gotten tired of Blade flirting with his wife? It got me back to thinking about the men with Blade at Gillganins that night. What about them and their wives? Frustratingly, I didn't know or have access to any of them. Maybe that was for the best.

I finished my coffee, stood, took one last look around for the Greens, and dumped the cup in the trash as I headed out the door.

I was home by eleven-thirty, and I fixed a fluffer-nutter sandwich for my lunch. After I finished it and washed the stickiness off my hands, I sat down to make phone calls. First, I called Vincenzo to see if his investigator had found anything. Since I hadn't heard from him, I wasn't surprised when he said no. Next, I called Awesome about the phone number I'd given him.

"Did you find anything out?" I asked when he answered. There was a pause. Not a good sign.

"Hang on," he finally said. "I wanted to get out of the squad room. They found some calls on the phone. A burner that we're trying to track down."

"Did they give you any new leads?" I asked.

"The only calls on the phone were to you."

Now it was my turn to pause. "Me? No one else?" Another letdown. The Greens had planned carefully enough to have a phone dedicated to me. The word *diabolical* floated through my mind. Followed quickly by why. Why me?

"Sorry. I know it's not helpful," Awesome said.

"I'm guessing not helpful is the best case. And the worst case, in the hands of the right prosecutor, is that they'll twist it to make it look like I bought the phone and called myself."

"I wish I could tell you otherwise," Awesome said.

"You and me both."

I'd been deliberately avoiding Mike Titone. Part of me hoped he was on to something, and part of me feared he was. I'd been watching the news closely to make sure two unidentifiable bodies hadn't shown up anywhere. None had. Since my options were dwindling it was time to check in with him. Calling Mike was usually a hassle of going through different people before finally getting to him. Today he answered after a couple of rings.

"Any luck?" I asked him.

"We tracked down a Kate and Alex Green in Indianapolis."

Finally. "That's great news. Were you able to trace them to here?" I asked.

"Kate and Alex Green are in their seventies. Three sons, eight grandchildren, and they've never been to Massachusetts. 'Why leave God's country?' to quote them."

"Is there an Alex junior?" Maybe he'd found a love named Kate, too. "One with a comma-shaped birthmark?"

"No. Sorry."

He did sound sorry. Mike liked to fix things even if I wasn't always sure about what motivated him to. "How in the world have these people buried"—*oh, not a good choice of words with Mike*—"hidden themselves so well?"

"No idea. Either they are very lucky or very clever."

"What about the picture? Was anyone able to de-fuzz it?" So much for technical terms.

"You need a miracle to make that photo any clearer. And I'm fresh out."

"Not lighting enough candles at church?" I asked.

"Lighting plenty. They save a whole section just for me." He paused. "These people are very good at blending in somehow."

Even Mike sounded frustrated. If Mike couldn't find them, what hope did I have? "I guess they'd have to be experts at hiding since it seems like they've been getting away with it for a while."

"You have anything else for me to go on?"

I racked my brain. What hadn't I told him? "I'm pretty sure they are military."

"I don't have a lot of connections in that world," he said.

Under any normal situation I would be glad to know that the Mob wasn't involved with the military. Today it was just frustrating.

"They also used the last name Fitzwater."

"Great," Mike said.

"Really?"

"No, but I'll run it down. But don't get your hopes up. It's probably a family in Poughkeepsie or Timbuktu."

"Okay. Thanks." I didn't know why I was thanking him. He was trying to save his own skin, not mine. I wondered if he'd help me with Michelle, though. In for a penny, in for a pound—whatever that meant.

"I have a friend who needs something." I waited for him to protest. When he didn't, I quickly explained Michelle's situation.

"Fuzzy pictures, grainy videos. Not very helpful," Mike said.

"Please," I asked. "Michelle's a good person. A good officer. I don't want to see her destroyed over something she didn't do."

"Send the video," Mike said. "I'll see if I can help her out."

"Thanks. And I know. I owe you."

Mike hung up without a denial. Perfect.

CHAPTER TWENTY-NINE

After I'd hung up with Mike, Eleanor called me to let me know that Michelle's squadron was having a darts tournament at a place called The Tavern, an all-ranks club on base, tonight at eight.

"Darts?" I asked.

"It's all the rage on base right now."

"What happened to Texas Hold 'Em?"

"They still play that, too. I think darts is some weird test of their manliness."

"Or womanliness?" Lest people forget there were plenty of women serving, too. "Let's just go with their warrior skills," I suggested. Military people were competitive, and this was probably one more way to one-up each other.

"It's an all-squadron event, but spouses are invited."

"Is it one of those mandatory team-building activities that everyone hates?"

"You've got it," Eleanor said.

"Yeah, I'm guessing if members of the squadron are killing each other, they might need something more than a darts game to resolve their issues."

Eleanor laughed. I wasn't sure I was trying to be funny.

"I thought there might be a chance that Joy and the other two wives you wanted to grill might be there."

"Grill seems so harsh," I said.

"But oh so true. If you want to go, I'll sponsor you on."

"And go with me?" I asked. Otherwise I'd stick out like the proverbial thumb.

"Of course. It's always a pleasure to see you in action."

But first I was due over at Kitty's house. It was almost twelve thirty, and I had promised her I'd be there by then. I grabbed my keys and hustled out.

As soon as I got to Kitty's house, I broke the bad news to her about the print. She was wearing leggings decorated with tiny white cats playing with each other. Her shirt had one big white cat with red and green balls of yarn. It looked like kids' clothes for adults.

"I figured I wasn't going to get it back. I hope the owners do."

"They should," I said. Eventually. "I'd better get to work."

"Me too," Kitty said.

Once Toulouse and I were all set up in the basement, I grabbed a box. The first one I opened was full of records. As was the next and next until I had seven boxes of albums ranging from jazz to rock to folk to classical. I went upstairs with Toulouse hot on my heels and called up to Kitty.

"I found seven boxes of records," I told her.

"I forgot those old things were down there. I kept meaning to donate them somewhere."

"Vinyl is hot right now." The Greens had bragged to me about their love of vinyl and their large collection. Probably all stolen. The Greens. I wasn't any closer to finding them than I had been a week ago. Next week was my pretrial conference. *Next week.*

"Sarah?" Kitty asked. "Are you okay?"

Loaded question. "Yes. Fine. Sorry I was just thinking about records." The one I was going to have if I didn't find the Greens. "Old records are popular. I think you should sell them. They would be a great draw, too. Something for people who don't love cats." I looked down at Toulouse, who meowed. "Sorry, Toulouse. I'm not talking about you. Everyone loves you." Good heavens, I was talking to him now.

Kitty cocked her head to one side, then looked down at Toulouse. It seemed like they had some kind of communication going on. Kitty straightened and looked back at me. "Okay. Great idea. Let's sell them."

After I priced the albums, I lifted a box and moved it over closer to my chair. It was heavy. I slit open the box with a box cutter and unwrapped a bunch of newspaper, wondering what weighed this much. It was an adorable cast-iron doorstop. A girl and boy kitten that looked like they were from the thirties with their rosy cheeks, bright smiles, and colorful clothing. I looked at the bottom. It was marked HUBLEY. Hubley, a company from Lancaster, Pennsylvania, was famous for their cast-iron toys. I examined it carefully. This could be highly collectible. I knew prices for these ran from forty dollars to five hundred dollars online. A prickle of excitement, the kind when I'd found something cool, swept over me. The downside was there were lots of reproductions out there.

I looked to see if it was one piece or two. Two didn't necessarily mean it was a reproduction. But the kind of screw used might. In newer reproductions they usually used Phillips-head screws instead of regular slotted ones. I also checked the paint job and the roughness of the edges of the doorstop, and looked for the markings Hubley used. After a thorough search, I decided this was indeed an original.

The next thing I pulled out was a boot scraper. Also cast-iron. The top part was a thin sleek black Siamese cat with a base to keep it steady while you cleaned the bottom of your boots or shoes. These were also very popular with collectors right now. After several more hours of work I glanced at my watch. It was already three thirty. All these cute cat things made me happy. Such a nice contrast to everything else going on in my life.

I was stuck in traffic on Great Road—rush hour could be brutal, as Great Road was a major cut-through from one freeway to another. But I didn't expect the traffic to be this bad at three forty-five. I finally remembered one lead I hadn't ever followed up on. The man who'd tipped off the police that his neighbor's household goods were being sold while they were away. I weighed the pros and cons of approaching him. Pellner had warned me not to. The man was obviously a law-and-order kind of guy, one who cared about his neighbors and neighborhood. I thought about his grim look, the folded arms. But maybe he knew something he didn't know he knew.

Or maybe he would call the cops if I showed up on his doorstep. The thought of meeting up with Officer Jones chilled me. By the time I finished arguing with myself, I was parked in front of the neighbor's house. It was now or never, because if I just sat in my car out here, he'd definitely call the cops.

The front door opened as I walked to his porch. I looked the man over and didn't see any guns or other weapons on him. He had a closely cropped Afro with a bit of gray mixed into the dark brown. His cheekbones were high, clothes neat, stance erect, and he looked to be in his seventies. Possibly former military. Maybe I could appeal to him on that level.

"Sarah Winston." He barked my name like he was giving orders.

I guess he recognized me from the day I'd been arrested. I resisted the temptation to snap into the attention stance like I'd seen so many men and women do when CJ was active duty. I did answer with a respectful, "Yes, sir."

"Come in, come in. I'm Ralph Garrett. I owe you an apology but didn't know if I should reach out or not."

We'd settled in a family room with big comfy furniture and a fire in the fireplace. "You owe me an apology?" I asked.

"Yes, ma'am."

I was astounded. In the scenarios I'd run through my head as I'd driven over here, I'd never pictured this one. "Please call me Sarah."

"Okay, Sarah. I figured you would be pretty darn mad at me for calling the whole thing in," Ralph said.

"No." I leaned forward. "I would have done the same thing if circumstances were switched around. You're the kind of neighbor everyone wants to have."

"I thank you for that. I've read the stories in the paper and believe you're innocent. I've known Officer Jones since he was a little boy, and he's always been bullheaded. Not to mention impulsive."

"Thank you. I hope there's a lot more people like you out there." Especially when it came to a jury of my peers. The ones I'd be facing after a trial date was set.

"Now, I haven't even let you tell me why you're here," he said.

"I just thought maybe there was something that you'd seen or heard that might help find the couple who set me up."

"I've pondered that very thing myself. Daily." Ralph frowned. "No one was eager to have our neighbors turn their house into a hotel, so to speak. It kind of turned neighbor against neighbor—those who thought it was fine and those who didn't. Then this happens."

"Did your neighbors ever meet the Greens face-to-face?" I asked.

"Nope. I called them after the police left. They did everything online. Even gave them a code to the fancy lock they have on their front door. It was a disaster waiting to happen."

I'd used a number of SuiteSwapzs over the years, so I knew that most of the time there wasn't any kind of disaster. Although with the statistics Luke had gathered, disasters happened at least part of the time.

"Did you ever talk to them? They went by the name Green. Alex and Kate," I said.

"I didn't. Not much help, am I?"

"Did you see what kind of car they drove?"

"Just the big rental truck they hauled everything over in."

All of this was so disappointing. I'd sort of pinned my hopes on this being my big break. I should have known better.

"Was anyone else ever around with them?"

Ralph leaned forward. "A young fellow did stop by the night before the sale. Pounded on the door and walked around the house before he took off."

I wondered what his definition of "young fellow" was. To me it was someone in their twenties, but to my grandmother it was someone my parents' age. "How old was he?"

"Hard to tell."

"How did you know he was young?" I asked.

"The way he moved," Ralph said.

I'd been hoping for something more. "Was there anything that stood out about him?"

"It was darn near dark when I noticed him out there. He saw me lookin' out the window and headed out."

I stood. "Thanks for your time."

"I sure do wish I could have been a bit more helpful." He walked me to the door.

"Did you notice what kind of car the man drove?" I asked.

"He was on a motorcycle. And don't ask me what kind. Unless it's a Harley, I'm hopeless."

I patted his arm. "Me too. I don't suppose you saw a license plate number."

Ralph was shaking his head again. "If only. Maybe I could help you out of this mess then."

I dug in my purse and gave him my business card. "If you or one of your neighbors thinks of anything, please let me know."

"I'll ask around again."

"Thanks, Ralph."

"It's the least I can do."

A glass of wine and a good hearty meal were all I needed to restore my spirits. Which is why after I parked my car at home, I walked over to DiNapoli's. This was a great time of day to be here, the lunch crowd was long gone, the after-school kids had dispersed, and the dinner crowd had yet to arrive.

"Angelo made something special for our dinner tonight," Rosalie said as soon as I dragged myself in. "Come. Sit. Eat with us."

Seconds later I was seated at a table with a glass of red wine, a basket of hot bread, and a steaming plate of risotto in front of me. I took a bite. "This might be heaven," I said.

Angelo beamed. "I agree with your assessment."

Rosalie shook her head. Angelo's statements made Rosalie shake her head a lot, but they made me laugh. There were bits of sweet potato, chicken, pancetta, and asparagus in the creamy goodness.

"If food can be love, this is it," I said. Then, oh jeez, tears formed. I blinked as hard as I could to fight them back. But of course the DiNapolis noticed. They both leaned forward.

"I'm just tired," I said. "I worked hard today."

Rosalie and Angelo just watched me. "Okay, okay. And it's the arrest. And the arraignment." My throat felt full. "And I have a pretrial conference next week."

"Your eyes can't be beautiful if you haven't cried," Angelo said. Then he repeated it in Italian.

"That's beautiful, Angelo," I said.

"He's paraphrasing Sophia Loren," Rosalie said. We all laughed.

"Hey, you can do worse than quoting a woman who says she owes everything to spaghetti." Angelo pointed his fork at me. "If you need anything, you let me know."

"Let *us* know," Rosalie added.

By the time I left, my stomach and heart were full. I carried home a box of risotto that I didn't plan to share with anyone. I wasn't looking forward to this evening, but I had to meet Eleanor.

CHAPTER THIRTY

The dart games were in full swing by the time I arrived at eight. Darts were flying everywhere—not everywhere, but it felt that way to me, and it made me want to run away. Frankly, I'd avoided darts since I was a child because of a near miss involving a drunken uncle. The whiz of the dart by my ear still gave me nightmares.

Eleanor sat at a table in a dark corner to one side of the bar with a pitcher of beer and an extra mug. I slipped into the chair across from her. My back was against the wall and about as far away from the dartboards as you could get without working behind the bar. The perfect place for observing the room. Five dartboards were set up on the other side of the room with three-foot intervals in between. Darts zoomed towards the boards. As I watched, a woman made a wild throw, and the dart embedded itself in the wall. I repressed a shudder. She cheered along with her friends. Someone handed her a half-full mug of beer. She chugged it down. Great.

"That's Joy," Eleanor said, lifting her chin toward

a redheaded woman on the far side of the room catty-corner from us.

The captain who'd been with Blade had an arm possessively around her waist. She had a lush figure like a fifties Hollywood starlet. Her enviable red hair tumbled in loose waves around her shoulders. As I watched her, she pulled away from her husband, swished past a group of young, single officers in a tight dress that seemed unsuited for darts, and winked at someone as she made her way toward the bar in three-inch heels. She didn't teeter or wobble on the heels.

Enviable. "Wowsa," I said. "She's something." I could see a husband getting jealous over a wife like her. And I could see Major Blade being interested. Almost anyone breathing would be.

"And she's nice on top of all of it. I'll call her over. Hey, Joy." Eleanor waved to attract her attention. When Joy looked over, Eleanor pointed to the pitcher of beer. Joy changed direction and joined us.

Eleanor poured her a beer and made the introductions.

"Your name sounds familiar," Joy said to me.

Rats. That wasn't good. "I volunteer at the thrift shop," I said.

She tossed her gorgeous hair back. "No. That's not it."

"My ex-husband used to be in charge of the security police here on base."

"Sarah has her own business running garage sales in Ellington," Eleanor said.

"Not my thing," she said, looking at me. "No offense."

Joy's husband walked up behind her. He didn't look happy. "I know why you've heard of her."

He leaned in close to Joy's ear but stared straight at me. "She's friends with the woman who murdered Major Blade." Joy's eyes widened. "Come on. You're up," her husband said. He held out his hand to help her up. As they walked away Joy glanced over her shoulder and mouthed *Sorry*.

"That went well," I said to Eleanor.

We watched them rejoin the group. Joy took a dart, put one foot slightly forward, and pointed the elbow of her throwing arm at the dartboard in what looked like a very awkward position. She let the dart fly. It landed just off center. There was another round of cheers. I noticed her husband was going from group to group. They took turns looking back at Eleanor and me. It wasn't hard to figure out what he was saying.

"I hope this doesn't create any issues for you," I said to Eleanor.

"Piffle. I could care less. My husband isn't in that squadron, and I'd stand up for you even if he was."

"Thanks. I guess that's going to put a damper on the sleuthing."

"I don't see the colonel's or the butter bar's wives here anyway. But we are staying put. I'm not going to let some vicious gossip chase us out of here."

"Maybe it's not vicious," I said hopefully.

Eleanor laughed. "You keep thinking that."

Eleanor and I were having a fun evening despite Joy's husband. Several people who had worked for CJ showed up and joined us. James came with his new girlfriend. A part of me felt like I was home. As much as I loved Ellington, I still missed the camaraderie of being a part of the military community. The excitement or disappointment of the next assignment. New places to live, new people to meet. The "we are all in this together" attitude—well, most of the time it was that attitude, Erin and Becky with their troubles with the Spouses' Club notwithstanding.

I guess that was part of my problem, sort of an every person who was attached to the military problem. No one had one place that was home; we lacked roots. But I was lucky. Ellington had become my home, and there was no other place I'd rather build a life. As soon as I figured out what to do about the Greens. And Michelle.

"Excuse me," I said to the people at our table. "I'll be right back." I went to the bathroom. When I was washing my hands, Joy came in. I didn't know whether to scurry around her or hide in a stall. Instead, I dried my hands in one of those horrible air dryers that was so weak it would take an hour to actually dry my hands. I turned, shaking the water off, and Joy stood there like she was waiting for me.

"I wanted to apologize for my husband," Joy said. "He's a little overprotective."

"If I had a wife who looked like you, I might be, too." I smiled, trying to ease her discomfort.

She waved her hand as if to wave off the compliment. "He's just been very upset since he found out Major Blade was murdered."

"I imagine the whole base has been."

"Yeah. But he respected Major Blade. More than the others."

Interesting. "So you knew him?" I might as well try to find something out.

"Yes. Major Blade even helped me with my homework for a statistics class I'm taking." She moved to the mirror and checked her lipstick.

Overprotective husband. Joy and Blade working together. That was interesting.

"We almost always just met at my house, so there wasn't any cause for gossip."

She said almost always, not always. I wondered where they met the rest of the time. But asking her seemed imprudent if I wanted to get Joy to tell me anything else.

"It must be hard for both of you to have lost him then."

Joy dug around in her purse, found a lipstick, and reapplied the hot pink to her lips. "It has been. Maybe we spent too much time with Blade since he was a rank over my husband. But we all just had the same interests."

"What did you guys like to do?" I wondered if she was going to tell me to mind my own business.

"Camped, sailed, and surfed in the summer. A bunch of us booked a ski lodge in Vermont for over Thanksgiving. I'm not sure anyone will want to go without Blade." She put her lipstick away. "He was a life-of-the-party kind of guy."

"I'll be blunt. I heard he was a womanizer." I decided to leave it at that instead of adding that I'd heard he especially liked married women.

Joy lifted one corner of her mouth. "He did love women."

I couldn't help a tiny flinch.

"Oh, not in a bad way."

Joy had been watching me closer than I thought.

"Blade was a good guy." Her eyes looked sad. "I'd better get back out there. Do you mind waiting a minute before going out? I don't want my husband to know I was talking to you."

"Not at all." I didn't want her to have problems because of me.

"I'm sorry about your friend being a suspect. I've met Michelle. She's a smart woman when it comes to work."

"I sense a but."

Joy dipped her head for a moment. "She could be overbearing. And aloof. It was a strange combination." Joy opened the bathroom door and left.

I leaned against the sink and thought over what she'd said. There were a lot of different views of the kind of person Blade was. Good man, churchgoer, womanizer. Filer of false IG complaints. It was confusing. What wasn't confusing was that Joy spent time with Blade. And her husband was overprotective. It didn't seem like a good combination at all.

The door opened and Eleanor popped her head in. "I thought you fell in."

I straightened up. "Not this time."

"Come on. Your beer is getting warm," Eleanor said.

I followed Eleanor back to the table and tried to get back into the flow of conversation. Joy's husband watched me from across the room, and he didn't look happy.

James followed my gaze. "Everything okay?" he asked.

I smiled at him. "Yes." It was for me. I just hoped it was for Joy and her husband.

Thirty minutes later I stood at the bar waiting to get our pitcher of beer refilled. Joy's husband came and stood by me. So close our shoulders were touching, until I shifted to the left. He leaned his forearms on the bar. I hadn't realized until then how muscular he was. Not tall, but his biceps were massive. He had a dart in his hand, the one closest to me, and he tapped it slowly up and down on the countertop. I watched it until he turned his head toward me with a pleasant smile.

"Stay away from my wife," he said. He chuckled. Anyone watching us wouldn't realize he'd just threatened me. "She tells me everything."

I wonder if he knew about the "almost always" Joy had mentioned about meeting with Major Blade. *What a blowhard.* He wasn't scaring me. Too much. Maybe only because there were so many people around. But that tapping with the dart was freaky. It's like he knew I was afraid of them. But he couldn't. "You're a lucky man then." I didn't think Joy was a lucky woman, though.

James came up on the other side of me. "How long does it take to fill a pitcher around here?"

His question was neutral and friendly, but his eyes and the set of his jaw focused on the captain with a steely determination. The captain stared back. It was almost like they were arm-wrestling with their eyes. There was so much subtext swirling around, we could have been mind melding. And while neither of them was in uniform, I didn't want James to get in trouble later. The captain outranked him.

The bartender set the full pitcher of beer in front of me. I put my hand on James's arm. "There it is now. Take it back to the table for me?"

James raised his eyebrows in an "are you sure?" look. I gave him a quick nod. After James left, I turned toward Joy's husband. I mimicked his earlier friendly smile. "You may outrank him," I tipped my head toward James, "but you hold no sway over me."

CHAPTER THIRTY-ONE

I sat in Kitty's basement with Toulouse Thursday morning at seven forty-five. This time last week I'd been arrested. A whole week ago and what had I found out? Not enough. But I had to focus on this task. Today was going to be my big final push to finish pricing everything and do most of the setup in the garage. In the light of day, or make that the basement, I wondered if my remark to Joy's husband had been foolish. Sometimes I carried the strong, independent female thing too far. But what choice did I have? I cared about Seth but didn't want to be dependent on him. Although there were times when that was very tempting.

Maybe I should tell Special Agent Bristow or Pellner about Joy's husband's threat. But was it even a threat? Did I just imagine the "or else" after his "stay away from my wife" comment? Maybe the strain of worrying about the pretrial conference, trying to track down the Greens, and worrying about Michelle were putting my imagination in overdrive. Although, James had noticed something in the captain's attitude or he wouldn't have come over. After I had sat back down at the table he asked if I was okay. I had assured him I was.

I straightened my shoulders and opened another box. "Toulouse, I'm going to miss you when I'm finished with all this."

Toulouse didn't answer, but he jumped in my lap and curled up. So maybe he did answer. I rubbed his ears. His purr throbbed through me. "I'll miss seeing Kitty every day, too." She was a little kooky, but in the best possible way.

A little after nine thirty my phone rang. Luke.

"I need Vincenzo's number," he said.

"What? Why?" I asked.

"I'm headed to the Ellington police station."

My stomach rippled. "Do you have any idea what they want to talk to you about?"

"Yes."

Luke had been like this as a kid, too, with the short answers. He'd perfected the "I'm not going to incriminate myself" by the time he was five. By the time he was six he was pleading the fifth whenever he was in trouble. He should have been a lawyer. "Tell me."

"I went up to visit my landlady before I left for the station. I always take her garbage out for her anyway. So I just asked if everything was okay."

"And?"

"She told me she'd seen that murderer hanging around and had called the police to let them know where she was." Luke paused. "So they could capture her."

I held back my "I told you so." It wasn't important

when he could be in trouble. I rattled off Vincenzo's number.

"They called Michelle in, too."

I didn't answer for fear I'd say something I'd regret, like *How stupid are you two?*

"I know what you're thinking. So I'll just say this once. You were right."

"As usual," I added. Any other time we would have both laughed because I'd been saying that to him since we were both able to talk. "Call me when you can. I love you."

"Will do. Love you, too."

Thank heavens I had so much physical work to do. It gave me a way to work off the worry and tension while I waited for Luke to call. I must have been up and down the stairs fifty times before he finally called.

"No one's been arrested," Luke said.

"That's a relief." Neither of us added the "yet." "What did they ask you?"

"How long we'd known each other. That kind of thing."

"That's it?"

"I could tell from their questions that they think Michelle and I had been seeing each other for a lot longer and didn't buy the 'we just met' story. Even though it's true."

"So they think you two worked together to kill Major Blade? Why?"

"Your guess is as good as mine. But I have an alibi for Thursday night."

"You do?" I couldn't have been more surprised. When Luke had dropped me off that night, he had been headed home.

"Yes."

"It can't be me," I said.

"It isn't. I spent the night at a friend's house." His tone was so neutral I knew something was up.

It didn't take long for it to dawn on me. "A *girl* friend's house?" It came out a little more shrill than I'd expected. It's not like I didn't know Luke was a bit of a ladies' man. He always had been. I remembered his first girlfriend. Margaret Mary. She lived down the hill from us with her nine brothers and sisters. She'd had long blond hair and big blue eyes. Luke always wanted her to come spend the night like other friends had and didn't understand why she couldn't.

"Yes. A friend who is a girl. I didn't know I was going to fall for Michelle the next day," Luke said.

"You fell for her?" I asked. I was astonished. Luke didn't fall for people. They fell for him.

"Yes. I did. Bad timing, right?"

"It is. But I'm happy for you." We chatted for a few more minutes before we hung up.

Thursday afternoon around two my phone rang. I had left Kitty's after I priced everything and hauled it out of the basement and up to the garage. Most of it was organized, too. I was patting myself on the back for all I had accomplished. I didn't recognize the number, but I was in a phase of answering all calls in hopes someone would get in touch about the Greens.

I'd hung up on a lot of telemarketers and reporters lately. This was probably another one.

"Is this Sarah Winston?"

"Yes." Ugh. Another telemarketer.

"This is the popcorn lady over at the flea market."

I gripped the phone harder. "Hi. How can I help you?"

"That couple you were asking about the other day?"

"Yes?" I almost dropped my phone.

"Plain popcorn and the caramel corn. They're here. Caramel corn is anyway. She looks kind of different. Her hair's short and she has more makeup on. A *lot* more makeup on. But she placed the same order. Couldn't fool me."

The change in appearance didn't worry me. I'd do the same if I was breaking the law. It was probably one of the reasons they'd been so hard to find. "Do they have a booth?" I asked.

"No. It seems like she's trying to sell some stuff to other dealers. I spotted her across the way chatting up some friends of mine. Regulars here."

I grabbed my purse, tucked my phone under my chin, locked my door, and rushed down the steps. "I'm on my way. If there's anything you can do to stall her, I'd appreciate it."

"Don't know what I can do. I have a business to run, you know."

I leaped into my Suburban. "I understand." I called Pellner as I sped over. It went to voice mail, but I hoped he get the message soon.

Twelve minutes later I was running across the flea market parking lot and into the building. I had to blink a couple of times to adjust to the dimmer light. I dodged left and right as I hurried to the popcorn stand. I pushed to the front of the line.

"Is she still here?" I asked the popcorn lady. I turned and smiled apologetically to the person behind me. He didn't smile back.

She nodded. "I sent a text to my friend telling her to stall her." She pointed diagonally to a booth. "See the woman with the short dark hair in the red shirt? That's her."

A group of people clumped around the booth she pointed to. But I spotted a woman in a red shirt. The popcorn lady put two fingers to her lips and let out a whistle that was probably heard over in Concord.

Her vendor friend jerked her head up, but so did everyone else. Kate Green and I stared at each other for a brief moment before she dropped her stuff and took off. She ran the opposite direction of where I'd parked. Go get my car? Or chase her? My feet took off before I'd realized I'd made any kind of decision. I ran after Kate.

I'd run through the flea market not too long ago. That time someone had been chasing me. "Look out. Look out," I yelled as I ran.

Two long blasts of a whistle sounded out. Probably from the popcorn lady. Other people shouted for security. A rolling cry for security followed me down the hall. Other feet pounded behind me. Kate ran faster than I did and made it to the west entrance. She disappeared from sight. I didn't slow down, and pretty soon I popped out into the parking lot on the west side of the building. An engine revved and wheels spun. Gravel sprayed.

A red car careened out of a parking spot. Kate sat in the passenger seat, and I got a quick glimpse of the driver. Alex. Sirens sounded in the distance. *Please let that be Pellner heading here.* I dug in harder and raced across the gravel parking lot, reaching the top of the exit as they flew onto the road. Another car was in their way. Both of them swerved. The driver of the other car flipped Kate's car off and drove on. The car Kate was in lost control. The back end slammed into an old oak tree. Bark splintered, limbs and leaves tumbled down.

I paused, staring at the car not quite believing what I was seeing. All was quiet except for the sound of the engine. I ran forward again. Gasoline permeated the air. Then I saw flames.

CHAPTER THIRTY-TWO

Shock stopped me. Flames swarmed toward the backseat. I could see the airbags had deployed in the front. Kate staggered out from the passenger seat and looked around like she didn't know where she was. The heat from the flames came at me in waves. I ran forward. Someone was yelling for me to stop. Kate turned back to the car, stared in toward the driver. She started to crawl back in.

A man grabbed my arm. "Get back. Get back. It's going to blow."

I tried to jerk away, but someone else grabbed my other arm and they dragged me back.

"The driver's in the car," I yelled. I started forward. Someone wrapped their arms around my waist and lifted me away.

"You can't. Fire department's on the way."

Another man darted toward Kate. He grabbed her by the arm and wrestled her away from the car. I tried to squirm free, but the arms were clamped tight around me. The flames brightened. Then the trunk of Kate's car exploded, lifting the back end up off the ground. A second explosion was far worse than the first.

Three hours later, I still couldn't stop shivering. I sat wrapped in several blankets on my couch. Pellner had pulled my grandmother's rocking chair up close and watched me. I kept seeing the blast over and over. Kate's screams echoed in my head.

"It wasn't your fault," Pellner said for the tenth or twentieth time.

He could say it a hundred times and I wouldn't believe him. "I shouldn't have chased her. I should have let you handle it."

Pellner looked down at his hands clasped in his lap. He knew I was right. "You couldn't have known that their trunk was full of gas cans. They were stupid. Thought they could run and would be far enough away using the gas in the trunk before they'd finally have to stop at a station to buy gas and risk being tracked on security footage."

"If I hadn't chased her . . ." My words hung there. Pellner had nothing to add that he hadn't already said. "Why was she even there?" I asked.

"Trying to get a last bit of money before they ran for Mexico."

"Mexico is a long way from Massachusetts."

"Exactly. Like I said, they were stupid."

"Still my fault." I didn't think I'd ever recover from seeing what I'd seen today. Kate's husband hadn't made it.

"They wouldn't have made it over the border. She

would have been AWOL. They would have been watching for her."

"Absent without leave." My voice sounded flat. Broken. Maybe I was this time. I'd thought I'd been broken when CJ and I split up the first time. But that was just a life blip compared to this. Dead inside. Empty. Maybe I'd died in the explosion and Pellner wasn't really here. This was hell. My punishment for killing that man. Wow, I didn't even know his real name.

Pellner gripped my knee. Dug his fingers in. It hurt. I guess I wasn't dead after all.

"The man you knew as Alex Green had a long criminal record."

"He did?" I pulled a blanket tighter around me. "What were their real names?"

"Ashley and Jeb Evans."

"How did Jeb having a criminal record work with his wife being in the military?" I asked.

Pellner shrugged. "It was a long time ago. Or so everyone thought. I guess they've been running this operation at every base they've been on. And when Ashley was on leave, too."

I pulled my knees up to my chest. There must be some way to get warm. If Stella was home, I'd be asking her for the scotch she loved so much.

"You'll warm up once the shock wears off."

"I'm not sure it ever will." I fought back tears. If I cried Pellner would never leave, and I wanted to be alone. I'd called Seth right after the accident so he'd hear about it from me and not someone else. He was at a political event in Boston and said he'd leave. I'd told him no. That I would take a nap once

I was done with the police. In the moment, when I was still so shocked from seeing the car explode, my voice had been calm and reasonable. I was thankful I'd convinced him to stay. He wouldn't believe me if we talked now.

"He worked as an auto mechanic. They both took one of those 'fun' lock-picking courses." Pellner had been getting constant updates since he'd brought me back here. "I think they were planning bigger and better things. You stopped them from whatever that was."

"Nice try." I shook my head. "I appreciate your effort. I'm done. I'm never going to sleuth again."

Pellner nodded. Looked relieved.

I felt a little twinge when I thought of Michelle. She'd be fine. Bristow was smart. Pellner was smart. Vincenzo was smart. I was the idiot. They'd figure it out. Faster than me. I shoved the blankets off me and stood. What I wanted to do was crawl under them and hide. Like I was in one of the blanket forts Luke and I made as kids. We'd been safe then. But if I was going to get Pellner out of here, I had to act normal.

"I'm going to make some tea. Do you want some?" I asked. Making tea sounded normal enough.

Pellner eyed me suspiciously. "No thanks."

He followed me into the kitchen. It took all my concentration to keep my hands, my whole body for that matter, from shaking while I made the tea. After I heated the water in the microwave, I added some honey and sipped it. Forcing it down. *See, everything is a-okay here.*

"Thanks for coming over, Scott." Oh dear. I never

called Pellner by his first name. But he didn't seem to notice. "I'll be fine."

"If you're sure?" he asked.

"I need to take a nap."

"That'll be the adrenaline leaving your body. A nap will be good for you."

I walked him to the door.

"Are you sure you don't want me to call someone for you?" Pellner asked.

"Stella's at practice. Carol has a class."

"What about Seth or the DiNapolis?"

I was surprised he mentioned Seth although there was probably plenty of talk about us around town. "They're all working. Besides, no one needs to be here while I sleep." I patted his arm and opened the door. "Thanks again."

I shut the door behind him and almost fell to the ground. I dragged myself down the hall to my bedroom. The shivering was back. It hurt. I climbed in bed, gathered the comforter around me, and curled into the fetal position to try to stop the cold.

I woke up when I heard Seth calling my name. Stella had a key, so she must have let him in. It was dark. But I didn't know if it had been dark for an hour or eight hours. When I'd come to bed I didn't think I'd sleep, but thankfully I had.

"Sarah?"

Seth was in my room. By the bed. I ignored him. Tried to keep my breathing even so he would go away. He deserved a better person than me. Instead of leaving, I heard him move around a bit. The comforter lifted and he curled himself around me, lending me his solid warm body for comfort. He didn't say anything. He just held me until he fell asleep. I hadn't felt so safe or loved in a very long time.

The next time I woke up a beam of sun was shining through a crack in my curtains. It seemed wrong to be in a warm, lighted place. Seth was gone, at least not in bed. I could hear someone moving around. Smelled coffee. I looked at my alarm clock. Eight a.m. My stomach had the nerve to rumble. Reminding me I was alive. I slipped out of bed and into the shower. I stood there letting the water beat down on me, trying to feel something other than numb. When the water turned icy I got out, dressed, and went out into my living room.

Seth sat on my couch, legs up on the trunk, working on a laptop. He shut it as soon as he saw me. We looked at each other, but he stayed seated waiting for me. I appreciated, no loved, his patience.

"There's coffee in the kitchen," he said.

I worked on a smile. "Sounds good."

I poured myself a cup. Drank right away. Scalded my tongue. Almost like I wanted to punish myself if no one else would. I took the coffee out into the living room and sat on the opposite end of the couch from Seth. He watched me.

"Pellner already explained to me what happened. Why the car exploded," I said. "Told me I didn't need to blame myself."

"So I heard."

"I know you need to get to work. Your trial starts next week. I'm fine."

Seth made a scoffing sound in his throat. "I don't think you are. If it's okay with you, I'll work from here today."

Tears. Damn tears flowed down my cheeks. "Thank you. I probably don't deserve it. But I'll take it. One of the only bright spots in all of this is that your opponent can't use me against you anymore."

"In my book he never could." Seth set his laptop on the trunk and pulled me to him. I nestled against his broad chest. His heart beat strong against my ear. When I woke up again an hour later, Seth held me firmly against him with one hand and texted someone with his other. I stirred and pushed away. Sleep had helped. I felt scarred inside but wasn't in the dark place I'd been yesterday. I'd made a foolish mistake. A man had died, but if the gas cans hadn't been in the back of his car he'd probably still be alive.

Seth put his phone down. "Hungry?"

"Yes. But there isn't much here."

Seth stood up. "I brought some supplies with me. I'll make us breakfast."

"I can help," I said.

Seth narrowed his eyes at me. So cooking wasn't my forte. At least all of my friends, including Seth, knew it.

"How are you at peeling potatoes?" he asked.

"I aced it in school."

Seth laughed. "Then you can help."

My kitchen was small so there was a lot of bumping into each other as we cooked. Maybe some of it was deliberate. Seth had brought eggs, potatoes, a loaf of French bread, and sausages. After I peeled the potatoes, he nudged me over to the small kitchen table. He rolled up his sleeves. I admired his strong forearms.

"Watch and learn," he said.

"I'll watch but am not so sure about the learning part." I put a fresh vintage tablecloth on the kitchen table. It was decorated with little hedgehogs. Seth chattered away about what he was doing, but I spent more time admiring his broad thick shoulders and his nice rear end instead of paying attention to what he was saying. I should get my phone. I'd sent Luke a quick text yesterday afternoon since I knew he'd hear what happened, and I didn't want him to worry.

Soon Seth set two plates heaped with scrambled eggs, French toast, sausage, and hash browns on the table. The scrambled eggs were so creamy. I ate like it had been a week since I had. It felt like that.

"How did you learn to cook?" I asked. He'd grown up in luxury. I couldn't imagine a scenario where he was in the kitchen helping the cook.

"I went off to college. Dorm food was awful. And yes. I was spoiled by our cook growing up." Seth added more maple syrup to his French toast. "I've lived alone for a long, long time." He looked at me intently before forking in some French toast. "I found out I enjoyed cooking. It relaxes me."

I'd always found cooking was stressful. I expected something to go wrong and it usually did. Maybe it was just a self-fulfilling prophecy. "That's how I feel about cleaning up after someone else cooks." Maybe that wasn't entirely true, but there was something comforting about putting a kitchen back to rights.

When my stomach was rounded like I had a food baby, I set my fork down. I reached across and took Seth's hand, interlocking our fingers. "Thank you. For this. For everything."

"Always."

My heart almost couldn't take the love in his voice and the way he looked at me. I pushed my chair back. "Now, I'll clean up while you go work."

"If you're sure?" Seth had looked past me toward the living room more than once during our breakfast. He was a busy man with a lot on his plate with his job as district attorney and running for the position so he could continue his work.

I pulled him up and pushed him out of the kitchen. "I'm sure." I didn't want to tell him I needed a little space. It had been almost two years since I moved here. I'd come to enjoy being on my own, to setting my own pace for the day. If Seth had a flaw, it was probably that he was more ready for us than I was. That wasn't exactly a flaw. More like a bit of a problem. A timing problem. He was a patient man, but for how long?

When I finished cleaning, I grabbed my computer and settled in my grandmother's rocker. "Seth, you don't have to stay. I have work to do. On my virtual garage sale and for a couple of clients with upcoming events."

Seth closed his computer. "I want to be here."

"You can come back for dinner."

"If you're sure?" he asked again.

"I am. I'd tell you I'm fine. But that isn't quite true." I set my computer on the floor and stood. "I appreciate that you haven't pushed me or tried to brush off what happened yesterday as nothing."

Seth nodded and gathered his things. He put on his suit jacket. Wow, he was handsome. And here I was with no makeup on, puffy eyes, and hair that had been washed but not blown dry or styled. A far cry from the model types he'd dated before me.

"Call me if you need anything. Or even if you don't." He hugged me fiercely and left.

CHAPTER THIRTY-THREE

I drifted to my bedroom and found my phone. I called Luke first.

"Have you heard how Kate Green, I mean Ashley Evans, is?"

"She's in the hospital for burns and a concussion. From what I've heard she's lucky it's only that."

My breath caught and I felt woozy. I wasn't as fine as I'd led Seth to believe. Maybe that was my flaw, putting up a good front. Not really letting people see me.

"How are you?" Luke asked.

I had to prepare myself for being asked that a lot over the next few days. "Recovering," I said.

"You might want to think about talking to a professional about what happened."

Luke had his share of demons. He knew what he was talking about. "I'll think about it," I said. "Did you ever have any luck with the footage of the runner I sent you?"

"The guy didn't have any luck. I'm sorry." He paused.

"How's Michelle?" I asked. I hadn't talked to her for a couple of days.

"She's okay. Doing the best she can," Luke said.

I might be off the hook with the police, but she certainly wasn't. I would call her after I finished working.

"I keep hoping something will come through to save her," Luke said.

"Yeah, me too," I said.

"I need to get back to it. Love you," Luke said.

"Love you, too," I said as he disconnected.

I made quick calls to Carol, Stella, and the DiNapolis, assuring them I was okay. James sent me a text asking how I was doing. I sent a short response saying I'd be fine. Eventually. Some day. Right?

I went to Kitty's house and worked for several hours so everything would be ready for tomorrow. It helped keep my mind off the horror of yesterday. After I got everything as ready as I could, I went back home and ate a late lunch. I made some cute signs to put up for the sale tomorrow and checked my listings for it on social media sites. My phone rang at two. Michelle.

"Can you come pick me up?" Michelle asked. Her voice was a little out of breath.

"Are you okay?"

"I need to talk to you."

That worried me. "Sure. Where are you?"

"At the Visitors Center for the Minuteman Park. The one in Lexington."

The Minuteman National Park had two visitors centers, one in Lexington and one in Concord. Basically on either end of the Minuteman National Trail. "I can be there in about twenty minutes."

"Great." Michelle hung up before I could ask her any other questions.

I hoped everything was okay, but I got the feeling it wasn't. I did a quick brush of my hair and swiped on some mascara before I drove over. The park ran along the approximate path that the British troops marched on in 1775 looking for weapons they believe were stored in Concord. I loved walking the wooded lanes.

I found Michelle huddled on a bench outside the building. A Patriots ball cap was pulled low on her brow. She was wearing her running clothes and shoes.

"What is going on?" I asked.

"Let's walk," she said. We headed west toward the Paul Revere capture site. There were lots of people on the path. Some were riding bikes, others walking dogs, and some like us were strolling. Although Michelle was moving quickly enough that I was almost jogging. Michelle kept glancing around and back over her shoulder.

"Michelle, slow down. What the heck is going on?"

"About forty-five minutes ago I heard two cars pull up outside my house and peeked out my curtains."

"And," I said when she paused. I spotted a bench just off the path and pulled her over to it. Once we sat down, I motioned for her to continue.

"I saw Special Agent Bristow, one of the cops from Ellington, and my commander in the first car. The second one was a security police car with two police in it."

"What did they say?" It must have freaked her out if she came out for a run. Part of the trail was right behind the fence that encircled the base.

"I left. I was all ready to go for a run anyway. I climbed out a back window and ran for the woods. Then I climbed the chain-link fence. Cut myself on the razor wire." She held out her right arm to show me the cut.

I put my head in my hands for a couple of moments. The fence was a good ten feet tall and topped with coiled razor wire. Michelle could have been seriously hurt. "You ran?" I asked when I lifted my head.

"I'm sure they were there to arrest me. I didn't kill the major."

"So what? You plan to go on the run?" It made me think of the Greens, and the gas, and the explosion. I guess I could give her some advice on what not to do.

"No. Of course not. I just panicked."

Michelle wasn't normally one to panic. She'd fought in wars, led troops, so the death of Major Blade must have had her more on edge than I'd realized. "They'll be waiting for you at your house. Maybe they just came by to talk." I didn't believe that, and I don't think I sounded too convincing.

"Right."

"We need to call Vincenzo and then he can take you back to your house," I said.

"Please. Not yet. You know me better than Vincenzo does. Let's just talk this through one more time. There must be something to help us figure out who killed Blade. I promise after we talk I'll call Vincenzo. If we come up with something, he can run with it."

I thought about my pledge yesterday to Pellner that I was giving up sleuthing. But this wasn't sleuthing. It was listening to a friend who was desperate. It's what

I would want someone to do for me if the situation was reversed.

"Okay." I hoped Bristow and the others just thought Michelle was out for a run and not that she'd run from them. "Tell me any little detail you can think of about Major Blade."

Michelle frowned. "He was well read. Especially military history. He was a runner and played baseball on the squadron intramural team. And Blade loved his single-malt Scotch whisky. I think he collected it. He certainly liked to show off his knowledge about it. Frankly, he liked to show off about everything."

"None of that seems to lend itself to murder," I said.

"We know he's a womanizer," Michelle said. "And that he likes married women."

I nodded. I'd been wondering if we'd been going down the wrong track with all of that. We knew he'd hit on Carol, but maybe the bartender had his own agenda and lied to us. Erin had called him a flirt but believed it to be harmless.

"What other jobs has he had in the Air Force?" I asked.

"He's mostly been a program manager. It's how he ended up here."

"Did he do a good job in his other assignments?" Michelle was above him in the chain of command, so she should know.

"I'd been working on his OPR, so reviewing his records."

His officer performance report.

"His past reviews were all glowing. He got commendations at every base. And if I'm being honest, other than the whole harassing issue, he worked hard here, too."

"Where else was he assigned?"

Michelle started listing his previous bases. I sat up a little straighter with each one.

"What?" she asked. "What are you thinking?"

I couldn't tell her what I was thinking because I didn't want to get her hopes up. Every base she'd mentioned was one the Greens—I had to quit thinking of them as the Greens and start thinking of them as the Evanses—had been at, too. I wanted to leap up and pace around. What if the Greens/Evanses were linked somehow with Major Blade?

The Air Force world could be small. People overlapped all the time at various bases. It's how I knew Carol and Michelle, from previous assignments. But we hadn't gone from base to base to base together. And maybe I was all wrong. Maybe the Evanses had been at the same bases as Major Blade but at different times.

"Sarah, what is going on with you?"

I shrugged, hiding my excitement. "Not sure. I was just wondering if there were any incidents at past bases with married women. But from the sound of his OPRs he must have been okay."

"Or they just passed him along anyway. Sometimes the good old boys protect each other. What's a little 'harmless' flirting among friends, right?" Michelle sounded bitter. Way more bitter than I'd ever heard her sound.

"Any chance you know or have ever worked with Ashley Evans?" I asked.

Michelle nodded. "She works for me."

"*Here*? At Fitch?" I asked.

"Yes. Why do you ask?"

"How did you get along?"

"I was her boss and I gave her a bad EPR, enlisted performance review, six months ago."

"Why?" I asked.

"I can't tell you. It was a personnel issue."

I formed a theory. One that might involve someone angry enough over a bad EPR to seek out some revenge. Placing a dead body in someone's car was one heck of a way to get back. I realized with a jolt that Kate/Ashley was only a couple of inches shorter than Michelle and had a similar build. Maybe she'd been the one running in the security footage. But why would Kate/Ashley kill Major Blade or have him killed?

I thought over everything I knew about both of them. Kate/Ashley was married, and Major Blade liked married women from everything I'd heard. Had they somehow been involved romantically? Had Major Blade known about the stolen goods?

"Why are you asking about her?" Michelle asked.

"I found out yesterday she, along with her husband, were the ones who set me up." I shook my head as the image of the car exploding flashed through it again.

"What? I can't believe I didn't hear about this." Michelle thought for a moment. "Ashley called in sick yesterday, and I worked from home today. I guess they are cutting me out of the loop. Are you all right?"

"Yes." I didn't want to focus on me. "And you're going to be okay, too," I said. I was more confident of that than I had been since the day we found Major Blade. "Did Blade have a motorcycle?"

"Yeah. He loved that thing."

I could almost feel my synapses pinging. "What kind was it?" I asked.

"A Honda, I think."

A Honda would fit with what Ralph had told me. I had a lot of theories and a few possible connections. But I needed hard evidence. Fast.

"I need to get you to Vincenzo." And then I had a couple of stops to make. So much for not sleuthing, but I had to make an exception just this once.

CHAPTER THIRTY-FOUR

Forty-five minutes later I was in Gillganins bar. It was early enough that the bar was fairly empty. Fortunately, the bartender I'd talked to the other night was there. I caught his eye.

"What can I get you?" he asked. "Cape Cod?"

"Not now. I have a favor. Would you please look at a photo and tell me if you ever saw the two people in it with Major Blade?"

"Sure, why not?" he said. "I want to help get this mess cleared up. I freak out every time I have to close and walk to my car by myself."

I opened my phone to the picture of the Greens/Evanses. A newer one that I'd seen online after the crash yesterday. The bartender took the phone out of my hand and studied the photo. He kind of nodded to himself before giving me my phone back.

"Oh, yeah. I remember them. I'm not sure what night it was but within the last week or so before Blade was murdered."

"Why do you remember them?" I asked.

"Because they were having one hell of a heated discussion over at that table in the corner."

"What about?"

"I couldn't hear what it was about. But Blade shoved the table so hard it almost fell over on them. Drinks went flying. Then he took off all red-faced. I had to clean up the mess. The couple kept apologizing for their friend's behavior."

"Thank you," I said. I put a big tip on the bar.

"Not necessary," the bartender said.

"Oh, but it is."

I called Special Agent Bristow from my car, but he didn't answer. Then I sent him a text telling him I needed to talk to him ASAP. Nothing. That didn't bode well for Michelle. I stopped by a florist's shop and bought a huge bouquet of flowers. A mixture of tiger lilies, daisies, and carnations with some baby's breath scattered throughout. Then I drove to the hospital in Billerica. The one where Luke had said Ashley Evans was a patient. Finding her room might be difficult, but as I recalled the hospital wasn't that big.

I roamed up and down corridors peeking into rooms. The flowers made it look like I was there to visit someone. Finding her room wasn't that hard but getting into it was going to be. A police officer was posted outside the door. And not just any police officer, but Officer Jones. He spotted me before I had a chance to reverse course. I thought about turning and running, but he'd probably just arrest me for something else. So I approached cautiously.

"What are you doing here?" we asked each other almost simultaneously.

"Ladies first."

"I was looking for Kate, uh Ashley," I said.

"Funny, I'm here guarding her instead of being out on patrol. Apparently, one shouldn't arrest the district attorney's girlfriend even if she is in possession of stolen goods."

I winced, realizing he'd been sent here as some kind of punishment. "I'm sorry if that got you into trouble. It wasn't my doing."

He shrugged. "Actually, this is an extra duty. I need the overtime." He got a pained expression. "And I realize I should have listened to you. But in the moment, you looked and acted guilty. Not to mention you were actually in—"

"Possession of stolen goods." I finished for him. "I'm making some changes to my business practices after this."

"Sounds like a good idea."

"Can I see Ashley?"

"No. No visitors."

I wanted to stamp my foot, but I refrained.

"I can give her the flowers," he said.

"Why don't you just keep them?" I suggested. "A peace offering."

He smiled. "It'll make my wife happy."

"That's good enough for me. Are you sure I can't—"

"You could bring chocolates, champagne, flowers, and money for a bribe. You still aren't getting in. Why do you want to after what she did?"

"I haven't been able to reason out why they would set me up." I looked down at the floor for a moment. "I'd never met them before they hired me."

"It's because you were an easy target," Ashley called from the room.

Officer Jones and I both turned and looked in. I stepped into the room.

Ashley sipped from a white Styrofoam cup with a bendy straw in it. Her face was pasty. Her hospital gown looked three sizes too big. There was a bandage over her left brow and on her right arm. IV tubing went from a bag on a pole to her left arm.

"And your husband was a jerk to my friend Tiffany Lopez," she said.

I took a step back and put a hand against the door-jamb so I wouldn't fall over as thoughts swirled through my head. Talk about a blow to the gut. Tiffany had caused the original rift between CJ and me.

"Are you okay?" Officer Jones asked me.

I nodded. I looked at Ashley again. She watched me with a glint of glee in her eyes. That woman was sick and not just from the explosion yesterday. My only light here was knowing if I was right that she'd be in prison for a very long time.

"What about Blade? Why kill him?" I asked. I assumed she wouldn't answer.

Ashley used a remote and raised the head of her bed. She set down her drink and smoothed the blankets. "I didn't need him anymore. He kept wanting more of the take from our little scheme."

So Major Blade *was* involved with the Greens/Evanses. "You call serial burglaries and setting innocent people up a little scheme?" For a minute I thought about looping that IV tubing around her neck and pulling it tight.

Ashley lifted a shoulder and dropped it. "But Jeb is the one who strangled him. Not me."

Officer Jones and I stared at each other.

"We can testify that you said that," I said. I tried not to sound too delighted.

Ashley lifted the arm with the IV in it. "No, you can't. I'm under the influence of painkillers."

A nurse breezed in. He wore light blue scrubs. The top had yellow smiley faces all over it. "There's no drugs in that, honey," he said. "It's just liquids because you're dehydrated."

Ashley's face flushed to a shade of red only seen in roses. "Any good attorney will have my statement thrown out," Ashley said.

"Not when Miss Winston and I both testify to it," Officer Jones said.

"I heard her, too," the nurse said. "I'll give you my contact information."

Ashley doubled over and shrieked. She clutched her head. "Nurse. My head." Tears welled in her eyes. "Help." She slumped back against the bed.

The nurse looked over at Officer Jones and me. "Get out." Then she pushed a button on the wall.

I backed out of the room and Officer Jones followed me.

"I can't believe she said those things," I said to Jones.

"Neither can I."

A doctor and another nurse pounded down the hall toward us and ran into Ashley's room.

"Figures," Officer Jones said. "Just when you think you have solid information."

"She's faking it."

"Why do you say that?"

"I glanced at her heart monitor before we left. Her heartbeat and blood pressure were normal. I don't think they would have been if something was terribly wrong."

"So she's trying to make a case that an attorney could use in court?"

"That's what I think. I need to get going. I hope I never see you again." I said it with a smile.

"Back at you," he said.

My phone *bing*ed. A text from Special Agent Bristow responding to my earlier call and text. But all it said was he was at the Ellington police station and too busy to talk right now. After what I'd just heard, we'd see about that.

CHAPTER THIRTY-FIVE

Forty-five minutes later, I had cajoled, pleaded, and threatened my way into seeing Bristow. I sat across from him in an interview room at the Ellington Police Department. I was fairly certain Michelle was sitting in another room down the hall as I'd seen Vincenzo's car in the parking lot.

Bristow didn't look happy. He probably didn't take well to threats, which had come in the form of me telling him if he didn't see me I'd go to my brother and Bristow could read what I had to tell him in the newspaper. Two chairs, one table, a big two-way mirror, and two glasses of water were all there was in the room. A security camera was up in one corner. As far as I could tell it was off, but I didn't care if it wasn't.

"I thought you'd given up sleuthing," Bristow said. He had a fresh haircut, but it didn't offset the worn-out look around his eyes.

Apparently, he'd been talking to Pellner about me. "You're interviewing the wrong person down the hall," I said. "I had to make sure you got it right."

Bristow just looked at me with the stoic look he was so good at.

"Ashley confessed," I said.

"What?" That took the stoic look right off of his face.

I explained what happened. Words tumbled out so fast that Bristow was having trouble following. I took a breath and went through it again.

"I'm not sure that will hold up," Bristow said.

"I have a theory to go with her confession," I said.

Bristow leaned forward and put his forearms on the scarred table between us. "Theories don't convict people. Evidence does."

Yeesh. I'd heard that from CJ more than once. "And some information from Ashley Evans. I think you'll find that my theory will fit the evidence." I sounded kind of snotty. I needed to take it down a notch, because without his help I had no way to prove what I was going to tell him. I paused. "You will have to fill in some of the blanks with information I don't have access to."

"I'm all ears." Bristow said it, but not like he meant it.

I blew out a puff of air. "First, I'll tell you what I think happened and then give you my best guesses as to why."

Bristow raised his eyebrows when I said guesses. I should have thought of a better way of phrasing it.

"Major Blade and the Evanses have been stationed together repeatedly."

"Not a crime," Bristow said, but he looked more interested.

"Major Blade had a thing for married women. Ashley Evans was young and married the first time I think they were stationed together. Maybe the fact she was forbidden fruit since she was enlisted and he an officer might have made her even more tempting."

I took a drink of water. My throat felt suddenly constricted saying all of this out loud. "So early in his career they had an affair. What Blade didn't realize is how twisted Ashley is. That she'd use the affair to blackmail him and get him involved in their robbery ring."

"Why would he put up with that?"

"She could end any chance of his ever doing well in the Air Force. Even a rumor of that could have ended his career. Look what's happening to Michelle because of the IG complaint." I leaned forward. "And from what I've heard Major Blade was ambitious."

Bristow nodded.

"However, I think he'd had enough of dealing with the Evanses. The bartender at Gillganins saw them arguing. Blade stormed out."

"That doesn't mean they killed him."

"When we first found Blade's body, I noticed there weren't any defensive wounds on his hands. He must have been strangled from the back. One person is in the front seat like they are going to drive him home. One is in the back and uses something to strangle him. Michelle couldn't have done that on her own."

"We always thought two people were involved. Michelle and someone else." He looked at me and I knew he was thinking about Luke. "Why involve Colonel Diaz?" Bristow asked. "Why use her car?"

He didn't refute my theory of how Blade was killed. I must be on the right track. "Ashley worked for

Michelle, and Michelle gave her a bad performance report."

"That hardly seems like a reason to try to set someone up for a murder," Bristow said.

"Not to you or me or anyone reasonable. But she's twisted." I filled him in on what she'd said at the hospital about CJ, Tiffany Lopez, and me. Bristow had been on that case, so it didn't take too much explaining. I also mentioned Blade being an inconvenience. "I don't think she spent a long time planning setting me up, but she saw an opportunity and took it."

"She has her own sick system of justice." Bristow sat back in his chair, folding his arms over his chest.

I just waited, letting what I'd told him sink in before I continued. "Ashley *must* have been at Gillganins the night Michelle and I drank there. She would have seen what went on between Michelle and Blade. After we left, they argued with Blade, killed him, and set up Michelle."

Bristow rubbed a hand over his face. "It seems awfully convenient."

"It was just a win-win for Ashley. Two birds, one stone." I drank some more water. "After they put Blade in Michelle's SUV, they broke into Michelle's house."

"Why?"

"To make it more convincing. Ashley dressed in Michelle's running clothes and ran off base to the car and back to Michelle's house. Then she left the dirty shoes at the top of Michelle's steps. Maybe hoping she'd take a tumble. That would have been the perfect ending for Ashley. Blade dead. Michelle dead.

And me in jail for her other crime of selling stolen goods."

"What shoes?" Bristow asked.

"The ones Michelle threw in a dumpster over by the TLF. With any luck it hasn't been emptied. If they are still there, maybe there will be some evidence on them that will seal the deal for Ashley." Even if there wasn't, I hoped there was enough other evidence to convict her. Knowing who killed Blade would mean it would be easier to process any trace evidence in Michelle's SUV.

Bristow stood up. "Excuse me for a minute."

I stood and stretched while I waited. Michelle was going to be in trouble for not saying anything about the shoes, but it sure beat being tried and imprisoned for murder.

Bristow returned a half hour later and we both sat back down. "I made some calls. It hasn't been dumped yet. I have someone going to the dumpster. But you have to realize it doesn't look good for Michelle."

Bristow took his water glass and swirled the water around. "I'll check to see when and where Blade's and Ashley's professional lives crossed paths." He pushed the water glass away. "But why did they argue now?"

"I'm not sure. Maybe he decided he was far enough along in his career and had enough support that a long-ago affair as a young officer would no longer hurt him. He'd proved himself to be a good officer." For the most part. "Or maybe he was tired of being involved with their burglary schemes." Unless Ashley suddenly confessed to everything we might never know. Somehow, after the scene at the hospital

I didn't think she'd do that. Or if she did she'd blame Jeb and Blade. Dead men really don't tell any tales.

"It seems very risky for her to have been in the bar the night you were there. You could have recognized her."

"I wasn't looking for her. Besides as the Greens they were friendly hipsters. As the Evanses, Ashley had short hair and wore a ton of makeup. No glasses."

Bristow looked thoughtful. "If Blade knew about Jeb and Ashley's extracurricular activities, he'd always be a threat to them."

"Exactly. It's the why of all of this. When Ashley saw Blade undermining Michelle and filing the IG complaint, she knew he couldn't be trusted." My phone rang. Mike. "I've got to take this. Will you excuse me for a minute?"

Bristow looked incredulous but motioned for me to go ahead.

I slipped out into the hallway. "What's up? I'm kind of busy here trying to convince Special Agent Bristow that Michelle didn't kill Major Blade."

"Then I'm going to make you very happy," Mike said.

"Did you enhance the security camera footage I sent you?" I asked. I could hardly breathe.

"No. It was worthless."

I was so disappointed. "Oh."

"I'm going to send you some dashcam video from a car that was traveling down the road the night Major Blade was murdered. It shows a clear picture of the face of your runner. And it isn't your friend Michelle."

"What?" This was amazing news. "And it's not doctored?" Okay, so I didn't quite trust Mike.

He didn't respond.

"I'm sorry. It just almost seems too good to be true." I remembered when I'd first watched the video at Patty Sanchez's apartment. A couple of cars had gone by. "How did you get it?" I hoped it didn't involve broken knees or any other body part.

"I twisted a few limbs," Mike said.

"Mike—" I felt dizzy.

"Not literally."

"Oh. Whew. But how?"

"Let's just say people are creatures of habit and leave it at that."

"And if Special Agent Bristow wants to talk to the person who owns the car and dashcam?"

"He can. There's no connection to me. It will look like it came through Vincenzo's investigator."

Good enough. "Thank you." Another check mark in the "I owe you" column for me. Sometimes I pictured Mike as Scrooge hunched over a desk with a big book. It only had two columns. One for "I owe you" and one for "you owe me." The "you owe me" column was full of check marks and the other practically empty. Someday I was going to balance that ledger in my favor. Somehow.

As soon as we hung up my phone *bing*ed, and there was the video with the name of the driver and his contact information. I watched the video because I wanted to make sure it was authentic before I showed it to Bristow. The dashcam showed a dark two-lane road. The car turned, and as the headlights swept around the corner it caught the face of the runner before they ducked their head. The video even had a date and time stamp.

"Ashley. Ashley *is* the runner," I said when I burst back into the interrogation room. I handed my phone to Bristow and sat back down in the chair across from him. He watched the video without comment and then watched it again.

"Where did you get this?" he asked.

"Vincenzo's investigator." I didn't like to lie to Bristow. He watched me with his cop eyes. I didn't have a good poker face, but I did my best to not look away.

"Okay, then."

Whew. If he didn't believe me, he wasn't going to call me out right now. I stood up. "That's all I have. It's in your hands." I thought about Michelle who must be sitting in a room down the hall. How scared she must be. I hoped with all of this information that she'd be home soon. I needed to call Luke when I left here and tell him all that had happened. He'd be relieved, too.

Bristow stood, too. "You're good at this you know. Investigating. Making connections."

I shrugged. This was the second time he'd said this to me. The first being the day we'd found Major Blade's body. I couldn't decide if he was serious or not.

"Why not make it official? It might keep you out of trouble."

Wow. Maybe I should be flattered. Or maybe Bristow was telling me to do it officially or not at all. "It's not for me. I can't picture me running around with a gun and a badge."

"You could be an analyst," Bristow said.

"No thanks. I'll stick to garage sales."

"Will you?"

"Of course," I said. It did boost the old ego when someone of Bristow's caliber thought so well of me. "Thanks for listening to me."

"I'll keep you posted," Bristow said as I left.

CHAPTER THIRTY-SIX

Becky called me as I drove over to Kitty's house at seven on Saturday morning.

"I talked to Erin yesterday," she said.

"How did it go?" I pulled over to the curb because I didn't like driving and talking even though Great Road was fairly empty right now. Ellington was just waking up. Although the Dunkin's had been crowded when I picked up a couple of boxes of coffee and donut holes to give out at the sale. Kitty's sale didn't start until nine, so a few minutes of talking to Becky wouldn't make me late.

Becky sniffed. Once, twice, three times.

Oh dear. That wasn't a good sign.

"She wasn't interested in my apology or trying to forgive me. She said that everyone on base knew what kind of person I was and that I should just get over myself."

Inside I sighed. "At least you tried." I thought about sharing some platitude about you can only control what you do, not what others do. "That's all you can do."

"I guess it is. But you don't agree with Erin, do you?"

I wasn't sure what I thought, and what did it matter anyway? I saw the good and bad in Becky and Erin. None of us are perfect. And I didn't have to deal with Becky in my daily life or worry about her husband hurting the career of anyone I cared for. "Sometimes it's very hard to be a military spouse."

"You're right." Becky sniffed again. "I'll just do my best. And try to ignore people like Erin."

"There you go," I said. I wondered if she noticed I hadn't answered her question.

We said our good-byes and I headed to Kitty's house, thinking about how I couldn't control how the Greens set me up to sell their stolen goods. And Major Blade hadn't been able to control them, either.

By eleven the Cat-tastic Garage Sale was in full swing. People milled about buying, buying, buying. Who knew people loved cat items so very much? I guess Kitty did. I looked across the driveway at her. Kitty wore tights with a cat head just below each knee. A sweater with dancing cats on it and her fifties "cat" skirt. She flounced from person to person in shoes covered in cat heads that matched her tights, asking them what cat things they loved and leading them to it. This was one sale that had something for every cat lover. The advertising I'd done with the cat groups was certainly paying off. If this kept up, it would be one of the most successful sales I'd ever run.

Michelle was home. Not out of trouble yet, but at least not in jail. It looked good that the IG complaint would be dropped because Major Blade was the one who filed it. It looked like he was doing it with extreme prejudice. Once that was taken care of her promotion would go through, which meant sometime in the next year she'd be moving. I wondered how Luke and Michelle felt about that.

My phone *bing*ed. Bristow sent a text saying they couldn't question Ashley until she was off the painkillers.

> Painkillers? She wasn't on them yesterday.
>
> She's had a relapse.
>
> Relapse, my rear end. She's faking it.

Ashley must be faking injuries to keep from being moved to jail and questioned. But that wasn't my problem. Bristow replied.

> I agree.
> But until the doctor does there's nothing to do but wait.

I put my phone away. This was so frustrating. She'd said all of those things she'd told Officer Jones and me when she thought she was on painkillers.

The day was overcast, and fall was definitely in the air. Clouds hurried across the sky. We had ten tables filled with cat items. And two baskets full of free cat figurines to go to good homes. I stayed over by the more expensive items because Kitty wasn't as comfortable with negotiating as I was. I still worried about what her neighbors were going to think when they found out she wanted her house to look like a cat. But it was her property to do with what she wanted.

There was a card table full of cat jewelry, some of it vintage, some of it new. None of it was that valuable. I'd taken flat, shallow box lids and lined them with terry-cloth towels. Then I'd put the jewelry in. It kept it all from rolling around. Kitty had hundreds of pieces of jewelry. It was a sight to behold. A woman in a Garfield T-shirt came up and started combing through the jewelry. She set the pieces she was interested in to one side.

Two other women came up and tried to crowd her out. One of the women started picking up the pieces the first woman had laid aside.

"Those are mine," the first woman said. She looked at me for help.

"Would you like a bag for those?" I asked. I'd brought some quart-size plastic bags to use for this kind of thing or for the miniature cat collection on another table.

"Yes, please. That would be great," she said.

I grabbed a bag and we put the jewelry in it. I offered the other two women bags, too. Then I set the box of bags at the edge of the table in case anyone else wanted to use them. All three of them crowded the table, hands bumping each other and glares getting fiercer. The first woman finally stepped away. She had one full bag of jewelry.

"Would you set this someplace while I continue to shop?" she asked. "I want to look through the records."

"Sure," I said. I set the bag next to the porch where I kept my water bottle, extra plastic bags, and a few other things that were sold but people were coming back for when they finished looking around.

"Excuse me," a man said. He wore corduroy pants, a cream-colored knit fisherman's sweater, and expensive shoes. "I saw in your advertisement that you had a set of opium weights. Have they sold?"

"No. They are over here, and the price is firm," I said.

He made a face. People didn't like not being able to negotiate at a garage sale. We walked to a set of white wooden shelves that had carved cats across the top.

"Here they are," I said. "And they are authentic, not reproductions." I had checked with a friend of mine who had an antiques business in Acton. "Also it's a complete set. All nine of them are here. Complete sets are hard to find, especially in as great condition as these." I picked the smallest one up. It was my favorite. Its expression reminded me just a bit of Toulouse, who I'd become very fond of.

He took out a pair of glasses and looked them over carefully. "I agree they are original." Then he offered me half of the price I'd put on them.

I shook my head. "I can sell them online for more than that."

He offered twenty-five percent more.

Apparently, this man didn't understand what the word *firm* meant. "No."

"You aren't going to counteroffer?" he asked. His face turned a little red.

Right now I was rethinking that whole having a badge thing. It would be lovely to whip it out and tell him to get lost. "No. I explained that the price was firm. It's a fair price. Cheaper than you could buy them anywhere else. So would you like them or not?"

"I drove all the way from Boston. Doesn't that count for something?"

"No." I set the smallest weight back on the shelf. I refrained from telling him I couldn't care less even if he'd flown over from London, England.

"You drive a hard bargain."

"So I've been told." I did have a modicum of empathy for the man. I knew what it was like to be shut down when you were trying to negotiate. Truth be told, it happened way more than I'd like it to when I was out shopping.

He took out his wallet and carefully counted the cash. He handed me the money and I recounted it.

"You're short twenty dollars," I said, fairly certain that was deliberate.

"And you aren't going to cut me any slack?"

"Again. No. See the woman over there? The one decked out in cat clothes? She has a dream, and she's selling things she loves to fulfill that dream. I'm going to make sure every dime, or in this case every twenty, counts."

"Oh, all right." He took his wallet out and got out another twenty. "If I ever have a garage sale, I'm going to hire you." He gave me a slight smile.

I tucked the money in the multi-pocketed carpenter's belt I wore around my waist. For a brief minute I thought about the last time I'd worn it—when I'd been arrested. "And I'll be just as tough for you as I am for my client today." I wrapped the opium weights individually in tissue paper with cats on it and put them in a bag. "Here you go."

The two women who'd been so aggressive at the jewelry table came over to me with their arms loaded with things, including several bags of jewelry.

"We are ready to pay you," one of the women said. "I assume you will do some negotiating since we're buying so much."

"Sure," I said. I took the first bag of jewelry, studied the front and then the back. I gave her a price. She asked for ten percent less and I said yes. The second bag was even more stuffed. I turned it over and over. This jewelry looked familiar. I glanced over to where I had set aside the first woman's jewelry while she looked at the records.

"Where did you get this bag?" I asked.

The woman frowned and then sighed. "From over there."

She pointed to where I'd set the bag for safe-keeping. I gave her a steely gaze and took the bag back. After that she and her friend didn't argue over the prices I gave them and left quickly. Sometimes I just didn't get people.

I drifted back over to where a man was looking at the jewelry. He had a jeweler's loupe with him and studied several pieces. He held up a necklace with an unassuming chain and enameled back.

"This is a Victorian mourning necklace," he said. "There's no price on it."

I took it from him and turned it over. The other side had an intricately woven hair preserved behind a piece of glass. How had I missed this?

"How much do you want for it?" he asked.

"I will have to check with the owner. Excuse me," I said. I took out my phone and did a quick search online. They were selling from fifty dollars all the way up to six hundred, depending on the condition and the hair. Some held just a snippet of hair, but the more expensive ones were more like the one I held.

"Kitty, a man found this Victorian mourning necklace in with the jewelry. I think it could be valuable."

"What is it?" she asked.

"It's a piece of jewelry with hair in it that during Victorian times people kept as a remembrance of their loved one who died. I'm so sorry I overlooked it earlier." I was kicking myself for missing it. It would have been terrible if I hadn't been there when the man had said that or if I hadn't taken a better look when he asked for the price. One of my biggest fears was selling something valuable for next to nothing for a client and then seeing it on an episode of *Antiques Roadshow*.

"It's beautiful and creepy at the same time," Kitty said.

I nodded. "Do you want to sell it? It could be a family heirloom."

Kitty frowned. "I should take it to my mom and see if she knows where it came from."

"I think that's a good idea. If you don't want to keep it after you talk to her, I can sell it for you online." That at least would ease my conscience a little.

"Why do you look so upset?" Kitty asked.

"Because I missed it."

"I think it's my fault. I found another bag of jewelry this morning and stuck it in with the others."

"Oh, thank heavens. I thought I was slipping."

Kitty patted my arm and turned to a friend who'd come up to her. I headed back over to the man who found the necklace.

"I'm sorry. It's not for sale after all." I braced myself for his reaction.

He smiled. "I get it. I guess I should learn to keep my big mouth shut at these things."

At three o'clock the garage sale looked like a wasteland. We'd consolidated the remaining cats onto two tables.

"I got two commissions for painting people's pets," Kitty said.

"That's wonderful." I'd helped design a brochure of Kitty's paintings.

"If I'm lucky someday I'll be able to quit my accounting job and paint animals all day. What a joy it would be to make people happy through my paintings."

"When do you think you'll start redoing the outside of your house?" I asked. Hopefully, it would be long enough from now that her neighbors wouldn't associate the garage sale with the construction.

"About that," Kitty said. "So many people from cat organizations were here today. I overheard lots of conversations. They have so many needs. I decided to donate the money instead of changing the outside of my house."

Kitty looked at me and laughed.

"What?" I asked.

"You look so relieved."

"I was worried about what your neighbors would think. It's a lovely neighborhood."

Kitty looked around. "It is."

"And I think Toulouse will approve," I said.

"So do I."

Back at home I stretched out on top of my blue and white comforter. It was fluffy and felt like a hug. My white curtains let the late afternoon light in. Garage sales were a lot of work, and I just wanted to close my eyes for a few minutes. My phone rang, so I rolled over to see who was calling. Erin. Great. I thought for a second about not answering, but since I'd talked to Becky this morning I felt like I should take Erin's call, too.

"Hey, Erin." I didn't ask her how she was, because from what Becky said not happy.

"You are never going to believe this, but Becky called me yesterday."

Actually, I could believe it. "She did?"

"She said she was calling to apologize, but instead she did one of those I'm sorry you felt that way. That's not an apology, that's blaming the person for being right. In this case anyway. Because she was wrong, and I was totally right."

I hated those kinds of so-called apologies, but I didn't want to get back in the middle of the two of them. I should have kept my big mouth shut about the whole thing. Lesson learned. I murmured some kind of noise that might sound like an agreement, but that gave me deniability if I needed it. I liked Becky and I liked Erin. It was hard when two people were at odds. And I had to be practical. A few people from base had hired me to do garage sales for them.

Unless something egregious happened, I'd chalk this up to *she said, she said* and try to remain friends with both of them.

"I might have forgiven her," Erin said, "but I will never forget. What she did originally or that phony apology. And frankly none of my friends will, either."

We talked a few more minutes before hanging up. I rolled over and closed my eyes. But instead of sleeping, I thought about the situation with Becky and Erin. Life was hard enough, and things like this made it harder when they didn't necessarily need to. It was like me being intimidated by Nichole. What good did it do? What would it matter in five years? We all fretted about a lot of stuff that wasn't that important.

CHAPTER THIRTY-SEVEN

At nine that night I sat at DiNapoli's with Carol, Stella, Rosalie, and Angelo. Angelo had fixed us a feast fit for thirty instead of five. Seth had begged off, saying he had some work to catch up on. I wondered if something else was going on. The table was still loaded with food. Calamari, garlic bread, two kinds of salad, ziti, meatballs. And that was after the antipasto plate and soup we'd started with. The last customers had left, and we had the place to ourselves. Angelo had kept our wineglasses full of Chianti and regaled us with stories of growing up poor in Cambridge. Maybe poor in money, but rich in family and friends. Loved. Isn't that all any of us really wanted? What was with me and the deep thoughts? Maybe it was because of the arrest and being set up by the Evans. Maybe it was from seeing a man get blown up. Or maybe it was the comfort Seth had given me over the last week.

I managed a final bite of my ziti and pushed my plate away. Thankfully, I'd worn a loose tunic top and leggings, so I didn't have to deal with a tight waistband. "Don't let me eat any more."

"But I have dessert," Rosalie said.

Rosalie's Italian cookies were amazing. I let out a small groan. "But I'm stuffed."

Angelo poured more Chianti in my glass. "Here's to you being off the hook."

We all clinked our glasses and then took a sip.

"Do you have any idea why Ashley and her husband set you up?" Carol asked.

I'd been so busy for the past two days clearing up my legal issues and working on the garage sale for Kitty I hadn't seen anyone. It had been such a fun evening that I hated to even talk about it. But these were my friends. My family. I wished Luke could have been here, but he had to fly out of town this afternoon on assignment. He'd told me before he left that he and Michelle had spent every minute together since she'd gotten home yesterday. Michelle even took him to the airport. I was happy for them.

"It was twofold. A matter of convenience and poor business practices on my part. But something creepier, too." I told them what Ashley had said about Tiffany Lopez. They all exchanged glances. "What is going on? I get the impression it's something other than just celebrating my freedom." All night they had been looking at each other. A raised eyebrow here, a shake of the head there. It seemed like they'd been waiting for dinner to be over.

"I'll clear the table," Rosalie said.

"I'll get the dessert and more wine." Angelo started to stand.

"Sit," I ordered. "Spill it. I'm a big girl."

"It's about CJ," Carol said.

"Is he sick? Hurt?" Being a police officer was risky even in a small town in Florida.

"No. He's fine," Stella said. She turned to Carol. We all did.

"You know he stays in touch with Brad," Carol said. I nodded.

"How do you feel about CJ?" Carol asked. They all watched me anxiously.

"Guilty. CJ said he'd die a lonely old man without me. It makes me sad. I want him to be happy. He thought he could be with me, but he was wrong. We were wrong for each other."

Carol glanced at Stella. "You don't need to feel guilty," Carol said. "CJ's seeing his high school sweetheart. She's a widow with two young girls. Her husband was killed two years ago in Afghanistan. It sounds like they are serious."

Wow. CJ always wanted kids and we couldn't have them. His mom must be over the moon. I'd heard enough about the high school sweetheart from her over the years. We'd actually met once when CJ and I were visiting his parents. She was a lovely, warm person, and her two girls had been adorable. I ran through memories of CJ and me. How we'd met, places we'd lived, the last two years of ups and downs between us. If CJ was happy, I could let the guilt go. There was a twinge of sadness for what we'd lost, maybe what we'd never had.

"I'm happy for him. He's a good man and deserves a good life," I said. "Is that why Seth isn't here? Because you were worried about how I'd react?"

They all nodded.

I smiled. "You are good friends. Thank you for

worrying about me. For loving me." My voice caught a little. "Now how about that dessert?"

An hour later Stella and I strolled home. I was too stuffed to move any faster. Seth was sitting on the top step of the porch.

"You should give him a key," Stella said while we were still out of earshot.

"I'm not ready. Have you given one to Awesome?" I asked.

Stella grinned. "Point taken." Stella greeted Seth and went inside.

The night was warm, the stars bright. I sat down next to Seth on the porch and leaned against him. "Do you know?" I asked. I had a feeling Carol had called him and told him she needed to talk to me privately.

"I know that I love you."

Little swirls of happiness surrounded me. I took his hand and squeezed it. "I mean do you know why Carol arranged the dinner at DiNapoli's?"

"No. She was a bit cryptic. Is everything okay?"

I looked over at the town common. The white church loomed large, glowing in the light of the almost full moon. I thought of a hymn that said *It is well, it is well with my soul.* It's how I felt sitting here in Ellington with Seth next to me.

"It's better than okay." I told Seth what Carol had told me about CJ. But also how it made me feel, including the twinge of sadness. Maybe it was time to quit holding back parts of me. Maybe that's why CJ and I had never completely worked. I thought about the Greens/Evanses and how they valued so little except money. Seth's arm was warm and steady against mine. The only things with any real value were the people in my life and my relationships with them.

I looked at Seth. "I love you, too."

ACKNOWLEDGMENTS

To my editor, Gary Goldstein, and my agent, John Talbot. Thank you both so much for all you have done for me. I love it when you tell me stories about each other from back in the day. Maybe I should write a book . . .

To the Wicked Cozy Authors—Jessie Crockett, Julie Hennrikus, Edith Maxwell, Liz Mugavero, and Barbara Ross. This publishing thing is quite the ride. Sometimes a roller coaster and sometimes merry-go-round. I wouldn't want to be on it without all of you.

To independent editor Barb Goffman—you do so much more than find plot holes and misspelled words. Thanks for always making me dig deeper and for making each book so much better.

To Mary Titone. Mary, Mary you're never contrary. Thank you for acting as my publicist, but more importantly for being such a wonderful friend.

To Clare—you now dance with angels while I weep. Thank you for working on each of these books with me. May you sit on my shoulder as I write and whisper encouragements when I have doubts. I miss you and our adventures.

To Bruce Coffin. Bruce Coffin is a retired detective sergeant from Portland, Maine. He writes the bestselling Detective Byron Mystery series. Thank you for encouraging me to go ahead and have Sarah arrested and for helping with those details. I love how it turned out. Any errors are all mine.

To Vida Antolin-Jenkins—you are the one who suggested a story focusing on issues women face in the military. I hope this makes you proud. Thank you for helping me understand the ups and downs, for sharing your personal experiences, and for letting me borrow some of them. You also talked me through the details of what an IG complaint could do to a career. This book wouldn't be a book without you.

To all the women who serve our country in the military. Thank you. A special thanks to two veterans, Stacy Bolla Woodson and Heather Reed. Your stories inspire me.

To the crime-writing community—especially to Sisters in Crime and Mystery Writers of America along with all the bloggers and reviewers. Thank you.

To my readers—thank you for reading my books and writing to me!

To my lovely family even though we are scattered around the country, I always hold you close to my heart.

Keep reading for a special excerpt of
The Gun Also Rises *by Sherry Harris!*

THE GUN ALSO RISES
A Sarah Winston Garage Sale Mystery

TO RECOVER A PRICELESS MANUSCRIPT . . .
A wealthy widow has asked Sarah Winston to sell
her massive collection of mysteries through her
garage sale business. While sorting through piles
of books stashed in the woman's attic, Sarah is
amazed to discover a case of lost Hemingway
stories, stolen from a train in Paris back in 1922.
How did they end up in Belle Winthrop Granville's
attic in Ellington, Massachusetts,
almost one hundred years later?

WILL SARAH HAVE TO PAY WITH HER LIFE?
Before Sarah can get any answers, Belle is assaulted,
the case is stolen, a maid is killed, and Sarah herself
is dodging bullets. And when rumors spread that
Belle has a limited edition of The Sun Also Rises in
her house, Sarah is soon mixed up with a mobster,
the fanatical League of Literary Treasure Hunters,
and a hard-to-read rare book dealer. With someone
willing to kill for the Hemingway, Sarah has to race
to catch the culprit—or the bell may toll for her . . .

Look for The Gun Also Rises. *On sale now!*

CHAPTER ONE

A drop of sweat rolled down my back as I rang the doorbell of the mansion. I wanted to blame it on the hot sun pummeling my shoulders, but it was nerves. As I listened to the deep gong echoing inside the house, I thought, *for whom the bell tolls; it tolls for thee.* I didn't know the rest of the poem, only that Hemingway used it for a title, or why the lines swirled through my head. They sure sounded ominous.

I'd been summoned here via a thick cream envelope delivered by a messenger yesterday at noon. The card inside read:

Mrs. Belle Winthrop Granville III
Requests the presence of Miss Sarah Winston
at 10:00 a.m., July 25

It was impossible to refuse such an invitation. Okay, so I could have, but curiosity would have killed me if I did. I'd been running a garage sale business for over a year and a half, here in Ellington, Massachusetts. But I'd never worked for someone as wealthy as Belle Winthrop Granville, III. Miss Belle,

as she was called around town, which was a very
Southern thing to do for a bunch of Yankees, was a
legend in Ellington. I couldn't imagine how she'd
even heard about me. Or that she needed me to do a
garage sale for her.

But I knew about Miss Belle. In fact, everyone in
Ellington knew her story because who didn't love a
good love story? She was from an elite Alabama
family. She'd met Sebastian Winthrop Granville III at
spring break in Key West in the early sixties. Sebastian
was from a wealthy Boston Brahmin family. Both
families were dead set against the union, but the two
snuck off and married. They were like Romeo and
Juliet without the entire star-crossed business.

The story went that Miss Belle had brought her
Southern hospitality up north as a young bride, but
never won over Sebastian's family. To escape the cold
disapproval, Miss Belle and Sebastian moved to
Ellington, where Sebastian opened a bank and made
his own fortune. This all happened in the sixties, long
before I'd landed in Massachusetts three years ago
when I was thirty-six.

I stared at the door, willing it to open. I was beginning to feel twitchy, which wasn't a good way to make
a first impression. When it finally swung open, a
twentysomething woman in a black knee-length dress
with a crisp white apron stood there. For a moment,
I wondered if I'd been invited to a costume party and
that I should have worn something other than my
blue and white sundress. "Hi, I'm Sarah Winston.
Mrs. Winthrop Granville is expecting me."

"Yes, ma'am, follow me."

I detected a bit of a Boston accent in her voice. We

trekked across what seemed like miles of marble flooring, under chandeliers, and past a staircase that would suit Tara from *Gone With the Wind*. She led me to a room with a massive desk near tall windows lined with dark green velvet curtains. For a moment, I wondered if I was on the set of a remake of *Gone With the Wind*.

"I'll go get Mrs. Winthrop Granville," the maid said.

"Thank you." I turned slowly around after she left. The room was two stories high and filled floor to ceiling with shelves of books. There were two library ladders and a small balcony. It was a reader's dream room. Except for a lack of comfy chairs.

"How do you like my library?"

I turned at the sound of the soft voice with a Southern accent, where the word *my* sounded like *mah* and the word *library* was drawled out from three syllables to about five. A petite woman with silver hair twisted into a neat bun stood behind me. "Mrs. Winthrop Granville," I said. I recognized her from photographs in the newspaper. "It's an amazing room."

"If you are going to work with me, please call me Belle," she said. She wore a twinset that looked like Chanel and tan slacks. A scarf draped gracefully around her neck.

I was going to work with her? She really wanted to have a garage sale?

Miss Belle laughed. "You look flabbergasted."

"Trying to keep my emotions from showing isn't my strongest suit. It's why I rarely play poker. Apparently, I don't have just one tell, I have a multitude of them. What did you have in mind?"

"Let's sit," Miss Belle said. "Would you like me to

have Kay get you something to drink? Tea or a Coke?"
She gestured to the maid, who stood in the doorway
of the room.

"No, I'm fine, thank you." The idea of having someone wait on me had always made me slightly uncomfortable.

Miss Belle sat in a leather chair behind a desk that
almost dwarfed her and gestured for me to sit across
from her in an equally massive chair. She ran a hand
across the smooth mahogany of the desk. "This was
my Sebastian's desk. He loved this silly thing. It's
ridiculously big, don't you think?"

"It's lovely." What else could I say?

"It was his grandfather's. One of the few things he
wanted from his family when we moved to Ellington
in the sixties." She sighed. "But I'm guessing you are
wondering why I've asked you here."

Boy, was I. I nodded. I realized I'd crossed my legs
at my ankles, had my hands folded neatly in my lap,
and sat more erect than usual, like I was in the presence of a VIP.

"It's time to do some downsizing."

I didn't realize rich people worried about downsizing too.

"We never had children, so there's no one to leave
all of our things to. Although a few pieces will be returned to Sebastian's nieces and nephews." She
wrinkled her nose on the last bit.

"I'm not sure I'm the person to do a sale for you."
I hated turning away business, but . . . "I think you
need Sotheby's, not me."

"Oh, dear. I'm not being clear at all. It's my massive

book collection. I want to put together a sale to raise money for the Ellington Free Library."

I craned my head around the room. The books were all bound in leather, some looked old, most looked valuable. I had no expertise with old or rare books. I didn't even know anyone who did. "I don't think I'm qualified to do that."

Miss Belle looked surprised. "Oh, not these books." She waved her hand around. "I have an expert coming in to deal with them."

"What books, then?" I asked.

Miss Belle's cheeks reddened. "I'm addicted to mysteries. Come with me."

CHAPTER TWO

"Nothing wrong with that. I love them myself."

Miss Belle smiled. I followed her down the hall and into an office. This one was a smaller-scale version of the first. Tall windows, a smaller desk with graceful curved legs, and paperback books everywhere, on shelves, on end tables, even some stacked on the floor. A bunch of hardbacks were on the shelves too. I spotted a complete set of Sue Grafton books, all Louise Penny's Armand Gamache novels, and books by Sara Paretesky. This room had several comfy chairs to sit in with a good book.

"I don't bring everyone in here," she said, "but you don't seem like the judgmental type." She took a quick glance at me, and I gave her my best nonjudgmental smile. "Some people look down on mysteries, you know."

I may be a lot of things, but snooty wasn't one of them. Besides, who wouldn't love mysteries?

"There's everything from Agatha Christie to Trixie Beldon to Donna Andrews in here," she said.

"I think I could handle this," I said.

"This isn't all of it," Miss Belle said. "Follow me, please."

We climbed the curving staircase to the second floor. Halls led off on either side with the plushest, longest Oriental rugs I'd ever seen. Their reds glowed against the dark paneling.

"There's another staircase at the end of this hall" —she gestured to her left—"but we'll go up here."

She opened one of the multiple closed doors and we climbed another set of stairs. The rug on this floor wasn't as plush but looked much loved. In the center of the hall, Miss Belle opened a door to a steep set of stairs to an attic. The big house was very quiet. I could hear Kay vacuuming somewhere on another floor.

The attic was as clean as or cleaner than my apartment. Not a cobweb or mouse to be seen. To the left was a room with large windows spaced evenly around the room and plenty of lighting from fixtures in the ceiling. It certainly wasn't like most attics I'd been in, with low-sloped ceilings, a light bulb on a string, and rickety stairs leading up to it.

Miss Belle showed me around the room. We passed what looked to me like a treasure trove of antiques: an old radio, a gramophone, and an ice chest. I would have loved to linger and explore. For a small woman, Miss Belle could move quickly, and I hurried to keep up with her.

We arrived at a small hall with three closed doors. "Kay, my maid and housekeeper, lives up here. It's her choice. There are plenty of rooms on the second and third floor."

She opened the door that was straight ahead of us. The hinges squeaked just a little, and Miss Belle frowned. It made me realize again how very quiet this house was. This room had dress dummies, suitcases, trunks, shelves of books, and boxes with books spilling out of them. I spotted a box of Nancy Drew books and another of Bobbsey Twins.

Miss Belle shook her head. "I should have parted with some of these long ago. It's silly keeping them up here, where only I can read them. And it's a bit of a mess. I'm not sure what's in the trunks and suitcases. Probably more books." Miss Belle looked me over. "Are you up to the task?"

"Can I just poke about for a bit before I answer?" I asked.

"Very sensible. Of course. There's a bathroom just outside to the left. Kay's room is on the right. Stop by the study before you leave."

"Okay." I watched as Miss Belle left. When she was out of sight, I turned back to the scene before me. Books, glorious books.

I found a box full of Agatha Christie's books, including my favorite, *And Then There Were None*, and a trunk filled with Mary Stewart, Phyllis A. Whitney, and Victoria Holt books, which my mom loved. I flipped through a few of them but had to stop myself, more than once, from sitting down to read. None of them were first editions, but this might be the best project I'd ever had.

I spent about fifteen minutes poking around in Miss Belle's attic before I headed back downstairs. I heard voices coming from the library, so I knocked lightly on the open door before going in. Miss Belle stood next to an older man in a black suit who wasn't much taller than her and at least an inch shorter than my five-six.

"Sarah, let me introduce you to Roger Mervine. He's an old friend and a rare book dealer from Boston."

Roger strode over to me and took my hand. For a minute, I thought he was going to kiss it with his waxed, mustachioed mouth. But he shook it instead. Vigorously. "Belle tells me you'll be handling the lesser books."

Lesser books? Yeesh.

"And of course I'll be here to answer any of your questions should you find something rare or valuable."

I managed to maintain a pleasant expression. "That hasn't been decided yet." If I had to work with this guy around, I wasn't sure I wanted to. Although I'd come down here with every intention of saying yes.

"Oh, Roger, don't be such a snob," Miss Belle said. "He's harmless, really. Roger has a fabulous book-store on Beacon Hill in Boston."

Beacon Hill was a neighborhood full of beautiful brick row houses, exclusive shops, and restaurants north of Boston Common, America's first public park, and the Public Garden, the first public botanical garden in America. It was a world for John Kerry and the Kennedys and Seth Anderson's family, but this was no time to think about Seth. Good grief, now I was starting to sound like Scarlett O'Hara. He had caused me a lot of heartache and I'd done the same to him. I shook it off. "I've been in your shop. Mervine's Rare and Unusual Books?"

He did a slight bow instead of saying yes. His thick white hair swept forward, momentarily covering his face. It was hard to peg his age, but I'd guess somewhere north of sixty-five. Jeez, it was like he was playing the role of lord of the manor. Roger probably had a smoking jacket and crystal decanters full of port at home. He'd probably never tasted a fluffernutter, my favorite sandwich, in his life. Although if he was connected to Belle, he might really be a lord of a manor somewhere, or at least the American equivalent of one. When he raised his head, his light brown eyes had a bit of a twinkle in them.

"So delighted you've been in. Did you purchase anything?" he asked.

I almost said no to be ornery. "Several things. My father was thrilled with a history of coastal California I gave him for Christmas one year. Also a book with early California maps. They were beautiful." I'd grown up in Pacific Grove, California, which was sandwiched between the more famous Monterey and Carmel. My parents still lived there.

"Wonderful. It's the best part of having the store, knowing that the books end up in the hands of someone who loves them. I must be off. Sarah, I hope we'll meet again, and Belle, *enchanté* as usual." He swept out of the room as if he was exiting stage left.

"Sorry about that," Belle said. "I was hoping to have you on board before you met Roger. He's always overly assertive when you first meet him, but then he's just a big old teddy bear."

"I don't scare that easily," I said. That might not be true, but if I said it out loud often enough, maybe it would be.

"Good. That's what I heard, and that you're clever."

Oh, dear. People had been getting the craziest ideas about me since I'd helped solve a few murders. "Don't believe everything you've heard."

"I did a lot of checking before reaching out to you. After all, you will be in my home all day for some length of time going through my treasured things. I had to find someone trustworthy."

"How did you hear about me?"

"Other than the newspapers? I asked around. I know your friends the DiNapolis, among others."

Angelo and Rosalie DiNapoli owned DiNapoli's Roast Beef and Pizza, my favorite place to eat in Ellington. They had become my extended family since I'd moved to the area.

Belle clasped her hands together. "Back to my books. What do you think?"

"I'd like to do it. If I find things I can't easily price, I can look them up."

"Or you can ask Roger."

"Yes, of course." Over my dead body. I explained to Belle that I'd have to work on an hourly fee basis. I hated charging someone when they were doing something for charity, but I'd recently done an event for the school board for free. I was still trying to recoup the money I'd lost by turning away other paying jobs during that project. I also had another charity function in the works.

"No problem," Belle said. "When can you start?"

I pulled out my phone and checked out my calendar. "I could come by for a couple of hours in the morning, if that works for you."

"Of course it does. Thank you so much. This is going to be wonderful."

At noon, I sat across a table from Stella, my landlady and friend, at DiNapoli's. We were sharing my favorite bianco pizza, a white pizza with four cheeses, Angelo's secret garlic sauce, and basil, and sipping a nice cabernet sauvignon. I kind of missed the days when DiNapoli's didn't have a liquor license and would sneak me wine in a plastic kiddie cup with a lid and a straw.

"How is practice going?" I asked Stella. She taught voice classes at Berklee College of Music, private lessons at home, and had a minor role in a fall production of *The Phantom of the Opera.*

"Good. The cast is fantastic. The director has a clear vision. So far, it's been amazing."

"I hope it stays that way," I said.

"They asked me to be the understudy for the lead role, Christine." Stella's dark green eyes were wide with excitement. And her olive skin was a bit flushed.

"That's wonderful news. Now we just have to figure out how to get rid of the lead actress. I could wish her good luck instead of saying *break a leg.*" It was a theater superstition not to tell an actor good luck.

"No. I'm content with my role. It's been so long since I've been in anything professionally. I'm fine with this." Stella had toured Europe with an opera ten years ago, when she was in her twenties. "What about you?"

I picked up a second slice of pizza. The piece was

about the size of my head. Angelo didn't believe in small slices. He thought it threw off the toppings-to-crust ratio. The cheese dripped over the edges as I slid it onto my plate.

"I have a new job I'm excited about."

"For who?" Stella asked.

"Belle Winthrop Granville. She has an enormous collection of mystery books she wants to sell and then donate the money to the Ellington Library."

"Miss Belle? Wow. How did you manage that?"

"She found me," I said. "Her house is amazing. Right out of a magazine. And her attic. It's a treasure trove. I wish I had time to explore it all."

"Let me know if you need any help. I'd love to see her house."

"That would be fun. I may just need an assistant for a day or two."

A police officer walked over to the table. Usually that meant trouble for me, but this time it was just Nathan Bossum, who I called by the nickname I'd accidentally given him, Awesome.

"Want some pizza?" I asked.

"If you have extra," Awesome said.

Stella scooted over a chair and Awesome sat next to her, flinging an arm across the back of her chair. They'd been dating since they'd met last February. After giving her shoulder a squeeze, he snatched a piece of pizza, folded it, and took a bite.

"So, how about those Red Sox?" I asked with a grin. Awesome used to be a NYPD detective and was a die-hard Yankees fan. They weren't doing well this year and the Red Sox were well on their way to making the playoffs, if they didn't have a fall collapse.

Stella laughed. "They're amazing this year."

Awesome just chewed and didn't take the bait.

I scooted my chair back. "I'll leave you two to the pizza."

"You don't have to leave on my account," Awesome said. "I have to get back to work soon."

"I have a meeting to get to at two." A meeting with Seth Anderson, onetime love interest, that had me on edge. Now there would be no avoiding thinking about him. "I'll catch you later." I waved goodbye to Rosalie and Angelo as I left.

Connect with Us

Visit us online at
KensingtonBooks.com
to read more from your favorite authors, see books
by series, view reading group guides, and more.

for sneak peeks, chances to win books and prize packs,
and to share your thoughts with other readers.

facebook.com/kensingtonpublishing
twitter.com/kensingtonbooks

Tell us what you think!

To share your thoughts, submit a review,
or sign up for our eNewsletters, please visit:
KensingtonBooks.com/TellUs.